TreeVolution

Tara Campbell

Lillicat Publishers

USA

www.lillicatpublishers.com

Because of the dynamic nature of the Internet, any web addresses or links contained in this book may have changed since publication and may no longer be valid. The views expressed in these works are solely those of the author and do not necessarily reflect the views of the publisher, and the publisher hereby disclaims any responsibility for them.

Cover design by Victor Habbick Visions
www.victorhabbick.com

First Print Edition: November 2016

Print ISBN: 978-1-945646-04-1
EPUB ISBN: 978-1-945646-05-8
MOBI ISBN: 978-1-945646-06-5

Printed in the United States of America

TreeVolution

Books from Lillicat Publishers

Visions Anthology Series
Visions: Leaving Earth
Visions II: Moons of Saturn
Visions III: Inside the Kuiper Belt
Visions IV: Space Between Stars
Visions V: Milky Way
Visions VI: Galaxies
Visions VII: Universe (2017)

The Future Is Short: Science Fiction in a Flash

Sunshine & Shadow: Memories from a Long Life

To my husband Craig, who gave me the time, space, and encouragement to start a treevolution.

Contents

⚘ ACKNOWLEDGEMENTS

WRITING ACKNOWLEDGMENTS IS almost as frightening as writing a book. Where do I start? How many people will I forget to mention?

So many people have shaped and encouraged the creation of *TreeVolution* over the years, but my editor Carrol Fix is the reason it's out in the world and lookin' so fine. Thank you, Carrol, for picking it up from the forest floor, polishing it to a shine, and holding it up for the world to see.

I have the great fortune to be part of an amazing community of writers in Washington, D.C. Thank you to Michele Lerner for opening the door, and to Carrie Callaghan, Beth Wenger, Josh Trapani, Lacey N. Dunham, and too many others to name for whipping my writing into shape in various writing groups. I appreciate the advice and encouragement of literary mentors like Amber Sparks, Rion Amilcar Scott, Laura Ellen Scott, Kelly Ann Jacobson, Virgie Townsend, and the whole *Barrelhouse* team. Volunteering at the children's literacy organization 826DC not only helped me focus my time, but also introduced me to an encouraging literary community (thanks, lowercase!). And I owe a super big debt to my intrepid *TreeVolution* beta readers Richard Agemo, Dorothy Reno, Andrea Pawley, and Bridget Grimes.

Kevin Zobrist of Washington State University, Forestry and Wildlife Extension was a great help to my research on the trees of Washington State, through his online course, books, and a delightful in-person visit. Thank you, Erik Holtzapple, for providing tips on how scientific research projects are structured, and for teaching me how to actually pronounce "mycorrhiza." Thank you to Diana Veiga for helping me relax and write Tamia, even if you didn't realize that's what you were doing at the time. And I'm very grateful to the Yakama Nation, upon which the Palalla Nation in TreeVolution is largely based, for providing opportunities to visit (Treaty Days, Yakama Nation Museum, Library, and Cultural Center) and learn about Yakama land and traditions. (See "Resources" for more information.)

Thank you to my warm, smart, funny, loving, and at times goofy family, for giving me the imagination to come up with these crazy ideas and the confidence to pursue them.

And lastly, life and writing simply wouldn't be as grand without my husband Craig Hegemann. You are both my rock and my wings. There's no one I'd rather dig a rental car out of a snowbank in July with than you.

CHAPTER 1

CHARLIE CROUCHED BEHIND a toppled fir, bracing himself against the wall of splayed roots that had once anchored the tree to the forest floor. He held his breath and listened to the thrum of a truck in the distance. No one else was supposed to be out here near his cabin, not even other tribal members. There weren't even supposed to be roads this far in from the main highway.

The engine's rumble grew louder. Charlie silenced his radio and yanked at his rifle sling—damn thing never sat right against his back—dislodging dusty clumps of soil from the tangle of roots he leaned against. He filled his lungs slowly and deliberately with crisp, pine-scented air to counter the adrenaline crackling through his body. His cousin had trusted him with this patrol. He was supposed to feel like a vigilante, the Palalla Nation's shot in the dark to catch timber poachers in the act.

Vigilantes stay cool, he reminded himself.

Charlie poked his head out and scanned across the sunlight-dappled forest. His nostrils flared at a current of sun-warmed earth and pungent scat. Bear dung? That would be all he needed right now.

The chug of the truck engine stopped. Doors creaked open and slammed shut, and the voices of two men drifted toward him. He closed his eyes, trying to trace their location, but his heart thumped against his chest and his blood carried the drumbeat into his ears. He struggled to concentrate over the throb—then a chainsaw rattled to life. Charlie's stomach lurched.

Cousin Eddie had told him about the poachers' technique. They traveled by twos, he'd said, and could take down an old-growth tree in less than 20 minutes. It was quick, but noisy; a real ballsy move when it's not your property.

The saw's raspy buzz changed pitch. Charlie imagined saw teeth biting into bark. He unlatched the radio from his belt and wrenched the dials. "Control, come in, this is Charlie. Come in, it's an emergency."

A blip broke through the static. "Copy, Charlie. This is Eddie."

"Eddie, send someone out here quick! They're cuttin'!" He scowled, imagining the saw chewing through pristine wood.

"Who's cuttin'? Where are you?"

"About ten miles northeast of the cabin. They cut in a new access road."

Eddie's voice scratched over the radio. "How many're out there?"

"I don't know. I think just two."

"Okay, just a minute."

"Eddie, they're cuttin' right now!" Charlie's teeth clenched at the whine of the saw and the crack of wood— the sounds of trees becoming timber on his watch.

"You think we got a chopper at the ready, Cuz? We have to send a truck over. What direction they come from?"

"I didn't see 'em, I just heard 'em."

"Okay, don't get any closer. Remember, some of these motherfuckers are mean. Blow your head off first chance they get. Now shut up for a minute and lemme get someone over there!"

"Copy. Out." Charlie clipped the radio back onto his belt and looked over the top of the downed fir. He put one hand on his rifle sling and balled the other hand into a fist, listening to the shouts of the poachers and the thunderous popping of a tree about to surrender. His frown deepened. The cracking was too loud to be from a sapling, but there was no way they could have felled a full-grown tree in the time he talked to Eddie.

The saw choked to a stop, but the yelling and crashing went on, like the tree was falling over again and again. Charlie stepped out from behind his cover of

6

upturned roots. These men weren't calling "timber"—they were screaming for help.

Charlie ran up the hill, clumsy with the rifle strapped to his back. He fumbled for his radio. "Eddie, I think someone's hurt!"

"What happened?"

Charlie cleared the top of the ridge and looked out over a wide, sloping expanse of forest. Bristling spires of Douglas fir and Ponderosa pine dominated the green carpet draped over the contours of the mountain. Leafy, rounded crowns of deciduous trees peeped out between the steeples of the evergreens that dwarfed them. Breaks in tree cover were barely visible, marked only by a thinning of color and a glimpse of rock.

A thousand steep yards downhill, a mass of treetops thrashed and bowed, cracking and popping. The yells turned into screams.

"Charlie, dammit." Eddie's voice crackled through the radio. "Come in!"

"I can't see 'em, but they sound hurt," he yelled back.

"Hang tight. I'll call it in. Serve those fuckers right," Eddie muttered.

"Eddie?" Charlie twisted the dial, amplifying the *fsss* of radio silence on the other end. "Eddie?"

What did "call it in" mean, cops or ambulance? And what was he supposed to do until they got here?

The screaming faded. Charlie raced downhill toward the poachers, blinded by alternating pools of sunlight and shade. He threaded a path between craggy tree trunks, his boots kicking up clouds of dust. Thorns pulled at his jeans as he wove between bushes and boulders, sidestepping roots that almost seemed like they were put there to trip him.

A moan reached his ears, soon eclipsed by the roar of a truck engine starting. The slope leveled, and he stumbled into a small, bright clearing. The air smelled like red cedar—freshly-cut.

The engine rumbled. Charlie spotted a road hacked out on the other side of the clearing, then saw the vehicle

7

bumping away thirty yards down the illegal access. He ran after it.

Another crack boomed through the forest. A moment later, a massive hunk of tree smashed into the cab of the truck. The vehicle veered off the trail and crashed into a young pine.

Charlie closed in on the truck as it sputtered against the tree. The front windshield was shattered. The top four feet of a Douglas fir stuck up and out of the cab, a spear thrown by a giant. Charlie pushed through branches, every movement setting off a tinkling shower of broken glass. He reached into the mangled cab to get to the driver. The man's head flopped back in Charlie's hands, revealing staring, motionless eyes. No breath. No pulse. Blood pooled on the vinyl seat. Charlie pulled metal and plastic away from the splintered trunk that had crushed the driver's chest. There was nothing left to push life back into.

Charlie shambled back to the clearing, shaking the glass off his sleeves and wiping the blood from his hands onto his jeans. There had only been one man in the truck, but he'd heard two. He stopped at the base of the felled tree and called out. Hearing no response, he moved into the calico shadows around the downed red cedar. It was covered in a jumble of branches and lay almost wedged between the other trees in the stand. Twigs and needles crunched under his feet as he tried to get close to the trunk. He stopped to listen for someone moving or breathing, but there was no sound at all. No wind, no birds, no drone of chirring, buzzing insects in the background. The forest held its breath.

He looked up into the canopy of leaves and boughs blocking the sky. The trees around him were ragged, some of them missing branches, which he guessed were now in the pile of debris on the ground. The remaining branches curved in close over his head, and the surrounding trunks seemed to bow in toward the fallen cedar, as though mourning their recent loss.

Why would the men have cut the tree to fall into the forest when there was more space in the clearing?

Charlie jumped when his radio bleeped.

"Chopper's on the way," announced Eddie. "There better be something for 'em to see."

"Yeah, one man dead."

"Goddamn."

"No sign of the other one," said Charlie, stepping over broken limbs to walk around the trunk. "He must have got away." He saw a glimpse of brown boot under a branch. "Hang on, I'll call you back."

Charlie freed himself of his rifle and tore at the branches, kicking and pulling to get to the man pinned underneath. He scrambled over the tree to try the other side, coughing in a cloud of dust. But the red cedar was immovable. He looked around for one of the saws. Nothing. He ran back to the truck. Nothing there either.

Chest heaving, he walked back to the felled tree and looked at the half-buried boot. No one could have survived that crushing weight.

Charlie dropped to his knees. A sudden fatigue rushed through his body. He looked down at his hands, scratched and bloody from digging. He tilted his head back, and his breath caught in his throat.

He could see the sky.

"Charlie!" barked the radio.

The canopy of leaves had parted; the trees around him no longer bent in over the fallen cedar. He now had a plain view of the cloudbank scudding overhead.

"Charlie, come in!"

Charlie could just make out the faint chop of a helicopter in the distance. The clouds shifted. The red cedar was flooded in sunlight.

CHAPTER 2

TAMIA BENNETT QUIETLY slid her desk drawer open and took out her purse. When she'd accepted the position at Governor Palmer's office, she hadn't considered the downside of working in a cubicle-farm, where everyone could hear everything she did.

She dug her compact out of her purse and slid a fingernail under the lid. It opened with a barely audible click. She angled the mirror up to the top of her head to check for the stray, wiry hairs that always seemed to pop up of their own accord. Between her father's straight, fine hair and her mother's kinky locks, she had inherited a head of hair that needed constant supervision.

"You look fine." Greg Dunlap smirked down at Tamia, his arm hooked over the flimsy wall of her cube.

"You know our briefing's today," she said, hating that this serial cubicle-roamer had caught her the one minute she wasn't focused.

"Yeah, but, you know," he said, shrugging. "Julie needed some advice on how to get rid of that asswipe she's dating."

"So you can swoop in and be the next one?" Tamia gave him her *just kidding* smile, dropped the compact back into her purse and slid the drawer closed. "You know she's, like, five years older than you."

"Whatever. How far are we on Tree-pocalypse?"

"*We?* Really?"

"Sorry."

Tamia twisted her lips. "*We* still have to pull together our talking points. It's already one o'clock and we're briefing the governor at two, remember?"

He grunted and dragged his chair over to her cube. "All right, let's get this over with."

Tamia pulled the screen around for him to see. "I'm thinking we can start with, 'Mr. Governor, we'd like to thank you for the opportunity to brief you on the series of reports surrounding—'"

"Oh for chrissake, Tam, just cut to the chase and say, 'We've put together a list of all abnormal tree-human interactions in Washington State.'"

"I'll think of something," she said, erasing her first line. She wasn't going to walk into another one of Greg's *me-boss, you-secretary* scenarios. He still kept trying, though, which was pretty messed up considering they had exactly the same job. Same poli sci degree, same year of graduation, and even though she couldn't afford to take any of those fancy unpaid internships he never tired of mentioning, she'd still landed the same Research Assistant I position. And she was going to show her bosses they'd been right to give her this chance, even if she had to throw Greg over her shoulder and carry him across the finish line with her.

Tamia read aloud from her notes, "April 30, a woman in Puyallup reports being assaulted by a tree. According to her statement, she was locking her bike to the tree when it 'slapped her.' No other witnesses. She took a picture of the tree, which was later identified as a Pacific yew."

"Whatsa matter for yew!" quipped Greg, pinching his fingers together and waggling his hands in mock Italian distress. Tamia shot him a disdainful look.

"July 12," he continued. "An Olympia man reports that his dog was kicked by a big-leaf maple. He was taking the dog for a walk and when pooch lifted its leg— pow, right in the acorns!"

"You can't brief Governor Palmer like that."

He rolled his eyes. "Dude, I won't. But it's all a bunch of urban legends. Kid gets spanked by a ficus, cat gets catapulted into the next yard. None of it substantiated."

"What about the guys who got killed out by that reservation last week?" she asked, pulling up an article.

"You mean the poachers?"

Tamia raised her eyebrows.

"Yes, I read the links you sent me," said Greg. "They were thieves, and wound up getting what they deserved."

"You don't think there was anything strange about what happened? They were supposed to be experts at cutting. So how does a log fly through a truck like that?"

He shrugged. "They cut the tree—illegally—and it fell on them. Case closed."

"So, if there's nothing to any of these claims, why is Palmer asking us to look into it?"

"Because *this*," he said, pointing to the name of a recent tree victim, "is Governor Palmer's cousin's wife."

"What, really? How do you know that?"

Greg patted her shoulder. "You've got to find a source of intel in this town, Tam."

"Ta-mi-a," she told him, for what felt like the billionth time. "And see, now that it's happened to someone he knows, he's taking it seriously."

"Yeah, not so much," he said with a smirk. "She's a raging alcoholic. This 'investigation' is a courtesy, a personal favor. Why else do you think they're having *us* do the briefing?"

She shrugged. "Staff development?"

"Seriously?" he snorted. "No, we're only doing it because it'd be a total waste of his advisors' time."

Tamia crossed her arms to distract herself from feeling foolish.

Greg held up his hands in theatrical modesty. "Intel. Anyway, let's wrap this up and move on. We have to get going on the Japanese trade delegation stuff for next week."

Five minutes before the briefing, Tamia was still putting the finishing touches on their document. Even if Greg was right, and their presentation was a joke, she still wanted to make a good impression. There were whispers about Palmer gearing up for a U.S. Senate run, and this was her chance to grab a piece of his coattails.

"All right, that's enough," said Greg. "Just print it out."

As he headed toward the printer, Tamia started closing the browser windows littering her screen. Her cursor lingered over the article about the dead timber poachers.

"Come on, Tamia," yelled Greg from the hallway. "Let's go."

Tamia left the article open and gave the philodendron on her desk a quick drink of water. "Okay, Harvey, here I go," she whispered to the little plant. "Wish me luck!"

CHAPTER 3

CHARLIE WATCHED THE state trooper raise a coffee mug to his sandy moustache and take a loud slurp. The cup's logo, like all of the county's official signage, featured the State of Washington's official spelling of Palalla: "Pilalla," with an "i" up front. Decades after the Palalla Nation had replaced the "i" to reflect the proper pronunciation of its name, the State had stayed its own course.

The trooper set down his cup and peered at his computer screen through the bottom of his glasses. "Mr. Meninick, we appreciate your coming in again this week. We just have to double-check some of our information. Need more water?" He nodded at the Styrofoam cup in Charlie's hands.

Charlie shook his head. His stomach was too tight to drink what he already had.

The trooper looked back at his monitor. "So you were in a closed tribal area, patrolling for illegal logging activity on behalf of the Palalla Land Enterprise." His eyes shifted to Charlie's.

"Yes."

"All right. We're used to seeing your Forest Patrol or Tribal Police folks perform that function; that's why we wanted to double-check." His moustache rose with his perfunctory smile. "Your cousin Eddie Washines hired you and you were living in a cabin owned by the tribe." He paused for confirmation and Charlie nodded. "And that was his rifle you were carrying?"

Charlie bristled at the question. He had every right to carry a rifle on Palalla land, or anywhere in the state for that matter, but he answered anyway. "Yes, sir, Eddie lent it to me."

The "i" on the trooper's cup seemed to stare right at him. His uncle Virgil—the "political" uncle, the one who wanted him to study law to help his people—always used to rail against that misplaced "i", the white man's "i" that stood for land grabs, broken treaties, and decimated tribes. *Only thing we have to thank the white man for,* he'd say, *is a chance to show our resilience.*

"So tell us again," continued the trooper. "What did Mr. Washines want you to do if you encountered poachers?"

"Radio him."

"That's all?"

"Yeah, just radio him and he'd take care of it."

"And by 'take care of,' what did he mean?"

"I don't know," said Charlie, trying not to sound annoyed. "He'd decide what to do, I suppose." *Why all the same questions again?*

Charlie watched the trooper's fingers stab the keyboard, wondering what those files could possibly be missing by now. *Charlie Meninick, Palalla, twenty-nine years old, average height, medium build, brown eyes, short black hair, just returned from Seattle, Washington, where he failed as student, construction worker, and boyfriend; recently witnessed—*

"What was the gun for?" the trooper asked. "Were you supposed to hold the poachers until help came?"

Charlie frowned, but then quickly relaxed his face. It wouldn't help to look too hostile. "Like I said before, Eddie gave it to me so I could hunt—animals for food. And for protection, from bears, mostly."

"Mostly?"

"Eddie said the poachers might have guns, so he wanted me to have one too." What the hell was their fixation on him having a gun? Those poachers were the criminals, not him.

"But you say they didn't have any firearms, that you knew of."

"No, sir."

"Mmm-hmm," murmured the trooper, scrolling through a file.

Was there some kind of rap sheet on him in there, Charlie wondered. Okay, so maybe he and his last girlfriend argued sometimes, loud, and the neighbors called the police once or twice. But that was in Seattle—the trooper couldn't see that in his record, could he?

"So you heard them talking," the trooper said. "Then you heard the chainsaws and radioed your cousin. What time was that, when you called him?"

"I don't know. I didn't stop to check my watch."

He noticed the trooper looking across the desk at the Styrofoam cup in his hands. Charlie hadn't realized he was rotating it between his palms. He set the cup on the desk.

"*About* how long after you heard the chainsaws did you hear the men yell?" asked the trooper.

"I don't know, five minutes, ten at the most."

"And they managed to cut down a mature tree in five to ten minutes?"

"I don't know." Charlie shrugged. "I don't know how they did it. That tree must've been four feet across."

The trooper stroked his moustache. "So, did you see the tree fall?"

"No. It was already down by the time I got there."

"Did you see any other tools they might have been using? Chains, for example; could they have used the truck to pull the tree down?"

Charlie shook his head again. He stretched out his fingers, still scratched up from digging around the fallen tree. One of the cuts on his thumb had started bleeding again.

"All right," said the trooper, scrolling through the report. "But you saw the truck leaving the scene."

"Yeah." He wiped at his bloody thumb with his other hand.

"And can you tell me one more time what happened next, Mr. Meninick? We're still trying to understand this part."

Charlie tried to keep impatience from slipping into his voice. "The truck was headin' away from me, and then I heard a big snap and this big branch came down on it."

"Straight down?"

"No, it kind of came at the truck, like..." He swallowed. "Like someone threw it."

"Must've been some powerful spirits in the forest that day."

Charlie remained silent.

The trooper cleared his throat. "When was the last storm out there, Mr. Meninick? I mean, strong enough to potentially cause tree damage that severe?"

"I only been out there a couple of weeks, but there haven't been any storms since I got there."

"You were in Seattle before, right?"

Charlie froze.

The trooper looked up from the screen.

Charlie concentrated on keeping his knee still. That's one of the things they look for, he'd heard, to see if you were nervous. "Yeah," he murmured.

The officer finished pecking at the keyboard and took a swig of coffee. "Well, just watch your head out there. Forestry folks are over there right now taking samples, trying to figure out why this timber was so unstable. Could be another beetle infestation, I suppose; but then, it's not my area of expertise." He leaned back in his chair and scrutinized Charlie. "Mr. Meninick, as you know, this is a very complicated situation, two men dead—one white, one Indian—on tribal land. Very complicated."

Complicated? thought Charlie. *Try just plain wrong.* The white poacher was bad enough. The Palalla man stealing from a tribal business: lowest of the low.

"I suppose you're speaking with Tribal Police too?" asked the trooper.

"Yep, tomorrow."

"That's a lot of driving."

"I'm stayin' with my cousin in Nakalish the next few days," said Charlie. "It's not so far."

The trooper leaned forward and cupped his hands around his mug. "We can send someone down there so you don't have to keep coming up to Pilalla City."

"No," he barked, instantly regretting his vehemence. "I just—I don't want to bother my cousin and his family."

The trooper stared at him a moment longer. "All right, Mr. Meninick. Thank you for coming in." He stood and extended his hand over his desk. "I think this is all we need right now. We'll contact you if anything else comes up."

"Fine," said Charlie. He wiped the sweat from his palm and accepted the outstretched hand. He'd keep coming in as long as he had to. There was no way he was going to bring the shame of a trooper's car to his cousin's door.

CHAPTER 4

TAMIA TIPPED A drink of water into her little cube plant before taking a sip for herself. Lauryn Hill crooned at her through her earbuds, and she bobbed her head and whispered along. Having just read an article called "Plant Volatiles—From Chemistry to Communication," she was debating whether her next read should be "Do Plants Think?" or "Trees Call for Help—And Now Scientists Can Understand." She took another bite of her sandwich and wiped the crumbs off her notepad.

Tamia felt a little guilty for reading this stuff at work. She hadn't been asked to do any more on it since last week's briefing, but at least she was doing it during lunch. She'd had no idea plants were so dynamic. They could send each other chemical messages; warn each other when they were under attack. Some plants could send out a beacon, like a Bat Signal, summoning wasps to attack the caterpillars chewing on their leaves. Trees had even been shown to exchange nutrients through their roots, trading sugars back and forth according to the season.

Mad respect, Harvey, she thought, looking at the philodendron on her desk. *So unassuming, just sitting there in your little terra cotta pot.*

Who knew, maybe she'd find something here to help her faltering garden at home. She probably should have become a botanist instead, because this stuff was much more interesting than all the number-crunching for the Japanese trade delegation.

The delegation had come and gone, with all the attendant hysteria from Protocol and her own awkwardness around important people. Whatever she did during high-profile visits, she always felt certain it was the exact wrong thing. All the stiff bowing and even stiffer smiling, and careful steering of guests down marble hallways to special meeting rooms with thick carpets and mahogany furniture. It was all such theatre, such *kabuki*. At least she knew that much Japanese.

Greg, on the other hand, seemed to know exactly how to exploit these opportunities. After dropping frequent hints about his Japanese minor at UW, he'd offered to refresh the governor's knowledge of the language, which had resulted in some nice one-on-one time with Palmer. And he had volunteered to help escort the delegation to and from the airport and draft the follow-up correspondence, planting the seeds for a grad school recommendation and overseas internship in one visit. Pretty slick. Just like the Career Development Center had said: offer to help on extra projects, build your network, make yourself a go-to person. But did he have to be so slimy about it, with that big, fawning smile and that syrupy voice?

Anyway, wasn't she supposed to be thinking about her own career instead of obsessing about his?

She felt a tug on the cord of her earbuds. It was Greg. She uncorked one ear.

"Does Palmer want more on the tree thing?" he asked, nodding toward her monitor.

"Oh, no. I'm just reading some articles."

He arched his back and stretched. "If you're just sitting here over lunch anyway, you could start working on e-mails."

"Constituent e-mails? And take that learning opportunity away from the intern?" she asked with mock innocence.

"Seriously, I know it sucks, but the intern isn't coming in today. Didn't you read Rima's e-mail?"

Tamia flipped over to her inbox and scanned the message from the staff supervisor. "Well, let's split 'em up," she said, taking out her remaining earbud and cutting off the music.

He shook his head. "Palmer needs me on follow-up for the trade delegation."

"Well, we can do that first." The Japanese trade thing was important, so she'd go ahead and help him out one more time.

"Tam, look." Greg pointed to the salient part of the staff supervisor's e-mail.

"Oh," she said quietly. There it was, in text and subtext: she'd been assigned to constituent e-mails again, while Greg would be taking on the more important trade work.

"Eyes on the prize," said Greg. "You keep wasting your time on trees, you'll never get to D.C.."

Tamia glared at him, seriously wondering what Richie Rich could presume to tell her about "eyes on the prize."

Greg shook his head. "You gotta keep up. You want to stay in Olympia forever?"

"Maybe I do," she shot back. "Maybe we don't all want the same prize."

Tamia sifted through constituent complaints about fishing regulations and hunting permits, wondering what her prize really was. If she really cared about being part of Palmer's Senate run, she should have tried to make her mark with the trade delegation. On the other hand, if she didn't really care about that stuff, she shouldn't be so pissed off at Greg for pulling ahead.

So... So what if she *did* want to stay in Olympia forever? Well, not Olympia in particular, but what if she actually *liked* Washington? What if she missed hiking with her friends and spending more time in the woods? What if she didn't want to move farther away from her mom and dad and brother in Seattle? And what if, contrary to her parents' beliefs, success wasn't synonymous with a big, important job in Washington, D.C.?

After an hour tackling constituent e-mails, Tamia took a break and walked to the lake at the edge of the legislative grounds. Heading down the twisting trail to Capitol Lake, smelling the wild roses along the path, watching the ripples sparkle on the water—this always seemed to help her think.

Greg said she was wasting time on the trees. Why was it a waste; she was interested in it. Did everything have to be about her career?

She looked uphill and saw the tip of the old plant conservatory at the top of the trail. The dilapidated greenhouse was closed and slated for demolition. Greg had teased her when she talked about joining the committee to raise funds to reopen it, making cracks about little old ladies and tea. She'd gotten annoyed at him for panning the committee—but had she joined it yet? No.

She sighed and turned back to the lake. After all the scholarships and loans and hopes that had been invested in her degree, she felt guilty for being so hazy on what she was going to do with it. What she really had to do was figure out exactly what her goals were—and stop wasting time being mad at Greg for going after his.

CHAPTER 5

RICKY NYSTROM ADVANCED down the middle of a cracked, deserted road, blaster at the ready. He whirled around just in time to blow a hole through a lunging zombie. More zombies materialized behind the singed, double-dead corpse, and he fired into them without pity until they were a quivering mass on the asphalt.

Over the gurgling of his victims, an unholy sound reached his ears: "Ricky, that's enough X-box for today."

Wincing, he unloaded his weapon against a new flank of undead. The zombies jerked and twitched, spewing forth gallons of bright green ooze.

"Come on, Ricky," his father called again. "Outside."

Out of ammo, he picked up a shovel and was about to clock a charging zombie in the head when the screen went black.

"Daaaad!"

"Go on." The pale blue eyes staring down at Ricky were the same shade as his. He also had his dad to thank for the bright red hair and fair skin that made him stick out at school.

Ricky exhaled loudly and threw the controller down on the couch. He looked out the sliding glass doors into the back yard. "Dad, it's pouring!" It was always raining in Tacoma.

"It's sprinkling, and it's almost over." He tossed his windbreaker at him. "That never stops you and your friends anyway. Bring 'em over for a game," he said, motioning toward the drooping soccer nets.

"Nobody's here. They're all on vacation." All his friends were off somewhere fun right before school started, while he was stuck here staring third grade in the face by himself.

"Well, go practice your drills. I'll come out and kick your butt in a few minutes."

"You wish," Ricky teased back. With a grudging smile, he put on his windbreaker and headed out to his soccer ball. He dribbled the ball between his feet and tried to kick goals across the long, damp grass. Then he heard a window slide open and looked up.

His father waved from the office window. "Don't run off anywhere, I'll be out in a minute." Ricky sighed and waved back before his dad pulled his head in and shut the window. *A minute* usually turned into longer when Dad was in his office.

He kicked the ball aimlessly around the yard, stopping in front of a stick that looked like a rifle. He picked it up and sighted down the length of it, then spotted a bird in a tree and lifted his weapon. The bird flew to another tree, and Ricky followed it into the woods at the edge of the yard.

After targeting the bird, and then another bird, and then a squirrel, Ricky rested his weapon against the trunk of a slender young birch. He always liked the fresh, clean smell of the woods after rain. Their house was on the edge of the neighborhood, so there was nothing but trees and more trees from here on out.

Ricky looked at the tree propping up his rifle, examining its black lines and papery white bark. He fingered the bark and started to peel it off in small strips. Dad had told him once how many acres these woods were, but he'd forgotten exactly. They were big, though; all the times he'd struck out into them, they went on for longer than his legs would take him.

Something moved beneath him, like a small animal burrowing. Maybe it was a groundhog. Ricky bent down and started to dig. He kept digging and digging, forging a broad, shallow ditch with his hands. He didn't see anything. He picked up a rock to help him go deeper, scraping dirt away from between the roots.

Ricky heard a squeak, then felt a soft thump on his head. He stood up too quickly and blinked through a wave of dizziness. When he could focus again, he saw a squirrel on the ground, looking as dazed as he was. He picked up a twig to nudge it, but it rolled onto its paws and ran away.

The ground beneath him shifted again, but all he could see was a jumble of dirt and roots. Were there squirrels living under the tree? He leaned over the hole he'd dug and felt a thwack on his behind.

Ricky whirled around. No one was there. And it was really quiet. Where were all the birds and stuff? There was no sound except the rustling of leaves.

Twigs cracked under his sneakers as he backed up. His foot seesawed on the edge of his ditch.

With a yelp he jumped away from the birch—something had poked him in the side. Ricky stood perfectly still, skin tingling, moving nothing but his eyes as he looked around the forest.

He jumped again at the crack of a twig in the distance. He went to grab his stick but tripped on a root and fell. Rolling onto his back, he looked up into the branches above him. All the leaves were rustling and whipping around, like in a big storm—except there wasn't any wind. He swallowed. The ground rumbled underneath him again.

Ricky scrambled to his feet and ran, pumping his arms, ducking around trees and stumbling through underbrush until he reached his back yard. He sprinted across the grass toward his house, plowing straight into his father.

"Dad! Dad! The trees!"

"Ricky, what's wrong?" His father knelt to his eye level and looked him up and down. "Are you okay? Where were you? I was looking for you."

"The trees, the trees!"

"The what?"

"The trees are after me!"

"Who's chasing you?" His father rose and looked around. Then he yanked open the glass door, pushed

Ricky through it, and locked them both inside. "Did someone try to hurt you?"

"No, it was the trees. They were chasing me!"

"The trees?" He peered through the glass into the yard. "I don't see anything."

"It was out there in the woods."

"What were you doing? I told you to stick around."

"But Dad—"

"No 'but'. You know you're not supposed to run around those woods alone." His father looked him over for cuts and bruises. "You hurt?"

He shook his head and looked over his shoulder into the wall of trees behind the back yard. Nothing was charging out of the woods to get him.

"Listen, Ricky." He paused until Ricky turned to face him again. "I should have gone out there with you sooner, like I said I would. I let something distract me, and I'm sorry. But you know how your mom feels about you going out into the woods by yourself."

Ricky looked down at his feet. "I'm sorry."

"I know, buddy. But you have to understand how nervous she's been since you fell out of that tree a couple of months ago."

"But I was fine!"

"But what if you weren't? And what if Micah hadn't been around to help you get home? Your mom's right, you should always bring a friend."

His father brushed some leaves out his hair. "You better get rid of the evidence before Mom gets home. She's bringing pizza, but not for kids who disobey orders."

Ricky turned toward the glass doors again and squinted his eyes. Nothing was moving out there. Just a little breeze tossing the leaves.

And they were having pizza.

Ricky kicked off his shoes and ran upstairs to clean up. He'd figure the forest out tomorrow.

CHAPTER 6

CHARLIE LIFTED HIS chin to greet his cousin Eddie, then descended the front steps of the Tribal Police Station. The sky was grey and the air smelled like rain.

Eddie was leaning against his car, smoking. Stocky and square-chinned, he had a sense of certainty about him that went deeper than Charlie's own bravado. Charlie found it hard to believe they were the same age. He supposed that was what settling down did. Eddie had stayed home, gone to the tribal college, and worked his way up at Palalla Land Enterprise. He'd earned a lot of trust and responsibility. One of the many differences between them.

"Hungry?" asked Eddie, dropping his cigarette to the sidewalk and stepping on it.

"Yeah, but let's get away from here."

Eddie nodded. "We'll take my car. I'll bring you back to your truck later." They got in and pulled away from the curb.

A light rain began to mist the windshield as they drove. "Sorry you got to talk to so many people," said Eddie. "But it's no problem for you to stay with us. And you're bringin' the rain from Seattle." He smiled.

Charlie watched the drizzle fall on the dusty Mexican restaurants and faux-Western storefronts of downtown Nakalish. After fifteen years in rain-soaked Seattle, he was still getting used to how dry it was east of the Cascades.

"Hey, don't sweat it, Cuz," said Eddie. "The cops just got to get all the information. At least the Feds aren't tryin' to stick their noses in."

"Why would they?" Charlie growled. "Aren't there enough damn police involved?" Despite all his interviews, nobody could explain what had happened. No one could have cut down that big a red cedar so quickly. And only a tornado could have chucked a treetop through the cab of a truck like that.

Eddie's muscular hands turned the steering wheel. "White man gets killed on tribal land, you never know who'll want to start stickin' their noses in. But Tribal Police got no reason to bring the Feds in on an accidental death. Now, if you'd been involved somehow—"

"I wasn't involved! Those guys weren't even supposed to be there in the first place, and they went and got themselves killed, and now I got to talk to all these police."

"Okay, okay, lighten up, Cuz." Eddie pulled into a parking lot. "Let's eat. This place here—nothin' fancy, but they got the best burgers in town."

Charlie glanced across the street as he climbed out of the car. Wagon Wheel Liquors was still there, one of too many places that had wrangled an exemption from the Nation's alcohol ban. He turned and followed Eddie across cracked asphalt toward the rustic, wooden façade of the Crossroads Saloon.

"Sit anywhere you like, gents," a waitress said as they entered.

On their way toward a booth, Eddie stopped next to a table where two men were having lunch. "*Áay*, brothers."

"Hey, Eddie. Is that your cousin?" asked the younger one. "Back from the city?"

Charlie held his hand out to them and introduced himself.

"He's helpin' me out with the damn poaching," said Eddie, clopping him on the shoulder. "He's gonna put a stop to it."

The older man shook Charlie's hand, looking at him appraisingly. "That so?"

"Well, I'm gonna try."

"Try, hell," said the younger man. "We all heard about those two got killed last week. Sounds like you're already doin' the job."

Charlie clenched his teeth.

Eddie cleared his throat noisily. "Well, we're gonna find a seat and get some lunch."

"All right," said the older one. "Till next time, brother." They all nodded their goodbyes.

Charlie and Eddie sank into spongy benches opposite each other at a booth by the window. The waitress brought them menus. Charlie looked across the street at Wagon Wheel Liquors.

"Hey." Eddie's voice was stern.

Charlie frowned at Eddie, then studied his menu.

They both knew Charlie had spent too much time in bars up in Seattle, telling himself he was just going to have a couple of beers with his buddies. He'd been so sure he wasn't going to fall into the same trap he'd seen so many of his brothers fall into before, but he'd found out the hard way that pride only gets you so far. He was as vulnerable as anyone, and his own stubbornness had sent him right to the bottom of the bottle. Time after time he denied he'd lost control and, instead, lost another job and another chance to provide for his girlfriend Jenna and their child on the way.

For all their differences, he and Jenna had shared the same weakness. They'd both drink and then curse themselves for drinking. They knew what it did to them, but they couldn't stop. Or maybe they hadn't really wanted to stop, not bad enough. Not even for the daughter she was bearing.

The daughter he would never get to hold.

Charlie and Eddie ordered and ate quickly. It was already afternoon, Charlie said, and he still had to stock up on supplies before tackling the winding mountain road back up to his cabin. The ride back to his truck was quiet.

The feeble rain had stopped by the time Charlie finished his errands. The dusty ground had absorbed the sprinkle of moisture, and there was barely any indication it had rained at all. As he rode out of town in his rusted black Ford, the sun penetrated the clouds without lifting his mood. He spent the drive trying to push things out of his mind: the image of the dead men in the forest; the flashing lights on the Trooper's truck; the questions, all those questions; the nods that told him they didn't believe him, just like all the times the cops had thumped on the door of his and Jenna's apartment in Seattle.

"You all right, ma'am?" they would ask. "The neighbors called."

Damn police, troopers, they were all the same. If there was trouble, their eyes always locked on the darkest face first.

But then, he hadn't always proven them wrong, had he? He always wound up losing control and showing them just what they expected to see. And hadn't he come back home specifically to break that pattern?

Charlie pulled over and unpeeled his hands from the wheel before cutting the engine and climbing out. *I don't have time for this,* he thought, walking tight, angry circles at the side of the road. *Past is past.* This felt like another one of his grandfather's lessons. Whenever Charlie got mad, the old man would simply ask him questions, poking and prodding, letting Charlie tangle himself up in his own contradictions. He would hang there, his grandfather watching him writhe in his own trap, until he calmed down enough to see the way out. Charlie would have liked to ask him exactly what he was supposed to be learning this time.

He stopped pacing and stepped into the woods alongside the road. *Calm the hell down,* he told himself. He tilted his head back and closed his eyes. The lilting song of some hidden bird swooped through the forest. The air smelled both damp and dry, like drizzle on dust. And sweet—a hint of the fat, ripe huckleberries nearby. It was August, after all, peak season. He and Eddie, when they were kids, would have picked all the bushes clean had his mother not taught them the right way, to only take what you need.

Charlie thought about what his mother had told him before he'd gone to live with his father in Seattle. Even when he was away from Palalla land, he should remember to thank the Creator for the gifts He'd given, the water and the land and all they provided.

Charlie kept his eyes closed and tried to imagine the forest through his grandfather's eyes. He pictured a web of green over his head, drinking in the sunlight above. He tried to feel the presence of the massive trunks surrounding him, tried to imagine them—how would Grandfather have said it—sustaining life in their knots and hollows, their sturdy branches reaching up, their thick roots spreading out into the soil, grounding each tree in the earth. *Mother Earth,* Grandfather called her.

Should he try saying something to Mother Earth now, or to the Creator? He stood and waited, trying to open his mind to peaceful thoughts.

His eyes snapped open at the blare of a horn. He turned around to see a giant logging truck curving around the side of his Ford. He should have pulled farther over. He jogged back to his truck, started it and pulled back onto the road.

Charlie shifted in his seat. "Get your head straight," he muttered. Even if those trees had moved—which he had probably just imagined—it didn't matter: he wasn't one with the land. Calling up the Creator for comfort wasn't like turning on a faucet, and even if it was, he didn't want to be that bum friend who shows up only when he needs something. He'd seen enough of that crap in Seattle.

Charlie slowed as he neared his cabin. He checked the clock in the dash. He and Eddie had looked at a map to figure out where the poachers' trail might have started. And he still had some daylight.

He rolled past his turnoff, staying on the main road as it wound through the hills. He took the second turn on the left and kept his eyes peeled for tamped-down grass and breaks in the treeline. Before long, he found a flattened patch with several sets of fresh tire tracks leading into the forest.

Charlie stopped and lowered his window. All quiet. He shifted into four-wheel drive, then bumped off the main road and followed the tracks into the woods. Pebbles and twigs popped under his tires and pinged against the undercarriage. The trail was narrow, but it looked pretty well-traveled.

Charlie heard the SUV before he saw it crawling toward him on the trail. "Shit!" he hissed, slamming on the breaks. Poachers wouldn't dare come back; must be an investigator. And they'd probably wonder what he was looking for back at the scene of the accident. He clenched the steering wheel. There was no room to pull over, so it was on him to make way.

Charlie shoved his truck into reverse and looped an arm around the passenger seat to back out of the forest. The maroon SUV rolled forward with him like a lumbering dance partner. As soon as Charlie angled out onto the road, the SUV rolled by him without stopping. He only caught a profile of the driver as he passed, an older-looking guy wearing a baseball cap and shades. It was odd that the man didn't acknowledge him, the only other human being for miles. But he didn't mind—he didn't need anyone stopping him and asking what he wanted there.

Charlie shifted into drive and rolled back onto the path. He passed the place where the truck had crashed. The vehicle itself had been removed, but the area still contained police tape and debris. In another forty yards he reached the clearing where the second poacher had lain. Broken strips of police tape hung from a couple of trees surrounding the entrance.

He pulled in and climbed out of his Ford, trying to ignore his nerves. What was it they said, *the killer always returns to the scene of the crime?* Wouldn't look good for him, after all their questions.

Charlie slammed his door shut and straightened his back. He shouldn't feel like a trespasser. This was Indian country, and he had his own questions that needed answering.

He walked up to the twisted, jagged stump of the tree that had killed the poacher. Just a couple of weeks before, there had been screaming, and thrashing, and cracking of trees. He squatted to get a closer look at the stump, just as he had knelt to look at the dead man's boot two weeks before. He hadn't known it at the time, but the body here had been the Palalla man, the one about to steal from his own people. Charlie wasn't a vengeful man, but he couldn't help but see some sort of justice there.

The mound of sawdust and splintered wood had been cleared away, and he could now trace the cuts in the stump with his fingers. The cuts were shallow, nowhere near deep enough to have felled the tree by themselves. He looked up at the pines and firs standing tall around him in the impossibly tight space where the tree had fallen. Frowning, he thought back to the videos he'd watched with Eddie. These men had sawed in the right places. Even if the cuts had been deep enough, that tree should have fallen out into the clearing, not into the forest.

"What happened here?" he whispered. His only answers were the twitter of birds, the crackle of a rodent skittering over ground cover, and the gentle rustle of wind in the leaves above.

CHAPTER 7

TAMIA SAT AT her desk, one hand holding the phone, the other hand propping up her head. She really shouldn't have called this woman. She should have just left it alone, but she hadn't, and now she couldn't get crazy tree lady off the line.

Maybe sharing her cubicle with a philodendron named Harvey had clouded her judgment. Tamia's curiosity had gotten the better of her, and she'd started tracking down contact info on some of the alleged "victims" of tree activity. She'd approached it with an arm's-length curiosity, like UFOs, until a rare quiet moment in the office had prompted her to call one of them. The first person on her list was Mrs. Lemuelson, the woman who had purportedly been smacked by a Pacific yew while locking her bike to it. The longer Tamia listened to her, the more sympathetic she was to the tree's alleged reaction.

"So I reported it to the city," harped Mrs. Lemuelson. "But they refuse to take action; say they examined it and it's perfectly healthy, and they can't just chop down a healthy tree. Wanted proof it was sick, so I showed them my bruise, but they said that wasn't sufficient."

"Yes, I understand, but—"

"What kind of government is that, that won't take responsibility for its own property? It's city property, you know, it wasn't on anyone's lawn. I wouldn't just walk up to someone's house and start locking up my bike, you know."

"No, of course not."

"So then the city should take care of it, right? Can you believe they asked me if I had a video of it? A video.

Like I'm walking around waiting for trees to attack me. Isn't that ridiculous?"

"Yeah, that is a little—"

"But now that I *know* to keep an eye out, I can't get it to do it anymore. I went back there, you can believe it. But it won't move anymore. I can push and kick all I want, but it won't budge!"

"Well, that's—"

"I know, that's strange. Very strange. I'm so glad you called me, Tammy."

"It's Tamia."

"That tree needs to be removed, Tanya, but the city council won't listen to me. I've even brought it up with the mayor, but he just sends me back to the city. Even my husband—my own husband—is telling me to drop it, but I won't. I can't! What if someone else gets hurt?"

Tamia had just about given up any hope of a graceful exit when her computer bleeped. It was an instant message from Rima, the staff supervisor, asking Tamia to come see her.

"Excuse me, Mrs. Lemuelson," said Tamia. "I'm being called into a meeting."

"Oh, but—"

"This has been very informative. If you manage to catch the tree in the act, please send me the video."

"But will you—"

"I'm sorry, I really have to go now, but feel free to get in touch if there are any future developments."

"Well, how can I reach you?"

Tamia gave her the governor's general constituent e-mail address. There was no way she was giving this woman her direct e-mail.

Tamia smoothed down her hair and headed to Rima's office. The door was open. She rapped on the doorframe.

"Hi, Tamia, come in. Close the door, would you?"

Uh-oh.

"Have a seat," said Rima, adjusting her glasses.

Tamia donned her poker face as she sat down.

"I'm sorry I've had to put you on constituent e-mails so often recently," said Rima. "Our current intern isn't working out, but we have another one coming in this week."

"That's okay."

"Well, I still want to thank you for your flexibility. But, while we're on the subject of constituent e-mails . . ." Rima laced her fingers together. "As you know, I spot-check these things, and I noticed a couple of typos."

Tamia's face felt warm.

"I realize general inquires can be tedious," said Rima. "But the job still has to be done right. This is the face of the governor's office here, and we can't afford to put out sloppy work."

"Yes, I understand. I'm sorry."

"If you recall, we have those special funds for training. We could sign you up for a course in business writing."

Yes, she remembered the special training funds. They were part of the diversity program they'd touted when they'd hired her, along with the mentorship program, which would actually be great, but had yet to materialize. "No, thank you, I don't think that will be necessary. I just wasn't as focused as I should have been."

Rima readjusted her glasses. "It's surprising, considering how well you did at school. Your transcript was excellent."

"I'm sorry. I'll pay more attention in the future," said Tamia, cheeks burning.

Rima nodded. "I'm glad to hear that. But I'd like you to start sending me a draft of your external correspondence before you send it out."

"Excuse me?"

"Not everything. Internal messages aren't an issue, just anything with external agencies."

"Is this a new office-wide policy?"

Rima clicked her pen. "Tamia, it's my job to supervise staff, and to step in when I see a need for correction. So, no, this isn't for everyone. And it's just until you can show me I don't have to worry about it."

All this over a couple of typos? She hadn't had to get her correspondence cleared since her first month on the job. Tamia racked her brain for anything else she might have done wrong.

"Well," said Rima, "that's what I wanted to cover with you. Do you have anything for me?"

"No, thank you," she answered, careful to keep her voice even. She rose and walked stiffly out of Rima's office, ignoring Greg's inquisitive glance on her way back to her cube.

Tamia raked her mouse across its pad and stared at her screen. What had just happened? She was a college graduate; she didn't need some kind of remedial writing class. And she didn't need to be micromanaged. Everybody made mistakes; she'd seen enough of the interns'—and Greg's, for that matter—in the constituent e-mail outbox to know. Were they all getting "special" training and scrutiny?

She shook her head and jiggled her mouse. She had to stay cool. She just had to keep working. Harder. This is what her mom meant when she said *you have to be twice as good to be equal.* No one was going to call her incompetent.

Her fingers hovered above the keyboard. Her head felt like a blazing coal, and she clamped her lips to keep them steady. She had fishery research to finish by tomorrow—but her brain was all twisted up.

Tamia stood up abruptly. She marched to the ladies' room and shut herself into a stall. *Count, breathe, don't overreact.* Rima was being extreme, but on the other hand, Tamia didn't want to risk the "angry black woman" label less than a year into the job. She was conspicuous enough in the virtual sea of whiteness at the office—"the label" would not help.

This wasn't necessarily about race, anyway. Maybe they just had to use up their "special" training funds. And she had been careless, after all; she'd let herself get distracted.

Tamia dabbed at her eyes and listened to make sure she was alone in the bathroom. She left her stall, ran cool water over a paper towel and pressed it to her cheeks. Her light brown skin had taken on a cinnamon tinge—light enough to betray a blush, but still dark enough to be an issue?

She closed her eyes. *Stop.*

Even if this whole thing was unfair, she didn't have time to waste sitting around being pissed off about it. It was up to her to prove she was focused and capable. No more wasting time on crazy tree ladies. She just had to concentrate and work her way out of this hole.

CHAPTER 8

RICKY TROMPED THROUGH the woods with Viola close behind. She was younger than him, and a girl, but she was the only other kid in town whose family was back from vacation—and he wasn't supposed to go into the woods alone.

"Come on, Ricky," she whispered. "Show me the secret!"

"Okay, stop here." He couldn't remember exactly where he'd been the other time anyway, so here was good enough. He looked up and spun around. "Okay, trees, go!"

Nothing happened.

"We're here!" he yelled. "Go!"

Still nothing.

"What do they do?" asked Viola.

"Just wait. It's a surprise. Come on, trees!" He picked out a greyish-brown oak and put both hands on its trunk. The scaly bark dug into his palms as he pushed against it.

Viola crossed her arms. "This is stupid. Let's play something else."

"No, wait!" Ricky frowned and kicked the tree. "Come on, tree!" He kicked it over and over until an acorn fell on his head.

Viola giggled and kicked the oak too. An acorn fell on her head. She squealed and kept kicking until another one came down.

Ricky smiled and kicked the tree ninja-style. More acorns pelted them from above, along with a shower of dust and leaves. Ricky laughed and kicked. The acorns kept coming and coming until he couldn't even look up anymore

"Ow! Stop!" Viola backed away, arms over her head.

Ricky had felt it too. The acorns weren't just falling anymore; it felt like they were being thrown. He stopped kicking, and the shower of acorns trickled to a halt within seconds.

"Wow!" Viola had stopped cowering. A grin melted across her face. Ricky was on a roll. He looked around to see what else he could do to impress her.

"Watch this." He picked up a rock with a sharp edge and thwacked it into the trunk. He got in a second hit before the ground started to rumble.

Ricky looked at Viola. Her expression hovered between excitement and terror.

The soil under his sneakers churned as he chipped into the bark a third, fourth and fifth time. A slender, white root plunged up from the earth and snaked toward him. Viola screamed. Ricky fell backward and the root wrapped itself around his ankle. He yelled and pulled at the root, which grew thicker in his hands and branched off into more tendrils wrapping further up his leg.

Viola ran and knelt next to him. She pulled up the leg of his jeans and tried to untangle the twisting ends of the root while Ricky banged at its fibrous stalk with his rock. Several saplings at the base of the tree began to flail, whipping around their faces. Viola shrieked and shielded her eyes. As the tips of the root twined up toward Ricky's knee, he pulled at them with one hand and whacked at the thrashing saplings with the other. He finally dropped his rock to cover his eyes.

The saplings swayed to a stop as soon as the rock hit the soil. Ricky froze and the root halted its march up his leg. Viola whimpered. Ricky raised his trembling hands toward the sky like a cornered criminal on TV. The root loosened its grip on his leg.

Viola stared at him with saucer-wide eyes, mouth frozen open. Once again, everything was still.

Ricky poked the root with his finger. Nothing happened. He touched it again. Nothing. He held his breath and pulled the floppy, white roots away from his leg. His heart was pounding, but not just from fear. Sure, that was scary, but they stopped, so maybe he tamed them.

And that would be so cool!

He grinned up at Viola. He'd discovered this awesome thing, and now she'd seen it too, so she could prove he discovered it. They could do experiments, he and Viola. They hadn't tried karate chops yet. Maybe he could borrow his mom's phone and film their experiments.

Viola screamed—and that was when Ricky knew he was going to be in *big* trouble.

Viola turned and ran away from the monstrous oak. Ricky jumped up and ran after her. "Viola!" He was going to be in *so* much trouble. "Viola, you're going the wrong way!"

She stopped and waited, shifting her weight from foot to foot.

"Viola, don't tell, okay?"

"Ricky, let's go!" she pleaded, scanning the ground for suspicious roots.

"Please, don't tell. I'll get in trouble!"

"Okay, let's just go!"

They ran back through the woods toward his house. Ricky stopped at the edge of his neighbor's yard and looked across to his own. *Dang!* His dad was outside with the weed whacker.

Viola plowed into his back. He turned around and put his finger over his lips. They'd have to sneak out to the street, then circle back around his house as though—

His father glanced up from his trimming. "Hey, buddy. Hello, Viola."

"Hi, Mr. Nystrom." Viola shot a glance at Ricky.

"Come here, guys." His father turned off the weed whacker and scrutinized them as they approached. "Weren't you supposed to be at Viola's house?"

"We were," said Ricky. And what could be safer, right? Viola lived just around the corner, and they really had been there—at first.

"So why are you all covered in leaves?"

Ricky looked down at his sweater and batted a leaf away. He held his breath, unable to look up at his dad. He could say that they went out to play in Viola's yard, which they did. And he could say that they decided to take a shortcut to his house, which they had. The shortcut just happened to be longer than the usual way.

"I . . . I have to go home now," stammered Viola. "Bye, Ricky!" She took off running around the side of the house.

Ricky's father looked after her before turning back to him. "Come here."

Ricky shuffled over and his father bent on one knee to face him. "Be honest: were you in the woods again?"

"Yeah, Dad," he admitted, his voice quiet. "But not alone."

He paused. "You're going to be a lawyer, aren't you?" He kept her eyes trained on Ricky's. "Listen, when I tell you not to go out there alone, that doesn't mean take a six-year-old kid. Got it?"

He nodded.

"All right. Because I'm not going to let you get both of us in trouble with your mom." His eyes softened. "Maybe I need to get one of those invisible fences." He circled his hands gently around Ricky's throat. "Collar should be big enough."

Ricky smirked and batted his father's hands away.

"You're right. No collar. The neighbors would talk. We could hide an anklet though."

"Dad!" Ricky couldn't suppress a giggle.

"Okay, then, not yet," he said with a smile. "Look, I think it's great that you like to be out in the forest, but not without a partner in crime." He stood up and swatted dirt off his pants. "Maybe your grampa can come over and go exploring with you, tell you all about the trees out there."

Ricky sucked in a breath. "Does he know about the trees?"

"Yeah, buddy, he's a botanist. And he specializes in trees. You knew that."

"Oh, yeah." Grampa knew about trees, but not about *his* trees. And after seeing Viola freak out, Ricky had second thoughts about sharing his secret with anyone else.

CHAPTER 9

A MERE SIXTY miles west of Olympia, Tamia felt like she'd driven straight into the Mesozoic era. After making good time on the highway, she'd spent the past twenty minutes jostling down a gravel road between walls of towering, moss-covered trees and ferns as tall as her old Toyota's windows. This was truly a fitting habitat for a retired botanist.

Dr. Barbara Block, Professor Emeritus of the University of Washington's School of Environmental and Forest Sciences, had finally contacted her. Tamia had written to her during her initial zeal about the plant project. She regretted it now, but given that she'd used the implied interest of the governor's office to get a response, trying to ignore her at this point might create even more complications.

And to be honest, the botanist's secrecy had intrigued Tamia. Dr. Block hadn't wanted to talk on the phone or exchange e-mails either. She only wanted to speak in person, and since this wasn't strictly government business, Tamia had canceled her Saturday hair appointment and scheduled a visit with Dr. Block.

Of course, this could turn out to be another waste of time, like her phone call with Mrs. Lemuelson. What if the scientist turned out to be a crazy old cat lady who just wanted company? Although, a botanist would probably have an army of houseplants instead of cats. Well, if nothing else, it was a chance to get out into a new forest she hadn't explored yet.

Tamia finally reached Dr. Block's driveway at the end of the gravelly road. She parked and smoothed her hair down in the rear view mirror before getting out of the car.

She followed a short path to a modest bungalow, then knocked on the door and waited. Given how out of date faculty directory photos usually were, she was expecting to be eye-level with a wiry halo of white hair. But when the door swung open, Tamia was surprised to have to tilt her head up slightly to look Dr. Block in the eye.

The botanist extended her hand. "Tamia, good to meet you."

Tamia smiled. Dr. Block actually remembered how to pronounce her name. "It's a pleasure to meet you too." She shook the scientist's hand. "Thank you again for seeing me."

Dr. Block's smile revealed straight, strong-looking teeth. Her eyes were bright and her salt and pepper hair was pulled back into a thick ponytail. She was wearing cargo pants and a T-shirt with a pocketed vest over it, and she looked down approvingly at Tamia's long hiking pants and sturdy shoes.

"Let's get going, shall we?" Dr. Block picked up a backpack by the door and stepped outside, waving Tamia over to her truck. "Hop in."

"Where are we heading?" Although, it was a little bit late to be wary now, wasn't it? She was already out in the middle of nowhere with someone she didn't know.

"It's not far," said the older woman. "It was right under my nose the whole time."

As the truck jostled down the gravel road, Dr. Block reached behind her seat to rummage around in her backpack. She pulled out a bottle of water for Tamia. "It's the closest I can get to offering you a cup of tea."

Tamia blushed, thinking about her mistaken image of Dr. Block as a little old tea-sipping cat lady. "Thanks."

"So tell me, why did you contact me in particular?"

"Well, to be honest," said Tamia, "I contacted a few people, but you got back to me first."

Dr. Block laughed tersely. "Who else did you try?"

"Um, a guy named Nelson and a woman—Brady."

Dr. Block nodded. "And they'll both hand you off to their research assistants, who will give you as much time as the governor's office should get, out of courtesy, but not a minute more. They're 'serious' scientists," she said, puffing up her chest in a caricature of pride. "They don't go in for a bunch of hocus pocus."

"Do you?"

"Maybe it's not just hocus pocus." Dr. Block glanced at Tamia before turning back to the road. "Don't worry, I'm not crazy."

"Of course not," said Tamia, wondering if this was the kind of thing people heard just before they disappeared forever.

"I can't verify any of the incidents you're asking about, but I can tell you that trees are capable of a lot more than most people think they are."

"Like what?"

"Like . . ." She glanced over at Tamia again. "Well, everyone knows that plants and trees respond to their environments in many ways. Flowers open to the sun, leaves turn color and drop in the fall, the growth rate and shape of trees are affected by water and wind as well as light."

She slowed to take a curve and went on. "Most plants react to their environments incrementally. But some reactions happen very quickly, noticeably enough for the casual observer. Think Venus flytrap, or the 'sensitive plant,' whose leaves curl up when touched. We usually think of these interactions as reactions, like when the doctor bangs on your knee during an exam. You wouldn't think of the leg as having made a conscious decision to jump, would you?"

"No."

"Well, what would you say if I told you that trees are not just passively responding to their environments? That they are actively communicating with each other— and maybe soon with us?"

Dr. Block pulled onto the overgrown shoulder of the road and climbed out of the truck. Tamia jumped out and followed her through damp, thigh-high weeds into a wooded area.

"Research has shown," said Dr. Block, "that when certain plants are being attacked, chewed on by insects for example, they release chemical signals into the air to 'tip off' neighboring plants, which then start mounting their own defenses. Even if they aren't attacked themselves, the surrounding plants produce their own chemical inhibitors to discourage attackers. The damaged plant is effectively warning its neighbors."

"I read about this," Tamia said. "I've also read that trees communicate through this network of fungus underground. It was described as the internet for plants."

"That's right, the 'Wood Wide Web'," Dr. Block said, crooking her fingers into quotation marks. She rolled her eyes. "I hate that name. Anyway, yes, trees share nutrients and information through these mycorrhizal networks underground. We can't actually tap the line to hear what they're saying, but we do know that they swap sugars, and they seem to signal changes in environmental conditions to other trees in the network."

Dr. Block unzipped her backpack and produced a small metal box attached to a flat, woven strap. "You may have heard about the Grenoble team—the university lab in France that has developed the ability to listen in on the xylem, or circulatory system, of trees."

"Right," said Tamia. "They hear a popping sound when trees aren't getting enough water."

Dr. Block smiled. "You've been doing your homework. Here, hold this up there for a moment." Tamia held the box against the smooth, mottled trunk of an alder while Dr. Block walked the strap around and cinched it up. "As you probably know, the pressure of the water being pulled up through the trunk creates air bubbles when there isn't enough water in the root system, like when you're drinking out of a straw and have reached the bottom of your drink."

"And you can hear it with this machine?" asked Tamia.

"Have a listen." Dr. Block hooked a clunky set of earphones into the box and handed them to her. The older woman spoke over the faint, burbling crackle streaming through the headphones into Tamia's ears:

"We call this machine a circulatory translator. It has an internal processor to slow down and magnify the sound so we can actually hear it. Now hold still for a moment, and tell me what you hear."

Tamia stood silently with the headphones on. In less than a minute, the fizzy popping subsided to nothing. "I can't hear anything now."

As soon as she spoke, the headphones started gurgling again.

"It started up again, didn't it?" asked Dr. Block. "Cavitation—that popping sound—isn't supposed to just stop and start like that. And with all the rain we've gotten this summer, these trees should not want for water. So why that sound? Listen again."

They stayed silent until the bubbling stopped again. "And now?" asked Dr. Block. The cavitation crackled back to life.

Dr. Block took the headset off Tamia. "Let's do a little experiment. Would you go over to that other Douglas fir and whisper something?" She pointed about 50 yards ahead. "Just whisper. Don't say it loud enough for me to hear. And don't say anything you wouldn't want me to hear."

Tamia felt a bit silly, but set off toward the tree Dr. Block had picked out.

"Oh, and face away from me when you say it!" yelled Dr. Block. "And make sure it's something I couldn't possibly know."

"Okay!" she yelled back. She usually had a pretty good sense about people, and Dr. Block didn't seem like a wacko. Her opinion might change, however, depending on what this little eco-magic trick was all about. Tamia whispered her piece to the fir and tromped back over to Dr. Block.

"Is this what you said?" asked the scientist, pointing at the display on the metal box.

AND I GAVE UP MY RELAXER FOR THIS

Tamia felt her face grow warm. "How did you—" She stopped and watched her new words populate the screen.

HOW DID YOU

"Not 'How did *I.*' How did *they*?" the older woman asked, gesturing at the trees around them.

"Someone must have mic-ed this forest," said Tamia.

THIS FOREST rolled out onto the screen.

"I thought you might say that," Dr. Block said, unstrapping the device from the alder. "Here, speak into it."

Tamia did, but her words failed to register. She narrowed her eyes and looked at Dr. Block.

"Take it. You try it." She pressed the box into Tamia's hands.

Tamia held the box up against the tree while Dr. Block walked away and whispered into the forest. Tamia couldn't hear anything, but the machine scrolled out the older woman's words:

OVER MANY A QUAINT AND CURIOUS VOLUME OF FORGOTTEN LORE

"What the hell is this?" Tamia breathed.

WHAT THE HELL IS THIS ticked out onto the display.

Dr. Block came back and took the machine out of Tamia's hands. "*This* is a very sensitive matter," she said softly, holding the metal box up for emphasis. "I'm not supposed to have it anymore, and if they knew . . ." She returned the machine to her backpack. "Come with me," she said, guiding Tamia toward the truck.

Tamia climbed into the truck and shut the door. She didn't know what to think. Dr. Block had seemed so rational until now. But secret equipment? Some mysterious "they"?

"I don't think anyone's listening," said the older woman, "but you can't be too careful. And since you contacted me, I believe now is the time to come forward— as long as I can get some cover from the governor."

Tamia's face flushed. "Cover for what? What is this?"

"I believe," said Dr. Block, "that this is the future of domestic surveillance."

"Come again?"

"Simply put, surveillance trees."

Okay, thought Tamia, *all aboard the crazy train.*

"You know the popping sound you heard?" asked Dr. Block. "My lab was working for a number of years on ways to harness and channel that sound. Our work was protected, whereas the French team was able to make theirs public."

"You're telling me you've been working on a secret surveillance project involving spy trees?" The air in Dr. Block's truck began to feel close.

"No, not directly," answered the scientist. "At least, not to my knowledge. But I have reason to believe that someone else was."

"Who?"

Dr. Block cocked her head. "Think about it. Who would be interested in developing an undetectable, untraceable way of listening in on people?"

"I don't know," stammered Tamia. "Lots of people. There are security cameras all over the place." She'd never thought much about it before, and now that she did, it made her deeply uncomfortable. Who exactly was watching those cameras?

Dr. Block nodded. "Yes, but who would have the resources to put into something as speculative and potentially dangerous as biological surveillance, something that would require a massive outlay of resources? And whose budget is always the last to get cut?"

Tamia thought for a second. "Defense?"

The scientist said nothing, but her grim look told Tamia she'd guessed correctly.

"I don't know, this is all so . . ."

"Far-fetched?" Dr. Block said. "Improbable? Unconstitutional? All of the above, if you ask me."

"Exactly," said Tamia. "So why would they even try it? Especially now. Can you imagine the backlash if people found out the government was trying to invent trees that picked up every word they said?"

"Not just trying, they already have. This didn't start yesterday. No, it started years ago, back when the ends justified the means. You remember, after 9/11 it was all about security. Nobody gave a flip about privacy."

"How long has this been going on?" Tamia asked. "I mean, assuming that it's really the trees—which I still . . ." She trailed off, unable to think of another explanation for what she'd just seen.

Dr. Block hesitated. "I have an idea how this might have happened, but I'd need some assurances before coming forward. I'd be risking, at the very least, my professional reputation—likely much more. In order to do that, I'd need some powerful people on my side. Like the governor."

Tamia swallowed hard. The cab was getting warmer.

"I know this sounds insane," said the older woman. "But this isn't just about one little patch of trees out in the boonies. I've traced this trait in several other sections of the forest, and with several different species. Every day that I go out there, I find new areas that have changed."

Tamia was silent. This couldn't be happening.

"I can't keep doing this alone," pressed Dr. Block. "It's too big. We need more people on this, more resources. Whatever mutation this is, we need to find out how far it's spread."

"We?" asked Tamia, eyes wide.

"You sought me out," Dr. Block reminded her. "You said the governor wanted my help, didn't you?" The scientist held Tamia's eyes for an uncomfortable length of time before she started the truck and pulled back out on to the road. "I'm sure he'll want a full report," she said deliberately. "So let's get back to my office and figure out where we go from here."

Neither woman spoke on the drive back to the cabin. Tamia had no doubt Dr. Block was perceptive enough to have seen through her. She must have figured out that the governor hadn't sent her out here. One call from the scientist to the governor's office, innocent or otherwise, would probably get her canned for misrepresenting the office. Tamia couldn't just slink out the back door and pretend her visit had never happened—and at the moment, she had too many questions to want to.

CHAPTER 10

CHARLIE PEERED ALONG the barrel of his Marlin 30-30 at one of the cans he'd lined up on top of a log. His legs were shoulder-width apart, left side facing the target, right finger hovering over the trigger. The stock of the rifle was pressed to his cheek, the butt snug against his shoulder, still tender from the previous day's practice.

He tried different stances, attempting to recall which one Uncle Virgil had said was best. How old was he on those hunting trips, eleven or twelve? All he really remembered was getting hammered by the rifle butt back then too. And then Eddie'd say something like, "Deer got nothin' to worry about with Charlie around," and then he'd laugh his laugh—*haw haw haw!* Charlie started calling him "Crow," then "Crow Butt," to which Eddie responded by calling him "Buckshot," then "Great Blind Hunter." The fists came out and his uncle tried letting them knock a little sense into each other before he stepped in to separate them. The nicknames stopped there, along with the hunting trips.

Charlie braced himself and pressed the trigger. Wood splintered next to his target. He swung the lever out and back and aimed again. This time when he pressed the trigger, the can flew off the log. He went on to hit six out of eight. His heart swelled. Here was something he could do without running to Eddie for help.

Charlie cleared up his target range, cleaned his rifle, and put it away. Hitting a couple of cans on a log didn't necessarily mean he could hunt down lunch, so he grabbed his fishing gear and climbed into his truck. As he wound down the series of switchbacks to the main road, he thought about his last conversation with Eddie. His cousin had asked a couple of times what he wanted to do next in life. It was almost like Eddie was trying to get him out of the cabin. Had someone hassled Eddie about hiring him? Why would he suddenly be a problem, now that they had proof of illegal logging? Deterring poachers was supposed to be the whole point of his being here.

He pulled over to the shoulder and grabbed his equipment from the truck bed, then pushed aside looping arcs of vine maple as he headed down the slope to the creek. When he reached the riverbank, he readied his pole and cast out, relaxing as soon as the line hit the water. This is exactly where he wanted to be. He wasn't ready to leave the woods yet. He still hadn't made a plan. No matter what Eddie suggested—the casino, construction, helping out at the Cultural Center—Charlie could always think of a reason it wouldn't work.

He just wanted to be out *here*, away from everything and everyone. He didn't even have a phone at the cabin, just the radio for emergencies. No one could stick their noses in, call him up and get into his head. Especially Jenna. She kept trying to track him down, but why the hell did she want him back? Sure, he'd loved her—maybe still did a little—but he couldn't think about her without going back to the drinking, the fighting, the tears running down her cheeks. The cops knocking on their door. The fury burning inside him as they scrutinized him, asked their questions. The fear in her eyes when they left.

A mosquito buzzed around Charlie's ear. He slapped at it and noticed his line had grown slack. He reeled it back in, set his rod by the bucket and climbed back up to the road, feet heavy with residual guilt. As he rummaged around in the cab for insect repellent, the sound of another vehicle raised his head. A maroon SUV rounded the bend. It looked like the same vehicle he'd seen before, and as it passed him, it looked like the same guy driving.

Forest Service? he wondered, dousing himself with bug dope. *Another investigator?* He'd have to say something to Eddie next time he was back in town. How much more snooping around were they going to do?

He headed back down to the river, cast out again and watched his line grow taut with the current. One corner of his mouth lifted. This was pretty much what Jenna would expect him to be doing, he supposed. "What's it like on the Reservation?" she would always ask. "I bet you do a lot of hunting and fishing, don't you? How do you say 'I love you' in your language? Can we go visit?"

He kept putting her off, saying it was so far away, or he didn't have time or gas money, or it wasn't a good time to go. But he finally relented. They took a long weekend and drove the three hours over the pass and down to Nakalish, where he'd grown up. Even though he'd told her what to expect, he sensed her vague confusion about this small, sunbaked Rez town ringed by a checkerboard of dusty sagebrush and lush, irrigated crops. There were probably more cows than humans, and of the humans, more Whites and Hispanics than Native Americans. What's more, the town council had embraced a Westward Expansion motif with murals of cowboys and covered wagons as a way to boost tourism—on an Indian Reservation. He'd waited in vain for her comments on the irony of that initiative.

They'd stayed with his cousin Sherman on the outskirts of town, where the houses were a little shabbier, the strays scrappier, the cars visibly third- and fourth-hand. Charlie had cautioned her against asking Sherman what he did for a living, and had told Sherman to lay off his usual jokes about living the high life on government cheese. And no, Jenna said, she didn't mind having to use a wrench to turn on the shower, in fact, she'd lived in a house like that once herself. Still, Charlie had spent the entire weekend on edge, tuned for the first sign of disappointment on her face, the slightest tone of pity in any glance or observation. The only time that weekend he'd felt relaxed was when they escaped the heat of the valley and took his truck up into the mountains. He'd never forget the delight on her face when he drove her past spring-green foliage flanked by snowbanks in June. He'd finally shown her something worth seeing.

Charlie's pole jumped in his hands, and he reeled in a nice, fat trout. He cast in again and was able to catch enough for that night and the next morning. After gutting the fish and slipping the entrails back into the river, he rinsed his hands in the cold current and climbed back up to his truck. Once he'd loaded everything, he cranked on the stereo and started back to the cabin.

As he steered up the switchbacks, he thought about trying some hot sauce with the fish, or maybe throwing in spaghetti sauce for a change. As thankful as he was for the trout and sunfish, what he really craved was a good steak and a beer. He grunted and shook his head. *Forget about the beer, dummy.* Better to obsess over food than think about drinking and Jenna and all the damage he'd done.

A white truck came into view, and as it passed him he saw the U.S. Forest Service insignia on the side door. Then, who was that other guy in the SUV? Lots of folks prowling around here, it seemed. Maybe Eddie was right about there being too much traffic since the accident to worry about more poaching.

Charlie pulled up to the cabin and cut the engine. He sat still for a moment, listening to the motor tick as it cooled.

Maybe he did need to start thinking about his life beyond the forest.

CHAPTER 11

"TAMIA, BABY," SAID her mother over the phone. "When are you coming home for a visit?"

Tamia stood in her little backyard garden in Olympia, nudging a wilted tomato plant with her toe. "I don't know, maybe in a couple of weeks."

"Why not this weekend? DeShaun's got a home game."

"Mama, why do you let him play?" Tamia worried about her brother every time he stepped onto the football field.

"You got to do your track. This is what *he* wants to do."

"Well, you can't get a concussion from track," grumbled Tamia, bending over to pull up a weed.

"Tamia, he's a kicker."

"Still. Anyway, I can't come up to Seattle this weekend, but tell De-De to be safe."

"I will, Sweet T," she chuckled. "So how's your garden doing?"

Tamia looked around at stunted lettuce and chewed-up carrot tops. "Oh, okay, I guess. So, you know this botanist woman I told you about? The one with the talking trees?"

"Oh, Tamia," sighed her mother, "I don't know why you had to go out there. You didn't know that woman. You could have wound up chopped into pieces!"

"Mama, I'm fine. She's not crazy." In fact, Tamia felt a little nuts herself for still not knowing what to think. Dr. Block had sounded absolutely rational while explaining something completely insane. "I don't know what to do now. I feel like I have to be at the office all the time to make sure she doesn't call up and talk to anyone else. I mean, it can't be for real, can it? What if she's just trying to get funding, and everyone finds out I got tricked by some woman with a microphone in a box?"

"Curiosity is not a bad thing." Tamia loved the rich, comforting sound of her mother's voice. It was like an audible hug. "And they gave you the assignment in the first place."

"But the assignment's over, Mom."

"And yet you're still paying attention to the issue, working on your own time. They should appreciate your dedication. Well, boss lady won't, but we already know what her problem is."

Tamia sighed. She really shouldn't have called home the same day as her talk with Rima. She should have let it settle first. "Come on, now, she's not really racist."

"Oh, did she apologize for singling you out?"

"No, it's not like that," said Tamia, leaning over to pull up another weed. "I messed up and she's on my ass. And I got mad because I was embarrassed. That's all."

"You said it yourself, you're the only black person in that office."

"Not the only one. There's the chief of staff, remember? Derrick Jones, I told you about him." Not that Tamia had ever actually talked to him. He was nominally her mentor, but the mentorship program seemed to exist only on paper.

"Well, you're one of too few," said her mother. "And you're the only one who's being called out on minor mistakes."

"I don't know that for sure. Maybe she talked to the others too. Not everything has to be about race."

"Baby, you can't just wish it away. I told you, you have to work twice as hard—"

"I know, Mom. But look, this botanist lady is the bigger problem right now. If she tells anyone else at work about 'the project,' they'll be like, 'What project?' and I'll be like, 'Dang, I wish I still had a job.'"

"So why don't you just tell her there's no project?"

72

"What if I tell her that, and she lodges a complaint?" Tamia asked. "That would be even worse. I mean, I kind of used the office to get her attention in the first place. Wouldn't you be pissed?"

"They gave you the assignment. All you did was research it more than you had to. I guess you just worked twice as hard in the wrong direction," she said, adding slyly, "But they didn't tell you *not* to contact anyone, did they?"

"No."

"So you should be okay, unless . . ." Her mother's voice went deeper. "Unless you think there might be something to it."

"What, you mean, do I believe in talking trees?" Tamia asked defensively.

"I don't know. I'm just trying to figure out why you can't let this go."

"Because . . . Because . . ." Why *couldn't* she just ignore Dr. Block? Had past government surveillance scandals made her cynical enough to believe they would actually develop "spy trees"? It was bad enough that everything you said or wrote could be traced through your phone or your computer. She didn't want to imagine a world where you could never get away from surveillance, not even alone in nature. Maybe she just wanted to debunk Block's theory so she wouldn't have to think about that nightmare anymore.

"I don't know," said Tamia, brightening her tone to change the subject. All this thinking in circles wasn't doing any good. "I just like to consider all sides of an issue. Anyway, don't worry about it." She pulled at more weeds, adding to the clump in her hand.

"Mm-hmm. Well, you're going to have to decide. If it were me," she said, slipping into her *I don't want to tell you what to do, but I'm about to tell you what to do* voice. "If this scientist called again and still didn't make any sense, I'd cut her loose. Just tell her I was doing research and now it's done. And then I'd go up to Seattle and visit my family, go to DeShaun's game, and let my Mama relax my hair. You said it's about time, didn't you?"

"I do need a touchup," said Tamia, fingering her kinky roots. "But I can't, Mama." She hesitated, knowing this wasn't going to go over well. "I'm going out there again this weekend."

"What? Why?" All playfulness left her mother's voice. "Tamia, what is it you're after?"

"Some kind of proof."

Her mother exhaled sharply. "Do you believe this botanist?" she asked. "Is it worth risking your job to work with her?"

"That's what I'm going out there to find out."

"And if you think she's on to something?"

Tamia paused. "Then I'll have to come clean to my boss and report it."

"That woman?" snorted her mother. "What about your mentor, can't you talk to him?"

Tamia shook her head emphatically. "No, I can't go around Rima. That would just make things worse. I'll write up my findings and submit the proof to her through proper channels."

"And if this Dr. Block is wrong?"

"I'll talk to her. And if she tries to cause problems—I guess I'll have to face that too." Tamia straightened her back. No, it wasn't a full plan, but at least it was some kind of decision. She tossed the weeds into a corner of the yard, hoping she'd pulled enough of the roots out. Sometimes even when you thought you'd gotten rid of them, they had a way of popping back up again.

☘ CHAPTER 12

"RICKY, GRAMPA'S HERE!" His father's voice cut through the house and right into the zombie apocalypse. Ricky's shoulders slumped. There was no messing around in front of "company." He turned off his game and stood up as his father led his grandfather into the playroom.

"Come say hello to Grampa, buddy."

Ricky slow-poked up to his grandfather. The older man towered over him, taller and taller with each step he took.

"Hello, Ricky," boomed the voice from above. Ricky remained still as his grandfather leaned forward and patted him on the shoulder. "How you've grown!"

Ricky examined Grampa Nystrom's green, itchy-looking sweater and the unfamiliar folds of his face. He hardly ever saw Grampa Nystrom anymore, not since Gramma Nystrom died. Ricky missed Gramma. And the few times Grampa visited, he always looked so serious. Mom said that was because Grampa missed Gramma too.

"That game's turning him into a zombie himself," said his father.

Grampa Nystrom chuckled. "Well, we'll see what we can do about that." He bent down stiffly to meet Ricky face to face. He smelled like wool and aftershave. "I'm looking forward to our adventure today."

Ricky nodded.

"Wish I could join you," said his father. "But these software reviews won't write themselves." He clapped both of them on the shoulder as they went out the back door into the yard.

"So, Ricky, your dad tells me you've been exploring the woods around here." The older man's knees cracked as he crouched to match Ricky's height. "Sounds like you've seen some exciting things."

"I guess." Ricky shoved his hands into his jacket pockets. His dad must have told Grampa about that time he thought the trees were chasing him.

Grampa Nystrom looked at him eye to eye. "Well, trees are a great thing to be interested in, but your dad and I think it's better for you to have a research partner. So how about it?" asked his grandfather, rising and waving a hand toward the trees. "Shall we have a look?

Ricky hesitated. He wished his dad hadn't said anything to Grampa. But when he looked up to his grandfather's expectant face, he had to point the way. He just hoped Grampa wouldn't freak out like stupid Viola.

He walked double-time through the woods to keep up with his grandfather's long strides. He remembered the story his dad had told him about the time Grampa shot a fox because it had rabies. What if he thought the trees were sick too? Would he chop them down?

Grampa turned to look at Ricky. Ricky pointed again, toward some trees he hadn't "met" yet. Grampa wouldn't know.

"Do you know how to tell the trees apart?" asked Grampa Nystrom. "Would you like me to show you?" He stopped in front of a slender tree with a smooth, greyish-white trunk. Ricky gulped. It looked a little like the one that had swatted at him before.

"See the nice golden color developing here?" asked the older man, pointing up at the leaves. "They're just starting to turn. Notice the simple shape of the leaves, rounded with one point at the end. Some trees have needles, others have leaves with a bunch of points or rounded lobes, but this one is very simple. And the bark—"

Ricky stiffened. "Don't pull on it!"

Grampa Nystrom stopped and examined Ricky's face. "Don't worry, I'm not going to hurt anything."

78

Ricky looked more closely at the trunk. Maybe it wasn't the same tree after all, but there was still no telling what it would do.

"Grampa's going to do a little work here," he said, lightly patting the tree trunk. "This part isn't very interesting, so you can go off and play."

Ricky hesitated.

"Go on," said Grampa Nystrom firmly.

"Can I climb?" he asked. His mother wouldn't have allowed it.

"Yes, yes, go climb."

Ricky looked around for a big, strong tree with low branches. He'd learned that as long as you were gentle, they stayed asleep. And Grampa would think he was too busy climbing to watch him working.

He clambered up onto the first branch and pulled himself up to the next one. As he reached for the third, he felt a twig snap under his foot. "Sorry!" he whispered. It must not have hurt, because nothing happened. He made it up to the third branch and held on to the trunk while he watched.

Grampa's backpack was open on the ground, and he was facing the whitish-looking tree with his back to Ricky. He was holding something up, and he was talking. This seemed to go on forever before Grampa stopped and moved to another tree. Ricky got a glimpse of what he was holding. It was a small metallic-looking box. Grampa leaned over it and talked into it for ages before doing the same thing with another tree. Every time he switched trees, he shook his head. Ricky's curiosity eventually drove him down from the tree and over to Grampa Nystrom.

"What's that?"

The older man started and grabbed the box to his chest. He glared at Ricky and made an exasperated sound. "Weren't you supposed to be off playing?"

"I was. What's that?"

"Oh, this?" He uncovered the box and replaced his scowl with a friendly smile. "It's just something I use to see if the trees are healthy. Like a doctor listening to your heart."

"Can I listen?"

"No," said Grampa Nystrom. "All the trees are healthy, so there's nothing to listen to." He went over to his backpack and put the metal box back into it. "Where else do you play, Ricky?"

"Nowhere, just here."

Grampa Nystrom frowned a little. "Are you sure?" Ricky watched him reverse his frown again, like he was trying to be patient. "Never mind. You won't be interested in all the testing anyway. I'll just come back later. Now, do you want to know what's special about this tree here?" he asked, pointing up to the slender, white tree he'd started with.

"Special?" Ricky's eyes opened wide.

"Yes, look up at the leaves."

Ricky didn't want to look. If Grampa Nystrom knew his secret, it wouldn't feel like a secret anymore.

"Look up, look closely."

Ricky lifted his eyes to the leaves overhead. He gasped. "They're moving! But I didn't do anything!"

Grampa Nystrom laughed. "Don't worry, Ricky, no one's blaming you. This is *Populous tremuloides*, the Quaking Aspen. See that? Just the tiniest little breeze sends its leaves dancing. Remarkable, isn't it?"

Ricky smiled up into the leaves. Grampa thought they moved because of the wind. His secret was safe!

"Come on," said Grampa Nystrom, "let's go back."

He guided Ricky back through the forest, describing the differences between the trees, pointing out their coloring, the shape of their leaves, the texture of their bark and so on; telling Ricky a million different names he wouldn't remember. Ricky was relieved that their outing was almost over, so he didn't mind pretending to listen. He just wished Grampa didn't have to pluck needles and snap off twigs to show him.

His dad was out raking leaves when they got back to the yard. "There they are, our botanists!" he called out. "Want some lunch?"

"No thank you, son," answered Grampa Nystrom. "I've got to get home. But maybe next time. I'll be coming back to do some more work."

Ricky's heart plunged.

The three walked around to the front of the house. Ricky's father gave Grampa Nystrom a brisk hug, and the old man patted the boy's shoulder again before climbing into his vehicle.

"Wave goodbye to your Grampa, buddy."

From the top of the driveway, Ricky lifted his hand and waved as his grandfather's maroon SUV pulled away.

CHAPTER 13

DAMN HIS SOFT heart. He shouldn't have called Jenna back.

Charlie steered his truck up the switchbacks to his cabin, his passenger seat crammed with bags of groceries from town. The late afternoon sun flashed sideways through the trees, hitting his eyes like a strobe light. Guitars screeched out of his speakers from a radio station fading out of range. He checked his rear view mirror and took a swig from a can of beer.

Fuck her. Why can't she leave me alone?

He should have ignored her. Eddie had told him she was trying to get hold of him. The whole point of being out here was to be away from phones, away from her. But Jenna was trying to reach him, and he missed her sometimes, and Eddie had a phone, and who knew when he'd be near one again.

The sun blinded him as he curved to the west. He adjusted the sunshade and took another swig from his can.

She was crying by the end of the call. Said it wasn't his fault, none of it. It was the booze, if they could just get off it—but he could tell she'd been drinking. He wouldn't go back to that life; and why would she want him anyway? No, he couldn't go back. Didn't matter whether the poison was Seattle, the alcohol, or her. Wasn't any separating the three, she'd pretty much proven that over the phone just now.

Charlie swerved back into his lane. He had to slow down anyway; the switchbacks got tighter from here on in. He'd driven the road dozens of times by now, but you can't get too cocky driving next to a sheer drop of a couple hundred feet.

She was probably still crying, for all he knew. He was a drunk bastard when they were together and a heartless bastard for leaving. Trapped at bastard. He tipped the can up to his lips and drained it before tossing it into a grocery bag and easing a fresh beer out of its plastic harness.

Charlie looked up and edged back into his lane again. He checked his rear view mirror and tucked the can between his legs to pop it open. No matter how far away he got from her, it wasn't enough. Fucking crazy bitch, why did she even want him back, after what he did that night, the night they fought and he pushed her too hard. The night she fell and, days later, lost their unborn daughter.

She never told anyone the whole story. And no one ever asked. He hadn't touched a drop since then. Until now.

Charlie's truck wasn't holding the curve. Panic cut through the fog in his head. He jerked the wheel to the left but it was too late. His pickup skidded over the shoulder and he was airborne.

An instant later, he was engulfed in his airbag. He couldn't say he'd felt the first impact—it was too fast— but he felt another one, then a third and a fourth, each one smaller than the last. As his airbag deflated, his head flopped back and forth with the truck's movement and his groceries danced around the cab. The truck rocked to a halt.

Dazed, he tested his arms and legs to make sure he was in one piece. His pants were wet, from beer or piss or both. The radio had gone quiet. Everything was still. For the first time since his tires had left the road, he focused on the mass of green outside.

Through the cracks in his front windshield, to the back, to the sides, nothing but pine needles. Where the hell was he? He unlatched the door, but it only opened a sliver. He stuck a foot out. If he could get one leg out, he could squeeze—his foot dipped up and down, finding nothing solid. He pulled it back in and looked down through the slice of open door. There were another hundred feet of branches between him and the ground below.

The crinkle of grocery bags broke the silence; the truck began to tip again. Charlie grabbed at the steering wheel, the ceiling, the dash, fumbling for something steady. As he looked out the windshield, he realized the truck wasn't falling out of the tree—it was falling *with* the tree. The pine was tipping over, leaning in to the one next to it. He braced himself against the wheel, but just before what would have been impact, the tree he was tangled up in slowed down. It leaned against its neighbor, lowering his truck into the second pine's branches. Then, slowly, creaking and popping, the second tree arced over and leaned into a third. His truck jostled from one tree to another, each time a little closer to the earth.

Charlie's head began to tingle. He was hyperventilating, he had to slow down his breathing or he would pass out. He must be hallucinating right now.

The vehicle came to a halt ten feet from the ground in a mass of tree limbs and needles. Charlie's whole body was tensed, waiting. This might be his best chance to get out. He tested the door gingerly, freezing as the branch bobbed with the shift in weight. As soon as everything stabilized, he rolled down the window and climbed out onto the limb. There was another branch below him, within reach. Carefully, he followed a tenuous path of limbs, letting go of the last one five feet from the bottom. He stumbled backward as his feet hit the ground, landing painfully onto his back.

Charlie lay still, wincing and sucking in air while waiting for the pain to subside. He was alive. He shouldn't be, but he was. A needle fell on his forehead, then another. He opened his eyes and looked up into the undercarriage of his truck. A small shower of needles pelted him. With a start, he scrambled to his feet. A loud pop grew into a series of snaps and creaks, and he ran. He turned around just in time to see his truck slip from the pine's hold and crash to the ground.

Charlie began to tremble. The last rays of sunlight shimmered gold between the trees, surrounding him, illuminating the cloud of dust his truck had stirred up. He walked stiffly to the vehicle and freed his backpack from the scramble of glass and food in the cab. His hands were shaking so hard he could barely unzip the bag. He grabbed his emergency radio and flicked the switch. The familiar red light and warbling bleep made him weak with relief.

"Eddie?" he called. "Eddie?

He felt dizzy. He sat down with the radio in the darkening forest.

"Come in, Eddie. I need some help."

Charlie eased himself onto his back. He looked up into the dark grey branches crisscrossing against the twilight sky. He could just close his eyes and wake up from this crazy dream where drunk people drove off cliffs and got saved by trees.

"Charlie!" barked the radio.

He jerked and sat up, sending his head whirling.

"What's going on?" asked Eddie.

This was real, the crash and the trees.

"Charlie, come in. Where the hell are you?"

Charlie described his location, and Eddie told him to sit up and stay awake until help arrived. Charlie sat and waited, trying to piece together how he'd survived the fall. He looked up into the sky. The first stars of evening peeked out from between the black lace of canopy. Charlie closed his eyes. He was spinning in blackness.

CHAPTER 14

TAMIA STEPPED OUT of Dr. Block's truck into a section of forest just north of the scientist's cabin. Tamia had done her homework, rereading old articles and digging up new ones. Suspicious tree-related accidents had been reported from Bellingham down to Centralia, but the only official investigation she could find was the one into the casualties down at the Palalla Reservation. And nothing about tree speech had come up at all.

Tamia checked her cell phone battery—full and ready to film. This time she was going in with more background and a healthy skepticism. She had to either disprove Dr. Block's theory and put it to rest, or prove it and . . . what then?

She pinned her hopes on disproving it.

She joined Dr. Block near a large hemlock and held out her hand, motioning for the metal box. "Can I see that for a second?"

Tamia turned the machine over in her hands, looking at it from every side. It had an LED display and some switches and dials on the face, and a clip on each end for the strap. She peered at the headphone jack on top, then flipped it over. There was a little stethoscope-like attachment on the back, but it didn't look like any of the spy equipment she'd researched online. The dish would have to be a lot bigger to pick up her voice as far away as she had been last time—and it would have to be pointed toward her instead of pressed up against a tree. She wished she knew an engineer, someone who could come with her and look at this thing. But this was supposed to be a secret. Tamia almost regretted having said anything to her mother.

"Here, let me get it hooked up," said Dr. Block.

"Actually, can I try holding it?" asked Tamia. She placed it against the hemlock. "Is this the 'on' switch?"

"No, this one." A stream of random letters and symbols appeared on the readout. "And you adjust this dial until . . ."

The monitor continued to scroll: %*A R$D XX* THIS DIAL UNTIL

"There it is," said Dr. Block. "You want to observe first?"

"Yes, please."

YES PLEASE

Dr. Block nodded and walked off, pointing out trees and plants, stating their scientific and common names long past Tamia's earshot. Holding the machine against the tree with one hand, she turned on her phone's camera with the other. Dr. Block probably wouldn't want her recording this, but she was going to need some evidence, whether to prove or debunk this phenomenon. She filmed the machine as it mimicked the botanist, spewing out the names of every tree, bush, moss and lichen around them. Then she pointed the camera outward to capture how far away the woman was.

Tamia kept the camera rolling while she experimented with pulling the machine away from the trunk, holding it in the air, putting it against her leg, a rock, a fallen log. No matter what she did, the machine only registered speech when it was attached to the tree. She turned the camera off when she saw Dr. Block turn around and start back toward her. From the display she noted that the scientist had switched to reciting *The Raven* again.

As Dr. Block got closer, however, Tamia could see that her lips weren't moving.

Tamia looked at the monitor again, and the words of the poem kept spilling onto the screen.

"Dr. Block! Come here!"

The botanist jogged the short distance back.

"Look!" Nobody was speaking, but the machine continued to scroll through Poe's *Raven*.

"I wasn't—were you reciting this, Tamia?"

She shook her head. "I never memorized it."

Dr. Block furrowed her brow and took the machine out of Tamia's hand. "Odd, it's never done that before." She turned it off and on again, then held it back up to the tree.

LENORE

"Hello? Hello?" Tamia called out. "It's not responding."

NEVERMORE

"Something's wrong with the interface," muttered the scientist.

"Hello?" Tamia repeated. "Hello?"

After a pause, the word HELLO appeared. Both women sighed with relief.

HELLO TAMIA HELLO HELLO TAMIA

Tamia gasped.

HELLO DOCTOR BLOCK HELLO HELLO

Tamia stepped away from the trunk, staring at the display.

Dr. Block cursed. She turned the machine off and on again. "It's broken."

NO NOT BROKEN

"Dr. Block, are you doing this? How are you doing this?"

HELLO DOCTOR BLOCK HELLO TAMIA COMMUNICATE

The translator shook in Dr. Block's unsteady hand. "This is impossible," she whispered.

HELLO HELLO COMMUNICATE

Dr. Block fished the translator's strap out of her pocket, and Tamia held the machine while the scientist strapped it to the tree.

HELLO DOCTOR BLOCK COMMUNICATE

"Yes, communicate!" yelled the scientist, patting her pockets. "Tamia, do you have—can you record this?"

Tamia dug her phone out and started taking video again. Dr. Block inhaled, as if to gather herself, then faced the camera and spoke. She was clearly struggling to remain calm as she stated her name and credentials, the date and their location. "Subject is a Western Hemlock," she continued. "*Tsuga heterophylla,* approximately one hundred and fifty feet tall, diameter about three feet, perhaps three hundred years old. This," she said, pointing to the box, "is the translator previously shown."

Tamia directed her camera to the machine's monitor. She shouldn't have been surprised to find out that the doctor had taken videos before.

"This specimen is displaying a new trait. Rather than simply repeating human speech, this hemlock seems to be generating sentences independently."

The biologist turned toward the tree and spoke in its direction. "Hello—tree?"

HELLO DOCTOR BLOCK HELLO

"Are you talking to me?" asked the scientist.

COMMUNICATE DOCTOR BLOCK

"And who else is here? Who else are you talking to?"

HELLO TAMIA HELLO HELLO

"Oh my god, oh my god," breathed Tamia.

NOT BROKEN

"I know," said Dr. Block. "The machine is not broken. Tell me, can you identify yourself?"

TREE

Tamia's whole body tingled and she could barely hold the phone still. She looked over at Dr. Block for an explanation—but the doctor's eyes were just as wide as hers.

TREE COMMUNICATE DOCTOR BLOCK TAMIA HELLO

"This is unbelievable," Dr. Block stammered. "Tree, how did you—how did you learn to speak?"

There was a pause.

"Tree, do you understand me?"

YES

"Ohmygod, ohmygod," Tamia whispered again. Her heart hammered in her chest.

"Did somebody train you?"

NO

Dr. Block looked down, deep in thought. "How did they manage this? Human language isn't a natural trigger for a tree—aside, perhaps, from the CO_2 we exhale when we speak. But even if a sensitivity to language were introduced, it would still have to be shaped—"

"Tree," interrupted Tamia. "Do you speak with other trees?"

NO

"But you *communicate* with other trees?" asked Dr. Block.

YES

"And *how* do you communicate?"

WIND EARTH MOVE

"Volatiles, root system, mycorrhizae, yes." The scientist nodded in confirmation. "But what do you mean by move?"

LITTLE LITTLE MOVE

Tamia raised her eyebrows even higher than they already were. The "move" incidents—rumors—she'd researched weren't exactly "little little."

"Vibrations?" guessed Dr. Block.

VIBRATIONS

She faced Tamia. "Do you realize this could confirm acoustic theories of plant communication?"

Tamia nodded, slowly enough to avoid shaking the video. But she wasn't exactly concentrating on the finer points of scientific research at this moment because *hello, a tree was talking to them!*

The botanist turned toward the tree again. "And how do you communicate with us?"

MACHINE

Dr. Block addressed the camera. "As you can see, the hemlock appears to be aware of its surroundings and interlocutors."

"Can I ask another question?" Tamia interjected. "Tree—hemlock—when you say vibration, do you mean you feel them, or you make them?"

FEEL MAKE VIBRATIONS

"So both. And when you make vibrations, do the 'little little' movements ever get 'big big'?"

The tree didn't answer.

Tamia bit her lower lip and asked again. "Tree, can you move? Is it true?"

IS IT TRUE

"That you can move, is it true?"

IS IT TRUE

"Tree? Hemlock?"

TREE HEMLOCK

Dr. Block frowned. "Looks like it's had enough for one day."

ENOUGH FOR ONE DAY

"Let's get our samples," said Dr. Block, digging around in her backpack. "We'll try speech again when we're done." She reached up and twisted off a broken branch, examining its short, flat needles briefly before putting it into a plastic bag. Then she unfolded a chunky Leatherman multi-tool and snipped off another small piece of branch with a cone on the end.

NO

"Then hemlock, can you tell me: have you been altered in any way? Has someone done something to you to enable you to communicate?"

COMMUNICATE

"Yes, but how?"

COMMUNICATE

The botanist sighed. She reconfigured her Leatherman and used a single blade to pry up a scale of the reddish-brown bark. After peering underneath with a lens, she wrenched off a bark sample and put it in a bag.

NO DOCTOR BLOCK

"Dr. Block?" asked Tamia. She was still filming as the scientist took a small shovelful of dirt from around the base and sealed it in a jar, then scraped down to the roots and shaved off another sample.

NO DOCTOR BLOCK STOP

Tamia stiffened. How could they be sure this tree wasn't of the "big big move" variety? "Doctor Block, I don't think it likes that."

"Well, sorry. Diagnostics aren't always pleasant for us either, but they're necessary." She glanced at Tamia. "Just wait till your first mammogram."

The botanist crossed her arms and stared at the ground for a moment. "I still need more information." She looked up into the tree's branches and asked, "Hemlock, how old are you?"

NO HOW OLD TREE

"Do you understand what I'm asking? Do you know how old you are?"

HOW OLD FOREST

"No, I mean how many years are *you*, as an individual?"

There was no answer.

Dr. Block breathed out sharply and trudged to her truck. She came back with a long, slim, metal instrument. Tamia kept filming while the botanist unscrewed the end of the metal rod and pulled two long sticks out of it. "What's that?" she asked.

"Increment borer," answered the scientist. She fitted one of the sticks into a hole in the hollow rod, creating a T-shape, and guided the bottom of the T into a crease between thick chunks of the hemlock's bark.

Tamia eyed the instrument warily. "It kind of looks like a corkscrew."

"Well, it works a little like one too. We need to extract a sample." Dr. Block pushed the tip into the trunk and twisted the handle. Tamia's stomach clenched at the soft crunch of metal biting through bark and wood.

The screen strapped to the tree flashed: NO NO STOP

"Do you have to do that?" asked Tamia.

Dr. Block continued to turn the borer. "Short of chopping it down, this is the only way to know exactly how old a tree is. The ring spacing will also tell us about growth rates over the years, perhaps helping us pinpoint when the tree changed, if not how it happened. Wish I had a full lab."

NO NO NOT NO

Tamia leaned over and put her hand on Dr. Block's, not caring that she was ruining the video.

Calmly but firmly, the older woman removed Tamia's hand and resumed drilling. "I'm sorry, I need this data, and unfortunately you can't tell me." Tamia wasn't sure if the doctor was addressing her or the hemlock.

STOP STOP PLEASE STOP STOP

Dr. Block stopped turning the handles. She switched off the translator, pulled the strap from around the trunk, and handed it all to Tamia. "This is a standard practice. When done correctly, it doesn't harm the tree." She turned back to the hemlock and kept on boring.

"We've known for decades that plants can 'hear' in their own way. It was just a matter of how sensitive they were to specific sounds. Remember Dr. Appel's research?"

Tamia nodded. According to the article Dr. Block had sent her, when merely the sound of caterpillars eating leaves was played to plants, they mounted their chemical defenses against the perceived invaders.

"Auditory stimuli are one thing," the older woman continued, "but human speech? Trees don't have the necessary structures to hear and recognize human auditory input, much less translate and repeat it. And even if they had the physical capability, language skills only develop with time and training. I don't know of any labs teaching saplings to speak English, and yet here we are with a whole forest of full-grown talkers."

She glanced at Tamia. "Look, boring into trees isn't my favorite thing either, but I don't see another way right now."

Tamia thumbed off her phone's camera and hugged the translator to her chest. Dr. Block returned to her sampling. Tamia looked up into the hemlock's flat, splayed branches and whispered to it that everything would be all right. She couldn't say for sure if it was just the wind that made the needles quiver.

CHAPTER 15

CHARLIE SLUMPED ON Eddie's couch, staring forward into space. Everyone else was away at work and school, but he—he was finished. How could he work without a vehicle? Eddie said he knew a guy, but there was no way to fix a truck that had dropped from a height of ten feet, even if he *had* insurance.

Eddie had saved his ass, coming up the mountain in the dark to get him. He cringed inwardly, remembering the look on Eddie's face when he saw the cracked up vehicle, and him all scratched up and reeking of beer. If he had it to do over again, he'd sooner carry that truck home on his back than have to see that look on Eddie's face again.

"You're a lucky son of a bitch," Eddie had told him on the way home. Must be luck. There was no other way a sane man could explain it, was there? But no truck, no job, just a shitload of shame. He was having a hard time feeling lucky.

There was a knock on the door. Charlie shuffled toward the entrance, his muscles sore from the accident. Pain shot down his arm when he lifted it to pull open the door.

A native boy in his early teens stood on the stoop, hands stuffed into the pockets of his jean jacket. "You're Charlie Meninick, right?" the boy asked. "I heard you was here. Can I talk to you?"

Charlie blinked in the bright light. "Who are you?" He glanced around the boy up and down the street. Kid was there by himself.

"I'm Louis Greyfox. That was my brother in the forest. In the accident." The muscles working at his jawline belied his stoic expression.

Charlie's mind flashed back to the carnage in the woods. The boy's brother was the one crushed under the tree. "I'm sorry," he said.

The young man lowered his eyes.

"Want to come in?" Charlie wasn't sure why he'd said that. He didn't want to talk about that day anymore. But the boy nodded, and Charlie brought him into the living room.

The young man declined his offer of refreshments— which was fortunate, thought Charlie, because they weren't really his to offer. The boy sat down quietly on the edge of a wooden chair. Charlie eyed the young man: slim, dark and shy; jean jacket stained with the signs of outdoor chores. He looked about fifteen or so, just a hair older than Charlie had been when he'd left for Seattle.

"I'm real sorry about your brother," said Charlie.

"Thank you."

Charlie waited. He didn't want to be an asshole; he just wanted to get this over with—whatever it was the boy wanted from him. He cleared his throat and asked, "How can I help you?" He liked the utility of this white person's phrase for "hurry up and tell me what you want."

"My brother." The boy swallowed. "Did you see him before . . . the accident?"

Charlie released his breath, not realizing he'd been holding it. "No, I didn't."

"Did you hear him? Was he sayin' anything?"

Charlie shook his head. "No, I'm sorry. I heard voices, but I couldn't tell what they were saying."

"Well, did it maybe sound like they were fighting?" asked the boy.

Charlie shrugged and shook his head again. "I don't know. Didn't sound like it." He wondered if he was even supposed to be talking to this boy, with the investigation still going on.

"But it could've been, right? He could've been fightin' the white guy, tryin' to stop him?"

Poor kid. "I don't know," he said. "I suppose, maybe."

The boy's eyes brightened and he sat up a little straighter. "Do you think maybe you could tell the Council—"

"No!" barked Charlie. "I already told them everything, I can't go changin' my story now."

"Please, everybody says he was stealing trees!"

Charlie shook his head. "No way, sorry. I can't go making up stories. I gave my statement and I'm done."

"But my family . . ." The boy's voice faltered.

Charlie clenched his jaw and wiped his palms on his legs. "Look, kid, I said I'm sorry." And that was the truth, he really did feel sorry for the boy, but he couldn't risk it. Drunks go changing their stories all the time. He couldn't afford to, not now. Damn this whole thing.

The boy tightened his lips to suppress a tremble, and Charlie cursed himself for letting yet another person down, a kid no less.

But then the boy's tawny face reddened and his eyes narrowed. "My people aren't the only ones got to worry about this."

Charlie opened his mouth, but nothing came out.

"You tell Eddie I was here," Louis spat. He jumped up from his chair and stomped out of the room.

"What the hell?" Charlie's bewilderment bloomed into anger as he tailed the boy to the front door. "You get back here!" he bellowed.

Louis stormed out and slammed the door shut behind him.

"Hey!" Charlie yanked open the door and stepped onto the porch. He spotted the boy running and launched down the stairs after him. The boy looked back and put on an extra burst of speed, flying by an elderly woman wearing a fringed shawl. She tottered on unsteady feet, and Charlie managed to reach her before she fell. He held the old woman and could only watch the boy run around a corner, out of sight.

"Thank you, young one," said the woman, gathering her shawl back around her.

"It's all right, Grandmother." She wasn't related by blood, but as a native elder, she was *Grandmother.* And the warm look on her face did settle his nerves a bit.

The old woman clucked her tongue. "That boy. Runs like a thief."

Charlie's eyebrows shot up.

"I know his people," she said, pointing a wrinkled hand. "And yours. You are from good people. Don't mix yourself up with that boy."

Charlie couldn't think what to say.

The old woman patted his hand. "Until next time," she said. She released his hand and headed on her way. Charlie looked after her for a moment before turning around and walking back to Eddie's house. He supposed it was the privilege of the elders to speak their minds.

A sinking feeling came over him as soon as he stepped onto the porch, and it was confirmed when he tried the handle.

"Fuck!" The door was locked and his keys were inside. His hand went to his pocket, searching for his phone.

"Fuuuuuck!" He'd forgotten he didn't have a phone anymore. He rubbed his hands together, noticing just then how cool the fall mornings had become. It had been a month now since the accident—the first one, with the poachers—and he was stuck out here in just a T-shirt and jeans. Eddie didn't believe in hiding spare keys under the mat. Nothing but to go into town and get a set from him.

First the dead guys, then the truck, now I lock myself out. But it was the trees that occupied his mind all the way to town. If those had been normal trees his truck had hit, he'd be dead. He couldn't believe all their strange movements were just chance. But who could he ask about it? Not Eddie. His cousin would just tell him to stay out of the bottle.

It was the middle of the day, people were at work and kids were at school. Delivery vans trundled up and down the street. Everyone had something important to do.

Everyone but him. He hunched his shoulders up toward his ears and kept on walking.

He passed the county elementary school that he and Eddie had attended. Kids squealed and laughed, lining up at the door to go back inside after recess. The building had always seemed so huge when he was one of those kids walking through its doors, as big as castle gates, and heading down long, cavernous hallways to class. He pictured the proud little man he was at six years old, chest all puffed out, making sure his little sister got to school safe. Lilly. She would have been all grown by now. Probably would have gone to college, maybe been the lawyer or politician Uncle Virgil wanted for the people. Maybe she would have gotten married and had some kids too. Charlie could have been an uncle by now.

A couple of teachers stood at the door of the school building, eyeing him. He nodded at them and continued on his way to Eddie's office.

Just keep moving, he told himself. *Lilly's gone. Dad is*—he didn't know what to call it—*cold,* like he blamed Charlie for everything he wanted that never happened. And Charlie's mother had left town while he was up in Seattle. No one knew where she was anymore. He cursed all those years he was too wrapped up in himself to notice her hurt, realize she was drifting away. Maybe if he'd paid more attention. Been sober enough.

Past is past. Just keep moving.

Head down against the chill, he jogged across the highway separating downtown from the Tribal offices. He found Eddie's building and asked the way to his office.

"Hey, Eddie," he said, knocking on his open door.

"Hey, Cuz, come on in. You here about that job with the Cultural Center?"

"No, I don't think you want me up there talkin' to tourists." Charlie stepped up to Eddie's desk. "I, uh, I locked myself out." His face flushed as Eddie had a good belly-laugh. *Haw, haw, haw!* Crow Butt was back for a minute before the laugh subsided to a chuckle.

"Here you go." Eddie handed over his set of keys. "Don't lock these in too."

"Thanks," Charlie mumbled, stuffing the keys into his pocket. "You know what, Eddie? Some kid came around to the house today. Louis Greyfox."

Eddie frowned. "Greyfox? What'd he want?"

"You know him?"

"I know his people. Everybody knows everybody out here. Ain't that kinda why you left?" Eddie's lips twisted into a wry smile.

Charlie couldn't help but smile a little himself. Eddie always was a good shot. "Anyway, this Greyfox kid—"

"Shut the door, would you?" asked Eddie.

Charlie closed the door and sat down in front of his cousin's heavy wooden desk. "So the kid was upset about his older brother. He was one of those poachers, the one who wound up underneath the tree that day."

"Okay."

"Well, this kid's worried about people calling his brother a thief. Wanted me to make up some story about how he was trying to stop the other guy from cutting down the tree before it fell on him."

"Oh?"

Charlie found the wary look in Eddie's eye a little unsettling. "Yeah, but don't worry, Eddie. I'm not gonna stir that whole mess up again. I said my piece and I'm done with the whole damn thing."

Eddie nodded. "Did he say anything else?"

"Yeah. He said to tell you he came by. Said something about his family wasn't the only one should be worried."

Eddie's face clouded over.

"Worried about what, Eddie? Is something going on?"

"Don't pay no attention to him," Eddie finally said. "That boy don't know what he's sayin'. He's just hurtin'."

There was a knock at the door. Eddie's face morphed into a welcoming smile as he called for the person to come in. A colleague entered and, seeing Charlie, asked if he should come back later.

"No, no, come on in, have a seat. Joe, this is my cousin Charlie." Charlie stood up and they shook hands. Eddie came around his desk and patted his cousin's shoulder jovially. "We were just sittin' here flappin' our jaws. But he was about to head out."

Charlie felt Eddie's hand on his shoulder subtly steer him toward the door. He stepped out into the hallway and turned around to face his cousin.

"Don't you worry about nothing, Cuz," said Eddie. "You just concentrate on gettin' yourself back together. See you at home."

And for the second time that morning, a door closed in Charlie's face.

CHAPTER 16

RICKY SAT AT the kitchen table with his after school snack while his mother looked at the letter he'd brought home.

"A field trip already?" she asked, eyebrows raised. "School just started."

"Can I go?" he asked through a mouthful of bread and jam.

"The Palalla Nation Cultural Center," she mused. "In Nakalish." Ricky's father walked into the kitchen. "Honey," she asked him, "where's Nakalish? Ricky's got a field trip there."

Ricky's father pulled out his iPhone. "Wow, that's at least three hours from here." He showed her the map on his phone. "Your field trip is way over there?"

"It's about Native Americans," Ricky explained. "We're going to Ms. Martin's reservation, where she grew up."

"Ms. Martin?" his father asked. "The one we met at Back to School Night? She's Indian?"

"Palalla, it says. She doesn't look Indian," said Ricky's mother, handing the letter to her husband.

Ricky swallowed his mouthful. "Ms. Martin says it's not *Indian*, it's *Native American*."

"Well, yeah, she's right," said his father. He scanned the letter and directed a wry smile at his wife. "It's an overnighter. She must be new." He handed the notice back to her. "As long as I don't have to chaperone."

"They want four volunteers," she read. "That's five adults with the teacher. Do you think that's enough for the whole class? There's, what, about thirty students?"

"Well, I doubt they'll all go."

Just sign it, pleaded Ricky silently. He took a swig of milk and wiped his mouth with his sleeve.

"Napkin!" said his mom.

He grabbed the napkin and wiped his already clean mouth. All they had to do was sign it. Why did his parents have to make everything so complicated? "Mom and Dad, can I go? Ben is going, and Micah, and Zach." Well, Zach hadn't said so yet, but Ricky thought he probably would.

His father held up a hand. "We're not saying no, but your mother and I have to talk about it first."

"Okay." Ricky knew better than to push, because that usually resulted in "no." His parents kept reading and speaking in low voices. He really wanted to go. He didn't mind the long trip. He could bring his sleeping bag and sleep anywhere. Ms. Martin was teaching them about Native Americans and their land. They prayed to the animals, the sky, the earth, and most importantly, the trees. Maybe they could teach him how to talk to the trees too. He didn't like having to hit them to get them to move, so he wanted to talk to someone who knew about these things. Sure Grampa Nystrom studied trees, but from what he'd seen on their outing, Ricky didn't think he actually knew that much about them.

Ricky took another bite of his sandwich. His mother asked, "Why can't they just take them to the Puyallups or something closer?"

"That's not where Ms. Martin is from," he blurted through his mouthful.

His father folded his arms. "Ricky, this trip is the same weekend Grampa Nystrom's coming."

Ricky stopped chewing.

"That'll be fun, won't it? You guys can go exploring again."

Ricky swallowed a big ball of sandwich. Grampa wouldn't explain anything to him. All Grampa would do was send him off somewhere to play, while all of the other kids got to go see the reservation. His stomach started to hurt.

His mother looked at him intently. "You really want to go, don't you?"

Ricky nodded.

"Well," she said, "I guess we can talk to your Grampa."

His father snapped his fingers. "Hey, maybe Grampa could chaperone!"

"What?" snapped Ricky.

His father frowned at him. "What's wrong with that?"

"Nothing," said Ricky. "I just . . . I just don't think he'll want to."

His mother put her hands on her hips. "Well, we'll let him decide, won't we?"

With both parents glaring at him, all Ricky could do was nod. He wanted to go on the trip, but how was he going to solve the mystery of the trees with his grandfather watching? All he did was name them and describe them—but did he ever stop to listen to them? No, all he did was strap machines to them and pull at their leaves and snip off their branches. Ricky couldn't explain it, but somehow he knew Grampa Nystrom would ruin everything.

CHAPTER 17

TAMIA GRITTED HER teeth and scrolled through every menu on her phone. Where the hell was the video? Just yesterday she'd played it for the chief of staff, Derrick Jones, and now it was gone. And it was her own stupid fault.

Here she'd thought it was luck—fate, even—that she'd bumped into him on her way into the office yesterday. She'd been so excited to finally meet her mentor, and he'd been so approachable. Her face flushed as she recalled how she'd blathered on about her extensive research, her initiative in contacting Dr. Block, and capturing the actual human-tree interaction on video. She'd intended to follow protocol and go to Rima first, but he'd asked her what she'd done over the weekend, and seemed so interested in hearing about it, and it was sure to impress him—and hadn't Greg always come out on top by taking his chances when they presented themselves?

She swallowed a lump in her throat and continued searching through her phone. She felt like such an idiot now, recalling how Jones' smile had faded as she'd shared what she and Dr. Block had discovered. She should have known from the quick invitation to his office and his stony expression while watching the video that all was not well. She'd even chided herself for feeling a pang of panic when he'd asked to borrow her phone. After all, wasn't it a good sign that he wanted more time to look at the evidence?

But now her little speck of doubt was confirmed. His assistant had returned her phone, and the video was gone. And Derrick Jones hadn't said a word to her since.

Tamia fanned her face with a memo and clicked in to the staff schedule. He didn't have any meetings just then, and his assistant left for lunch at the same time every day like clockwork. This was her chance. She stepped quietly down the hallway toward his office, blood pounding in her ears. Bad enough to break protocol once; now she was forced to do it again.

She smoothed a hand over her hair and knocked on his office door.

"Enter," he said, his tone sharp and formidable.

"Excuse me," she stammered. "I hope I'm not interrupting."

"Yes, Tamia?" His face, so friendly the day before, was unreadable now.

"Well, I was wondering . . ." She clutched the doorframe. "I wanted to see if I could follow up on yesterday."

"Come in," he said curtly, waving her into a chair.

"Thank you." She closed the door before sitting down in front of his spotless desk.

"You did get your phone back, didn't you?"

"Um, yes, but . . ." Tamia looked up from his superior, paperless workspace. "I wanted to follow up, to see what the next steps are."

"Next steps?"

"Well, you said you'd look into it, what we talked about, and I just wondered if you'd had an opportunity to discuss this with anyone else."

The chief of staff's face pinched into a brief, almost imperceptible frown before he heaved a large sigh. "Yes, Tamia, we'll look into it. I'll let you know if we need anything else."

"So that's it?" How could he not care? Had she landed on a bizarre parallel planet where talking trees were as common as potholes?

He shook his head, condescendingly it seemed to her. "Tamia, until we have evidence of anything . . ."

"But I saw it myself! And the video—"

He raised his hand to silence her. "The video I saw shows an impressionable young woman believing everything she's shown."

She desperately wished she could stop the heat climbing to her cheeks.

"Tamia, really. Talking trees?" He looked at her with a mixture of pity and mirth.

She clasped her hands even more tightly on her lap.

He shook his head and tilted his smile ruefully. "I was trying to be kind, but as your mentor I should have been direct. I can't do anything with this. It's so . . . fantastical. I don't know how this professor created her illusion, but it's just not possible."

"But that's why—"

He raised his hand to stop her again. "I am convinced that you believe this. I have no doubt about that. But listen." He leaned forward and held her gaze. "I want you to succeed. I want you to do well, not just because I'm your mentor, and you're a talented young woman, but also because it's important for us to provide an example."

He paused to let "us" take hold.

"You are on your way up, Tamia. You are on the first step to a great career for yourself and a fine example for your sisters and brothers coming up behind you. And I need you to reflect on that when you make your decisions in life."

She held her breath and blinked.

"Now," he said, his eyes flicking away to release hers, "if you still want to pursue this . . ." He waited.

Disappoint him by saying yes, or betray herself and Dr. Block by saying no? She couldn't speak at all.

". . . then you need to trust me to pursue this quietly," he continued, "to spare you and the governor's office any potential embarrassment."

She nodded stiffly. She was not an example, then. She was a potential embarrassment.

"All right," he said, with thinly veiled disapproval. "But you are not to speak with anyone else about this, you understand? This will not work otherwise. I will shut it down if we can't handle it properly, with discretion."

She nodded again, clenching her teeth to keep them from chattering.

"Good. Now, I know we both have work to do." His quick, grim smile was her signal to leave. Her legs felt so numb she had to look down to keep from tripping on her way out. She was getting what she wanted, wasn't she? They were looking into it. But if this was what success felt like, she wasn't sure she was cut out for it.

And so much for Derrick Jones taking her seriously. Was he saying he'd look into it just to get her off his back? Would he even bother to pursue it at all? She felt a sudden need to reach out to Dr. Block. Instead of going back to her cube, she left the building and dialed the scientist's number.

"So, where do we stand?" asked Dr. Block. Tamia guessed from the background noise that she was in her truck somewhere out on the road.

"I'm not sure," she murmured, looking around for anyone else from the office. "I met with the Gov—*his* chief of—people." Dr. Block was still paranoid about phone surveillance, so Tamia had to choose her words carefully.

"Yes?" said the botanist expectantly.

"Well, he said they'd look into it."

"That's all?"

"That's all, really." She cleared her throat, trying to shake off the shame of how Jones had dismissed her. "We just have to be patient, and discreet."

"Patient? Discreet? About trees that—about something like this?"

Tamia shrugged helplessly. "I've talked to him about it twice already."

"Well, you'll just have to talk to Governor Palmer directly," Dr. Block said matter-of-factly. Apparently she'd grown tired of their cryptic, anonymous conversations. "You have to make sure Palmer sees the evidence himself. Can't you show him the video?"

Tamia couldn't suppress a bitter little laugh. "Look, it's not that easy. Even if I could get in to see him, I . . . I don't have it anymore. It's gone."

Dr. Block gasped. "I hope you don't mean 'erased' gone."

She gritted her teeth. "Jones borrowed my phone to review the video, but when I got my phone back, it wasn't there anymore."

"You can get a copy from him, can't you?"

"Nope, no way," said Tamia. "I can't go back to him again."

"Do you have a backup?" pressed the scientist. "You must have some kind of backup."

"I don't know."

Dr. Block made an exasperated noise. "I'm on my way out there again, and I've got my camera. I just hope it wasn't a one-time occurrence."

"Me too." Tamia switched the phone to her other ear and shook out her hand. She hadn't realized how hard she'd been gripping it. "But even if we get more video, I don't think it would matter."

"That's impossible," snapped Dr. Block. "They can't just ignore this."

"Well, they might if . . ." How could she say this? "If they think I got taken in by some quack scientist."

Dr. Block was silent for a moment. "Or perhaps," she said carefully, "they're already aware of this and don't want anyone else to know."

Tamia bit her lip. That ghost of a thought had been flitting around her mind, poking its head up between her embarrassment and shame. She felt a little light-headed just thinking the word *conspiracy*, but why else would Jones so quickly and definitively dismiss her video as a hoax? Why was no one being sent out to investigate the reports of anomalous tree activity, and why wasn't there any new information on the investigation about those poachers who were killed down at the Palalla reservation? People had been hurt, and two had died. Would Jones actually be able to suppress such a serious investigation?

"Hold on," said the doctor. "There's a roadblock up ahead. They're not letting anyone through."

"Why? What is it?"

"Fire crews. Smoke. Oh god."

"What?" Tamia pressed the phone to her ear. "Dr. Block, what's burning?"

"It's the trees," said Dr. Block, voice cracking. "*Our* trees. I've got to go. Our trees are burning!"

Tamia slowly lowered her phone, stunned and helpless in the silence Dr. Block left behind.

CHAPTER 18

CHARLIE WAS OVERSTAYING his welcome. Eddie hadn't said anything, but he was. How else could he have wound up at the Cultural Center on a Saturday afternoon babysitting a bunch of kids from Tacoma?

"Come on, Cuz. It's just for the weekend," Eddie had told him. "All you need to do is keep the kids together, make sure no one runs off."

He couldn't say no to Eddie, but something kept nagging at him. Something felt different between him and Eddie ever since that Greyfox boy came by. But then, his cousin probably just wanted his own house back. Things would get back to normal once he moved out on his own.

Charlie stood with his hands on his hips, surveying the group of children in the Winter Lodge. They were all sitting in what folks used to call "Indian style," looking up at a storyteller dressed in regalia. The beads of her wingdress clicked as she shot imaginary arrows into the air, telling how Beaver and Eagle stole fire from the Sky People to give to Man. The story slowly came back to him as he watched her. He remembered how grossed out and thrilled he'd been that Beaver could stay alive after being half-skinned by the Sky People.

The storyteller finished by handing a beaver paw around to the kids. She told them to look for the special claw Beaver used to carry fire down to Earth. Some of the students grabbed for it, others squealed and refused to touch it. The commotion forced a grin out of Charlie. He glanced up at the children's teacher, Ms. Martin, and was startled to find her beaming right at him. She looked so excited to be there. Her lean, pretty face was all lit up; her smooth, almond skin practically glowed against the ivory-colored ribbon dress she'd worn for the occasion. Two dark, shining braids framed her face, held in place with intricately beaded hair ornaments in colors matching the vibrant red, blue and yellow ribbons flashing across her chest and down her arms. He turned his eyes quickly back to the children.

The storyteller continued with more tales about brave Eagle and trickster Coyote; about *Pahto* and *Wyeast*, known to them as Mount Adams and Mount Hood; about the shadowy *Stick-showers* who kidnap small children when they stray too far into the woods at night. From the looks on their faces, Charlie didn't think he'd be needed to keep them in their sleeping bags that evening.

After story time, the children raced outside to play. Charlie stood by the edge of the field, watching the cultural guide and the teacher lead the kids through the stick game and ring-and-pin, then red rover and tug of war. Yelling and cheering floated over the cloud of dust kicked up by their sneakers. The plumes of dry earth smelled just the same to Charlie as the last time he'd played tug-of-war himself.

It was the spring before he moved to Seattle to live with his father, at some big picnic his school put on for the end of the school year. He and Eddie were both pretty strong, and they pulled next to each other each match. One of them always seemed to know when to hold on extra tight so the other could adjust his grip. But once the teachers caught on that all the Native kids had gravitated toward the same team, they moved everyone around. Charlie felt weird holding the rope opposite Eddie. He remembered digging his toes into the rocky dirt to set his stance. The teacher yelled *Go!* and as Charlie grunted and pulled, he glanced up at his cousin, expecting him to pull a face or do something to make him laugh. But Eddie's face was pinched with determination as he strained against the rope. He didn't look at Charlie once.

Ms. Martin released the kids into free time before dinner. Some of them went into the gift shop to look at jewelry. Others stood around in small clusters giggling and whispering. Those who had smart phones sank into them, while a couple more swung from nearby trees.

Charlie noticed a red-headed boy standing by himself, very still and very close to a pine with swooping branches and long, curved needles. Did he have to remind the kid where the bathrooms were? As he approached, the boy leaned even closer to the trunk, whispered something, and slapped his hand against the tree.

"Hey," said Charlie quietly.

The boy jumped and looked up at him. The strawberry blonde lashes framing his blue eyes were almost translucent.

Charlie smiled. He leaned forward to breathe in the sweet, vanilla scent of the pine bark. "You smell that? That's *Táp'ash*, Ponderosa pine."

The little boy stuck his nose close to the tree and sniffed.

"Pretty cool, huh?"

The boy nodded and looked up at Charlie expectantly. "Native Americans can communicate with nature, right?"

"Yeah, I suppose, in a way. You want to ask the storyteller some questions?"

"How do you communicate with trees?" the boy pressed.

Charlie shifted his weight from one leg to another. He'd told Eddie he wasn't really an expert on all of the spiritual stuff. "So, what's your name, kid?"

"Ricky. What's yours?"

"Charlie." The two shook hands. "You enjoyin' your visit?"

"Yup."

"Is it what you expected?"

"Well," said the boy scrunching up his nose, "I kinda thought we'd be out in the woods or something."

"Yeah." He smiled. "That's what most people think."

"So how do you talk to trees?"

Charlie stuffed his hands into his pockets. "You're pretty into trees, aren't you?"

"Yeah, I guess," said Ricky, shrugging. "Yeah."

"How come? What do you like about 'em?"

"Well," he said, lowering his voice, "I like when they move."

Charlie raised an eyebrow. "When they move? Like how they blow in the wind?"

Ricky shook his head. "No, I mean, move. You know, don't you?"

Charlie froze.

"I didn't like it at first," the boy said, "when they would poke me or throw things. But now . . ."

"But now?" he prodded.

"But now they help me," said Ricky. "They lift me up, you know, when I'm climbing. And if I slip, they catch me."

Charlie's heart skipped a beat. "Maybe you're just a really good climber."

The boy shook his head.

"How about this?" Charlie glanced back at the group of children. "Maybe you could show me what you mean. There's lots of trees to climb around here."

A smile stole across Ricky's lips. "Really? You believe me?"

"Well, maybe, if I could see what you're talking about." Charlie moved over to a twisty, grey oak with thick, broad branches. "How about this one?"

"Okay." Ricky grunted and pulled himself up onto the lowest branch. "No one's ever believed me."

"No one? Who have you told?"

"Oh, just my mom and dad." Ricky wobbled to a stand on the first branch and reached up for another one.

"Now, don't *try* to fall," warned Charlie. "We just want to see the lifting part, not the slipping and falling."

"I know." Ricky hopped and grabbed the limb above, swinging precariously.

"Maybe you should just stop there."

"I'm okay," said the boy. His shoes scuffed the trunk as he scrambled up to the second branch. Charlie braced himself for a catch as the boy climbed to a third. "What should I do now?" he asked.

"What do you mean? Aren't you the one who knows how to make 'em move?"

"Well, it doesn't always work."

"Now you tell me. Why don't you come on down, now?"

"I'm okay." The boy propped a hand against the bark and moved away from the trunk in a crouch. He tried to bob up and down, but the branch didn't move. "This isn't working." He sat down and scooted farther out on the limb.

"Hey!" yelled Charlie.

"It's okay!" he yelled back, moving farther and farther from the trunk.

A different voice, sharp and commanding, pierced Charlie's ears: "Ricky!"

Charlie swiveled and saw an elderly man glaring up at the boy in the tree. In the same instant he heard the boy yell. He looked up and saw Ricky hanging from a branch ten feet above the ground, feet flailing. Charlie opened his arms and braced himself for the child's fall. The older man's footsteps pounded closer.

"Ricky, what the hell are you doing?" yelled the man.

The boy grunted and twisted.

"I'm right below you!" shouted Charlie. "Go get help!" he called to the old man. Charlie's eyes remained on the boy as the footsteps thumped away. "Hold on, Ricky. Help is com—"

The cracking of wood filled his ears. *Shit!* But something was off. It was all happening in slow motion. The very branch that had been too thick to bounce was bending—but not breaking. The branch angled downward and to the left, amidst a shower of leaves and twigs, guiding the boy toward the closest branch below. At the same time, the lower branch rose toward Ricky until his feet came to rest on it.

Charlie stood transfixed, his arms still raised. He dimly registered the commotion of grownups and children approaching behind him. By the time they arrived, Ricky had maneuvered himself back to the trunk and begun climbing down the tree.

"Ricky!" yelled the older man.

"I'm okay, Grampa," said the boy. "Did you see it?"

"I saw you almost kill yourself. What were you doing?"

The boy hung from the lowest branch and let go, landing neatly on his feet. "Did you see that, Charlie?" he asked. His face was bright with excitement and the last traces of fear.

"What was this, some kind of dare?" The older man gripped his grandson's arm. "Don't ever go up that high, you hear me?" Ricky looked over his shoulder at Charlie as his grandfather led him away.

"Sir," said Charlie to the grandfather's back, "I didn't . . ." But the man wasn't paying attention to him, and the small crowd was already heading back to the clearing.

"Thank goodness he's safe," breathed Ms. Martin. "But let's not have any more students climbing this weekend, okay, Charlie?"

"Sorry," he mumbled, noting the golden flecks in her hazel eyes.

She smiled and patted his arm. "I know you didn't mean any harm. These kids always find a way to get us into trouble, don't they?" Her knowing smile triggered equal measures of embarrassment and relief.

One of the volunteers nodded in the direction of the old man. "That guy a chaperone?"

"Yes," said Ms. Martin. "He's the boy's grandfather."

The volunteer grunted. "No wonder the kid ran off on his own. That guy's just been snoopin' around the forest all afternoon, hasn't spent more'n a minute watchin' the kids." The volunteer ambled away, shaking his head.

The teacher folded her hands in front of her. "Everything's all right," she said quietly. She and Charlie watched the last couple of people head out of the forest. She looked up at him. "Come on, let's go eat."

He followed her back into the clearing, watching as she herded the children into the restaurant for dinner. The late afternoon sunlight brought out reddish highlights in her long, brown hair. He tore his eyes away from her to look for any stragglers to direct inside. He was just wondering if Ricky had already gone in, when the grandfather caught his eye and scowled at him. Something about the older man itched his brain. He'd seen him before somewhere.

"Charlie, you coming?"

He hadn't realized he'd stopped walking. Ms. Martin was halfway between him and the Cultural Center, looking back at him over her shoulder. A breeze tossed the multicolored ribbons and rippled the ivory skirt of her dress. A momentary gust pressed the cloth against the back of her legs, divulging a hint of the supple body underneath.

He cleared his throat. "Comin'."

Don't get sidetracked. He had to figure out who the old guy was and how to get past him to talk to the boy again. That kid was the only other person who knew anything about the movements of the trees.

CHAPTER 19

TAMIA FIDGETED AND took a sip of coffee from the thick, white mug in front of her. The heavy cup was definitely old school, like everything else in the rustic little coffee shop halfway between Olympia and Dr. Block's cabin. She would have found the place charming if she weren't so stressed out.

Dr. Block stared into her coffee. "ArborTech paid me a visit."

Tamia remembered that name from all the faculty bios she'd read while looking for tree experts. It was an agricultural engineering firm that most of the prominent faculty seemed to have worked with. "What did they want?" she asked.

"Oh, they just wanted to ask about any research I might be up to now and remind me of all the NDAs, CDAs, and MTAs I'd signed—non-disclosure and confidentiality agreements," she explained. "They wanted to see if there might be any materials or equipment that had slipped my mind, anything that should be returned. Something like this." Dr. Block handed Tamia a cloth bag under the table.

Tamia's eyes widened with recognition of the metal box inside. She glanced around nervously. "What? Why are you giving me this?" she hissed. "It's yours."

"Technically, it's ArborTech's. And they're going to come back looking for it, which is why I can't keep it right now."

"What am I going to do with it?" asked Tamia. It was bad enough she'd lied about having a doctor's appointment to come here. She hated lying, especially under Rima's watchful eye and with no backup from her *mentor* Derrick Jones. And now she was supposed to hold on to contraband as well?

Dr. Block lifted her mug with measured nonchalance. "I need you to keep it for a while. Just until things calm down and we can start our work again."

"*Our* work? Look Dr. Block, I think I'm in way over my head."

"We're both in over our heads." The scientist's voice was stern and low. "But that doesn't mean we can simply play dead and hope everything goes away. I thought we might get help from the governor. I know he didn't send you out to see me, but I thought he might be concerned when he saw the evidence. Now it appears he's part of the problem."

"What? How would he be involved in this?"

"I don't know, but the moment his chief of staff got the video, those trees burned to the ground. And now ArborTech is at my doorstep. These weren't just friendly people in lab coats, Tamia; they looked dangerous. And they'll be back."

Tamia clutched the box under the table, not even wanting to look at it. She couldn't say for sure this went all the way up to the governor, but the queasy feeling in her gut told her it wasn't impossible.

"ArborTech is a big deal," said Dr. Block. "They have a hand in billions of dollars' worth of research. Anyone in my field who aspires to a serious research career needs to be connected to them. Between their capital and their government connections, like USDA, DoE, DoD—"

"Defense?" asked Tamia. Her stomach fluttered.

"Yes, I told you from the start they were involved."

"Yeah, but . . ." *But I didn't really believe you then.* Tamia shifted in her chair.

"ArborTech will do whatever they have to do to protect their investments," continued Dr. Block. "And those trees aren't the investments—the technology is. Those trees are just objects to them."

Tamia's chest tightened. The trees they had connected with, actually spoken with, were all gone now. "But do we have any proof it was ArborTech?" she asked.

"I know it was them," the scientist insisted. "And mark my words, there will be more fires. They wouldn't think anything of threatening a retired faculty member, or even burning down a whole forest to do it. Bullets can be traced, but fires are trickier. If they can destroy evidence of illegal testing and eliminate a whistleblower with one match, they'll do it." She swiveled her cup on the tabletop. "We need to get through to Nystrom," she muttered.

"Who's Nystrom?"

"Richard Nystrom. We worked together at UW. That thing you're holding is mostly his creation."

Tamia remembered his profile from the University of Washington faculty list. She hadn't even tried contacting him. His photo had looked too imposing. "Then why can't you just give it back to him?" she whispered.

The scientist looked down and twisted her watch around her wrist. "He won't answer my calls. I think he knows something—and he knows I'm more likely to say to hell with ArborTech than he is. But I understand his concern. He *does* have a family."

The bag in Tamia's hands felt heavier by the minute. "Well, why can't you just give it back to ArborTech? Maybe they won't set any more fires if you give it back."

Dr. Block shook her head. "It's not just about the translator. They also have to wipe out the samples—the trees. God, if they got access to my notes, they'd have a veritable treasure map to all the areas they need to destroy."

A chill ran down Tamia's spine. "Where are your files?" she asked.

"I'm handling it. You just worry about keeping *that* safe," she said, nodding toward the bag under the table.

"Refill?" asked the waitress, startling them both. Dr. Block politely declined and the waitress drifted off.

"But Dr. Block, what if . . ." It was hard for her to say this, after having spoken with the trees. "If these trees are mutated, I mean, what if they *are* dangerous. Maybe they *should* be destroyed."

"Assuming for a moment they should be destroyed," replied the doctor. "It's still not that easy. We can't just let ArborTech burn up acres of forest without knowing how widespread the phenomenon is, or even *what* it is. Do they know for sure that every tree in a stand is affected? Could they wind up burning more natural trees than engineered ones? And what if the post-burn topography favors reproduction of the genetically manipulated trees over the unchanged ones?" She cupped her hands into the shape of a pinecone. "Did you know the extreme heat of fire actually triggers the cones of the Lodgepole pine to open and release its seeds?" she asked, splaying her fingers. "Where would we be if the 'wrong' trees gain the upper hand through our actions?"

The barrage of questions overwhelmed Tamia. "But if they created this thing, shouldn't they know how to contain it?"

Dr. Block lowered her hands and stared at Tamia.

Tamia looked down and sighed. She set the bag on her lap and rubbed her face with her palms. "I don't know. I'm not a scientist, and I'm not a spy."

"Well, I'm not a spy either," said Dr. Block. "But right now we both have to act like we are. Did you find a copy of the video?"

"Yes, in my auto-backup."

"Well good lord, girl, why didn't you say anything? Send it to me!" she demanded, poking the tabletop with her finger. "We need to get this out to the public. It's too late for those trees, but we can protect the others."

"So you want to save them? You don't think they're a threat?"

"The original intent for them was an abomination. But everything changed as soon as they spoke for themselves." Dr. Block's face softened into an expression of wonder. "Just think of everything we could learn from them. What started as the ultimate means of mass surveillance could turn into the ultimate means of understanding our environment."

Dr. Block continued, her voice harder. "Now, could they be dangerous? Certainly, in the wrong hands. But that's why everyone needs to know about them. Bottom line, we can't let ArborTech be the ones to decide what to do with them. We have to get as many people on this as possible. That's why we have to get that video out immediately."

"Okay, but, Dr. Block," Tamia said cringing. "I watched it again, and it looks kind of crazy. I mean, like not-credible crazy. Like . . . Excuse me, but kind of crazy-old-lady crazy."

Dr. Block's shoulders slumped slightly.

Tamia went on. "Seeing that video reminded me of what I thought the first time I talked to folks about this tree stuff. I didn't take them seriously at all. If we're going to do this, we can't just put the video out there on our own. We have to get it in front of the right people, reputable people, and get *them* to put it out there, too. Which means . . ." Tamia swallowed. "The message can't just come from one of us."

Dr. Block spread her hands. "Well, from whom, then?"

"It has to come from the governor's office."

"And how are we supposed to accomplish that?"

"I have access to the office's general e-mail account," said Tamia. Her pulse quickened just thinking about it. "If I send it out from there, people will actually look at it."

"But you know what would happen."

Tamia nodded. Her head felt light. She would get fired in a heartbeat—and who else would hire her after that?

Dr. Block pursed her lips. "Right now, let's focus on what we're going to send out and to whom. Then we'll revisit exactly how it goes out."

"All right," said Tamia, although at the moment she didn't see another solution. "If you can work on a statement, I'll start putting together a contact list." She checked the time on her phone. It was late now, much later than a doctor's appointment should have lasted.

Dr. Block raised her hand for the check. Her eyes settled on Tamia's face. "I'm sorry you had to get involved in all this."

"It's not your fault," Tamia sighed. "I sought you out, remember? Curiosity killed the cat."

"Well, these two cats still have some lives left." Dr. Block patted her hand and gave her a small, determined smile.

Tamia nodded, but she wasn't so sure.

CHAPTER 20

A FEW DAYS after the schoolchildren's visit, Charlie found himself back at the Palalla Cultural Center. He was just going to talk to Ruth, the manager, to see about picking up a few hours here and there. Better than hanging around Eddie's living room all day, trying to ignore his ex's calls. He had to get back on his feet, and all they would do was drag each other down again. Plus, Eddie was still acting strange around him. Something was going on with the Greyfoxes, something involving family, but Eddie wasn't telling. Seems Cousin Charlie wasn't family enough to know.

Charlie walked by displays of woven baskets, cradleboards, and beaded moccasins on his way to Ruth's office. He couldn't really say what was particularly Palalla about the designs—probably not the best qualification to be working at the Cultural Center. Maybe he should have boned up on some of this stuff before coming by.

Ruth emerged from the hallway just as he reached the reception area. "Hey, Charlie, I thought I heard someone. Good to see you," she said. "Thank you for helping out last weekend."

"Oh, sure," he said.

"Glad you're back. Eddie might have mentioned that Bobbie just left for college." She gestured toward a desk and empty chair. "We're a little short-handed."

"Mm-hmm."

"I think we'll keep you busy," she said. "There's daily stuff like answering phones and checking e-mails. We also lend a hand with the elders when we can, getting them to medical appointments and events. And the powwow's coming up, so I'll be needing some help with that."

"Oh. Does that mean I'm hired?"

Ruth laughed. "As of Saturday. You can fill out the forms this afternoon."

"Well," said Charlie uneasily, "I wasn't really thinkin' about full time. I mean, I haven't been around this cultural stuff in a while."

Ruth waved away his arguments. "Eddie recommended you, so I know you'll be fine. And Ms. Martin, the teacher who brought her class in over the weekend? She's one of our regular volunteers."

"I see," said Charlie, keeping a straight face. Sure, he wouldn't mind seeing Ms. Martin again, but his people were resourceful; they could turn any little thing into grist for the gossip mill.

"Yep, visits her family here every month," she said. "I'm sure she'll be glad to see another familiar face next time she's home." He saw a hint of *Speel'yi* in Ruth's eye. You never knew when sly coyote would come out to play.

Ruth showed him around the facilities, smiling up at him. She mentioned Ms. Martin a couple of times while talking about the Center, her voice dripping with faux discretion. It didn't matter what he did; he was going to be the star of the next round of gossip. *Oh,* she would say, *you should have seen how quickly he said yes when he found out who else he'd be working with!*

Eventually Ruth sat him down at his predecessor's desk. "I'm going to have you start answering calls now, but don't worry, Bobbie put together a binder." She gave him the packet with the staff list, calendar of events and information for visitors. "I'll be right in that office," she said, pointing down the hall.

Charlie flipped through the manual. This Bobbie person was pretty thorough. No doubt she'd be a lot better at college than he'd been. He leafed through the tourist info: statistics, local history, stuff he should know already but didn't.

Something lying on top of a pile of documents caught his eye. He picked it up. It was the visitor list from the weekend. He'd thought he might get in touch with the tree kid here, but hadn't expected it to hit him right in the face the first day on the job. He scanned the list of students for Rickys or Richards. There were two, but only one whose last name matched one of the chaperones. Ricky Nystrom. Now he knew who he was trying to find.

He sifted farther into the pile to see if there was any emergency contact information for the kids. Nothing—not that he would have known what to do with it if he'd found it. He still had to figure out how to contact the kid without looking like a stalker.

The phones were quiet, so he started to leaf through the visitor materials. He wondered if the storytellers ever treated the kids to his grandfather's versions: how Eel lost his bones through gambling; how a magic buckskin tied to Ant's middle came to life and ran away, squeezing his waist into the shape it has today. He wondered what visitors would think of *Speel'yi* bartering fish for wives, or of Coyote's sisters living in his stomach in the form of huckleberries. Eddie used to claim that's why his own sisters were such little shits, at least until his father heard him. Then they both got a whooping, Eddie for saying it and Charlie for laughing.

It'd been a long time since he'd thought about the stories. His mother would tell him and his sister as much as she could remember, and read them the rest out of books. His grandfather never needed books. Charlie missed getting caught up in those stories, one tale leading into the other. He always felt warm and safe snuggled up on his mother's lap with Lilly, even when hearing about men crawling into caves after bears or people coming back from the dead. He would jump and giggle when his grandfather growled like a hungry wolf, and his mother, his constant protector, would hug him tighter. Back then he never questioned whether the stories were real.

But at some point he decided they weren't. He didn't remember when or how. It was sometime after Lilly died and his father left; probably around the time his mother started to drink, and he started to get angry. By the time he left for Seattle, the transformation was complete. It embarrassed him now to remember how superior he felt back then, thinking he was too old for the stories anymore, calling them myths, legends, anything but real. But as usual, the joke was on Charlie, too stupid at the time to recognize another one of his grandfather's lessons.

Now he realized that his mother and grandfather had believed in the *telling* of stories. It wasn't a matter of "right" and "wrong," or what other traditions one learned alongside them—it was handing them down that mattered. That's what made the stories real, and in the end they had bubbled up through all of Charlie's anger and mistakes. Maybe in some way the stories had led him back home. But what good did all this wallowing in the past do if he couldn't go back and fix it? He couldn't bring back his baby girl, or make Jenna want to get clean, or understand his father or magically bring his mother back home.

If only the stories could tell him where to go from here.

CHAPTER 21

TAMIA SAT HUNCHED over in her cubicle, pressing her cell phone to her ear. She always felt conspicuous taking personal calls at work, even though she could hear other people doing it all the time. Or, more precisely, *because* she heard other people doing it all the time.

"Did you get it?" asked Dr. Block.

"Yeah," whispered Tamia. "I have it open right now." And she couldn't believe what she was reading: *The emergent communicative functionality may have propagated through the mycorrhizal network . . .*

"We can't send this out," she told Dr. Block. "No one's going to understand it. It has to be punchy, but solid." Tamia wedged the phone between her shoulder and cheek and started to edit the document. "Something like, 'The trees' remarkable new ability to communicate with—'"

"Yes, yes," said Dr. Block. "Make whatever changes you need to for the layperson. But not over the phone. And nothing in the body of the e-mail either. Attachments are safer, I'm told. I'll send you some more names for the distribution list too."

Tamia was overwhelmed. So much to rewrite, and she still had to edit down the video, and they also had to come up with a mailing list from scratch. The governor's media list would be perfect, but that database was off-limits after an unfortunate occurrence with an intern a couple of years ago.

"Maybe we need to shorten the statement," Tamia suggested.

"I don't think so. People need the complete context of what they're seeing, otherwise it comes off as a bad magic trick." Dr. Block paused. "You were right about the video. I look crazed. I'd go out and make a better copy if I could."

But they both knew this would be impossible because, as Tamia couldn't forget for an instant, she had the translator now. "Look, I can't miss work again this week, but if we can wait until the weekend—" She was cut short by her supervisor's sudden appearance at her cubicle. "I'll call you back."

"Tamia, I hope you're feeling better," said Rima solicitously.

Tamia's hand froze. Rushing to close the document would only draw Rima's attention to it. "Oh, I'm fine. It was only a check-up. I just forgot about it until the last minute, so I had to hurry."

"I see," she replied, sounding unconvinced. "You got a minute?"

"Sure." As soon as Rima turned, Tamia closed the press release document and followed her down the hall to her office.

"Tamia, are you sure everything is all right?" she asked as they both sat down. "You seem a little preoccupied."

"Really? I don't feel preoccupied." She wondered if she sounded as guilty as she felt. "Is something wrong?"

Rima clicked her pen. "No, not that I'm aware. But the chief of staff just asked to speak with you." She paused. "I normally coordinate everyone's work, so I'm not sure why he's asking to speak with you directly."

"I don't know either," she answered, shrugging as innocently as she could. "But he *is* my mentor."

"Indeed." Rima pressed her lips together. "Go ahead," she said, motioning toward the chief of staff's office. "But I want to see your work on any projects Mr. Jones might assign to you, before you submit it to him."

Tamia nodded and left Rima's office as quickly as possible. What the hell, the higher-ups didn't seem to have a problem looping Greg in on Japan. So why did Rima think it was so crazy for someone important to want to speak directly with her? Maybe she'd been too hasty in defending Rima; maybe her mom was right about her boss' *problem.*

She stopped outside the chief of staff's office and patted her hair for strays before knocking on the door.

"Yes." Jones' voice was businesslike—intimidating.

Tamia smoothed down her shirt and opened the door. "You wanted to see me, sir?"

"Come in, Tamia." He motioned for her to sit on the couch, then came out from behind the desk to occupy a chair across from her. The *I'm just a regular Joe* seating arrangement. "Everything okay? Rima said you were out sick yesterday."

"Oh, I'm fine, thank you. It was just a doctor's appointment." *Great, now I'm lying to the chief of staff.*

"Well, that's good. Listen, I have a project for you. Remember the big report we did on aquatic invasive species?"

"Yes, sir." How could she forget? She'd started at the governor's office just as they were wrapping up the project the staff called "the longest, boringest report known to man." She'd spent her first few days hearing how thankful she should be that she hadn't come earlier.

"I'm sure you're aware that every environmental reporter in the state has taken a whack at it." He brushed non-existent dust off his trousers. "We're putting out an addendum this week, and our environmental team needs support. You'll be helping them. Briefing on Thursday, release that evening. I'll inform Rima you won't have time to work on anything else this week."

And Tamia was sure that was the whole point of the assignment. "Yes, sir," she said, and started to rise from her seat.

"One more thing," he said.

"Yes?" She settled uncomfortably back onto the couch.

"You seem a bit—distracted lately."

"Oh? No, I'm fine." Was there some memo going around regarding her attention span? "Everything's okay.

Well, other than my tomato plants." She smiled, trying to diffuse the tension.

"Well, I'm sorry for your tomato plants," he chuckled. "Do they complain as much as your trees?" His condescending smile hardened. "Have you heard anything more about your talking trees lately?"

She took in a deep breath as she considered how to respond. "I heard about a fire where some of them had been observed," she said. "It was in the news."

"Yes, forest fires are always a tragedy. What have you heard about this one?"

She swallowed. "Well, they say it was probably arson."

"Yes, that's one of the theories," Jones said, looking at her appraisingly. "But the investigation isn't over yet. We'll have to let the experts do their work. No use in speculating."

She steeled herself. "Do you—were you able to find out anything more about the video?"

He examined his fingernails before looking up at her. "Tamia, I hate to embarrass you, but as I suspected, the video wasn't real. I mean, what you thought you saw wasn't real. The scientist, Dr. . . ."

"Block."

"Yes, Dr. Block. She worked up quite a sophisticated device, but that's all it seems to be. There's no evidence that trees could have any of the abilities she purports they have."

"I—I don't understand. I was there, I saw it."

"No, Tamia, what you saw was a very clever trick. Our analysts couldn't tell how she did it. But if you could get that machine, whatever it was she used, if you could get that to me, I could run it by our people and we could try to figure it out. Do you think you could do that?"

Tamia's heart began to pound. "Well . . . if it's not real, there's no point in looking at the machine, is there?"

"I wouldn't say that," he said, pursing his lips. "I'm actually curious now. You're still in touch with her, aren't you? Would you bring it in?"

"I suppose, if you really want to spend the time—"

"Tamia." His voice was quiet but firm. "Get me that machine. Please."

She nodded weakly, wondering if he knew she already had it. "Yes, sir. But can it wait until after the invasive species addendum goes out?"

He nodded and thanked her with a tone that marked the end of their meeting. She left his office in a daze. Two days on this new project, and then she was supposed to hand over the machine. What would he do with it? And what would happen if she didn't give it to him? She was desperate to call Dr. Block, but knew Rima would be watching. *Keep your nose down, do your work and figure it out later.*

But there wasn't much time left for later.

CHAPTER 22

CHARLIE GLANCED AT the number flashing on the screen as he reached for the Cultural Center's phone. It wasn't Jenna's number, but that would only be a matter of time.

"Palalla Cultural Center."

"Hi, this is Liz Martin from Tacoma Elementary." Her voice was low and sweet. Sexy.

"Oh, hey, Ms. Martin, this is Charlie Meninick. I don't know if you remember me."

"Certainly, Charlie, I remember you."

His chest swelled.

"Please, call me Liz," she said, a smile in her voice.

Charlie's mind went blank. "How can I help you?" he asked. He winced, imagining the scratch of a needle on a record.

She cleared her throat. "I was just calling to thank you guys for organizing our visit. The kids are working on a card for you all."

"Oh, sure. Glad they enjoyed it." *What do I say now?* "Do you have our address?" A game show buzzer sounded in his mind.

"I think I've got it somewhere," she said, sounding more amused than put off.

"So," he said. "It's nice that you brought your class."

"Well, they didn't all get to go. I'd like to do it again for those who couldn't make it this time."

"That's a good idea," he answered. "I—we'd like to see you again. You and your class."

During the pause that followed, he pictured her trying to contain her laughter at his awkwardness.

147

"So, Charlie," she continued, a lilt in her voice. "You remember Ricky, the one who was climbing?"

"Yeah, nice kid."

She laughed. "He's still jazzed up from the visit. He's been pestering me to get in touch with you ever since the trip."

"Oh yeah? Why's that?" He couldn't believe it—finally something was opening up for him.

"Well, he's got quite an imagination," she said. "And as you saw, he's kind of obsessed with trees. He really connected with that part of the lesson plan, you know, about our relationship with our land, so now he's trying to be that way too. He's going around saying he's friends with trees."

"He told you that?"

"Not at first. I found out about it when I broke up a shoving match on the playground. It seems he went a little overboard with his 'tree friends' and now the other kids are teasing him about it."

"Huh," said Charlie. "What does he say his 'tree friends' do?"

"He says they help him. Keep him safe. He said they helped him during the field trip last weekend when he climbed too high."

"Did he show you?"

"No, we can't let the kids climb trees here," she said wistfully. "The woods are outside school grounds."

Charlie scoffed.

"I know," she said. "Anyway, Ricky's frustrated because no one believes him—well, only one little girl, he said—and he wants you to come to the school and show everyone you're friends with the trees too. You really made an impression on him."

"Well, if you want, I could talk to him."

"That's sweet, Charlie, but we're not supposed to put children in one-on-one contact with non-approved adults. Regulations."

"Oh, right."

"Sorry. It's not about *you*, per se," she said. "It's just for safety. I mean, we could schedule a meeting with the three of us, but his parents would need to be notified, and then they might wonder why he's being singled out, or the other parents would want special visits for their kids too, and on and on."

"Jeez."

"I know. It's almost easier to organize a whole event than to have a simple meeting with a student."

Charlie spoke before he thought. "I'll do it."

"Excuse me?"

"I'll come in," he said, scrambling for an idea. "You know, do a little talk, like a follow-up."

"And what exactly would you talk about?" she asked playfully.

"I could do a talk on . . . 'Native Americans Today.'"

"Right, because their teacher doesn't fit that description at all," she teased.

"Oh. No, I meant more like . . ." His mind raced. "Like . . ."

"Mr. Meninick," she said coyly, "it almost sounds like you're fishing for an invitation to Tacoma."

"You sure that's my hook in the water? I hear Palalla women like to fish too."

Silence. Had he gone too far?

"Yes," she finally said, "we've been known to cast a line now and then." He could imagine the embarrassed little smile on her pretty, brown face. He wished he were looking at it right now. "Well, I have to go," she said. "Homework to grade."

He only had a second to keep her from slipping away. "Can I call you tomorrow? About the visit?"

"Yes," she said, "I'd like that."

For that one moment, everything was right in Charlie's world.

CHAPTER 23

TAMIA TURNED AWAY from Capitol Lake and headed back up the winding path toward the Legislative Building. Soon she'd pass the old plant conservatory and be reminded once again of the committee she still hadn't joined. But then, that wasn't exactly the most important thing going on in her life right now.

The aquatic species briefing that morning had been rough, but at least it was over. They didn't need her for the final draft, which confirmed her suspicion that they hadn't actually needed her in the first place.

No matter, now she had to finish Dr. Block's press release, and then decide on the best way to send it. She didn't see any way around using the general governor's office e-mail. If she or Dr. Block used their own e-mail accounts, the message could wind up in spam filters or relegated to the loony private citizen trash folder.

And she also had to decide what to do about Derrick Jones and the machine he wanted her to hand over.

Tamia's phone sang and she dug it out of her purse. "Hi, Dr. Block."

"Tamia, someone broke into my house."

"What? When?"

"Last night. I was out at a dinner, and when I got back—it was a disaster."

"Oh my god, are you all right?" She kept her voice low and hurried up the trail, glancing around at the trickle of tourists on the path with her.

"Yes, I'm fine, but they completely ransacked the place. I'm sure it was ArborTech. And I know what they were looking for."

Tamia's hand shot up to her mouth. "Did you call the police? Can they track them down?"

Dr. Block sighed. "Yes, the police came out. But these guys are good; I'm sure they know how to do this without leaving a trace. They took a few valuables to make it look like a robbery. And they took some of my files too."

Tamia gasped.

"It's okay," said Dr. Block. "They didn't get anything important."

Tamia had reached the top of the path. She needed privacy, and she wouldn't get any in her cubicle. She looked over at the dilapidated conservatory.

"You have to be careful," the scientist warned. "I was the first target, and they didn't find what they were looking for, so I'm afraid you'll be next."

Tamia stiffened at the last three words.

"Tamia?"

"Hang on." She unrooted her feet and tried to walk casually toward the greenhouse. *I'll be next.* Her skin prickled. "This is crazy," she whispered. She turned to see if anyone was watching and jiggled the front door handle. Locked. "I'm just going to give the machine back to Jones, and this whole thing will be over."

"No!" barked Dr. Block. "You can't! That machine is the only way we can keep doing our work."

Tamia slid behind the box hedges around the side of the conservatory, crouching below a row of large, cloudy windows. "It's *your* work, Dr. Block," she hissed. "I'm not cut out for this." She crept farther along the wall, careful to stay below the windows and hoping the bushes would provide cover from the path. "And it's not just about me. I have a housemate, what about her? And what about my family?"

"I understand you're afraid, Tamia. I am too. But it won't stop with the machine, you know. I doubt ArborTech believes your mentor deleted the only copy of the video."

"Well, what am I supposed to do? I can't spend the rest of my life looking over my shoulder." Tamia tensed at a murmur coming from the path. As soon as the voices trailed away, she moved behind a rusty dumpster wedged against the wall.

"That's why we have to get more people involved," said Dr. Block. "We can't wait for perfection. We have to get this message out today."

"Won't that just encourage them? I mean they burned down a forest! What'll stop them from coming after us?"

"Scrutiny, Tamia. They can't do a thing if they're in the spotlight. And we're running out of time."

"I'm sorry, Dr. Block, but I'm out. I can't do this anymore. I have to think about my family." Though her head felt so faint she couldn't think about much of anything.

"Don't be rash," pleaded Dr. Block. "At least give the translator back to me and let me worry about it."

"Okay, but what if I give it back and they still think I have it?"

Dr. Block sighed. "I don't know."

The groan of a heavy door inside the greenhouse caught Tamia's breath. "Hang on." She held the phone to her chest as footsteps clicked across a grimy floor.

"Look, can't this wait till I get back to my office?" said a voice from inside the conservatory. Then, in a low growl, "You did what? God dammit, I told you to wait!"

Tamia held her breath. *Is that the chief of staff? What is he doing in there?*

The voice continued, angry and low: "She was going to bring it right to me. Yes, I was going to get the documents too, until you went and fucked everything up."

Tamia peeked up briefly through a cracked window. *Holy shit, that's him!* She quietly cut off her call and put her phone on mute before turning on the record function. Hopefully she hadn't missed everything.

"But did you get what you needed?" asked Jones. "Can I tell Palmer we're done here?" He muttered another expletive. "I'll talk to her again. Block must have given everything to her."

Tamia's heart lodged itself in her throat.

"Jesus, no, stand down! Just wait for my call. And don't you lay a hand on her, you understand?"

The footsteps clicked again and the heavy door creaked. Silence. She turned the recorder off and finally paid attention to Dr. Block's worried messages, texting back with clumsy fingers: *I'm okay. Talk later.*

She needed time to think. But how much time did she have? What if they were at her house right now? Jones had told them to hold off, but they didn't seem to be in the habit of listening to him.

Her housemate was going out of town this weekend. This might all be resolved by the time she got back if Tamia gave up the machine. Or it might not be, if they thought she still had Dr. Block's files. She couldn't give them something she didn't have. But what could she do, other than sit around and wait for them to break in—or do something worse? The only thing she actually had any control over was the press release.

She checked the time on her phone. Jones and Rima would be in their weekly meeting soon. She hurried back to the office and sat back down in front of her computer with as much nonchalance as she could muster. She had about an hour. She scanned the press release. Was it good enough to throw the spotlight on ArborTech? She could either spend the hour scraping up a few more contacts, or . . .

She clicked on a folder called "Communications." There had to be another version of the governor's media list floating around somewhere. In all the offices where she'd had summer jobs, she'd never known of a document having just one incarnation. She clicked on "Press Releases" and various subfolders organized by fiscal year and topic. Would it be in "Wildlife" or "Environment" or "Coastal Health"?

Fukushima! Everybody and their dog had called in about that one. Two more clicks and—her stomach fluttered as she opened up the governor's press list. It was old, but there it was, with hundreds of solid contacts. Journalists, pundits, business leaders, lobbyists, association chiefs—people who would definitely read a message from the governor's office and get the word out.

Tamia swallowed hard and copied more than 300 e-mail addresses from the spreadsheet into the bcc field of a new e-mail. What the hell was she doing? Was this really worth getting fired over when she could just turn over the machine? She'd never find another job with something like this on her record.

Tamia jumped at the chief of staff's voice down the hall, followed by Rima's. *They're out early!* With jittery fingers, she cut and pasted the text of her press release into the open e-mail. She thought about the phone call in the conservatory. Would Derrick Jones really be able to protect her from ArborTech?

Her hand felt numb on the mouse. She could have sworn she heard her name from down the hallway. Tamia double-clicked on the paperclip symbol and attached the video file. She moved her cursor over to the send button and held her breath.

❧ CHAPTER 24

RICKY PICKED UP his cereal bowl and drank the rest of the milk while his parents thumbed their phones. "Can Charlie come over tomorrow?" he asked.

"Charlie again?" asked his mother. "You've been talking about him all week."

Ricky's father furrowed his brow. "Grampa said this guy is a lot older than you, like in his twenties, maybe early thirties."

Leave it to Grampa to ruin everything, Ricky grumbled to himself.

"Your dad's right. We don't know this man," his mother said, looking back at her screen.

"Well, then let's all go out there and you can meet him!"

"Ricky, honey," she sighed. "We can't just drop everything and run over to Nakalish."

"Why not?" pouted Ricky.

"It's three hours away, and you were just there last weekend."

"And you have other things to do," his father added. "Like visit with your grandfather."

"Well, where is he?" asked Ricky, throwing his hands open in the grampa-less room.

"Hey, watch your tone," warned his father. "He's out doing his research now. But he'll be back for lunch, and your attitude had better improve by then."

"Why don't you go outside for a bit," suggested his mother. She didn't have to ask twice. He left the house as fast as he could pull on his windbreaker.

He stomped off into the woods, brooding. No one believed him! He knew he shouldn't have told anyone.

His teacher, his parents, everyone thought he was making it all up, even when Viola told them it was true. And all Grampa did was hook machines up to the trees, which they probably didn't like, and say a bunch of nonsense like "check, check, testing." He never really talked to them, never asked how they were feeling. The only person who probably knew how was Charlie.

He reached up and pulled himself up into a stout, twisted oak. He knew how to pick the right ones now, the ones that leaned and had little creases and divots for his fingers and toes, so he wouldn't wind up tearing off bits by accident. He got up to the second branch okay, but was still a bit too short to reach the next one.

"Can you help me, please?" he asked. He stepped a little farther away from the trunk to where the branch was a more flexible. With a creak, it carried him higher while he crouched and balanced like a surfer. At the same time, another limb dipped down from above. Ricky stood and stretched toward the limb, grabbing it to test its strength. "Okay!" he yelled. He gripped the branch as it pulled him up onto another broad, sturdy limb. He scooted on his butt along the limb to the trunk and settled into the crook.

Ricky dangled one of his legs in the air and looked out at the birds flitting from tree to tree. Squirrels ran up and down the trunks with nuts, getting ready for winter. If he waited and was quiet, he might even see a deer. He stopped moving his leg and settled into a comfortable position to wait. Pretty soon something crunched through the leaves below—but it wasn't a deer.

He looked down onto the top of Grampa Nystrom's head moving toward the house. Was it lunchtime already? His grandfather stopped and his head swiveled, as though he'd heard something. Ricky held his breath.

Grampa seemed to dismiss whatever he was listening for and strode toward a prickly-looking pine. He hooked his machine up to the trunk; but this time instead of just talking nonsense, he was actually trying to talk to it like a person.

"Hello?" said his grandfather. He was speaking quietly, so Ricky could barely make out what he was saying. "Can you hear me? Say 'yes' if you can. Please confirm, say 'yes' if you can hear me."

Ricky couldn't see Grampa Nystrom's face, but the older man clutched his head like he was excited or nervous. "My god, it's true," he said. "How is this possible? How long have you had this capability?" There was a pause. "How long, how many years?" After another pause, "I see, we need to start slowly. That's fine. Do you have a name?"

Ricky sat still in the twisty tree while Grampa Nystrom peppered the pine with questions. His legs felt stiff and he desperately wanted to shift position, but he didn't want to make any noise either. His right foot fell asleep.

"How many of you are there?" asked his grandfather. "How far away can you—see? Feel?"

Ricky finally had to shift his leg, grimacing as hundreds of invisible needles pricked his calf. He wiggled the sleeping leg, keeping an eye on his grandfather below. As he got to his feet, he realized the other leg was cramped too. As if on command, the oak dipped a branch toward him from above. He tried to wave it away, afraid it would attract his grandfather's attention, but suddenly the branch he was standing on tipped downward. Ricky had no choice but to grab the limb hovering over his head. Yellow leaves swirled lazily down around him. Ricky strengthened his grip on the branch and looked down at his grandfather—who was by then looking directly at him.

The branch Ricky was holding ferried him lower, until he was able to step onto the next one. With his left leg stiff and his right leg still asleep, he relied mostly on his arms to descend, hanging from one branch after another like a monkey. When he could afford to, Ricky stole a glance at his grandfather, who stood with his mouth open. Ricky was almost at the bottom when Grampa Nystrom, as if in a trance, gently reached up and carried him down to the forest floor.

Grampa Nystrom knelt down in front of Ricky, gripping him by the shoulders. Ricky squirmed a little at the look in his eye. His grandfather stared at the oak, then back at the pine with the machine strapped to its trunk before returning his unnerving gaze to Ricky.

"This is impossible," he whispered.

"It's okay, Grampa, they're my friends."

Dr. Nystrom shook his head slowly. He rose and looked at the forest around him, clutching Ricky to his side.

"It's okay, Grampa," Ricky repeated. "They won't hurt us. They're our friends. Charlie's friends too!"

"Charlie? Who's Charlie?"

"Charlie, the Palalla man." Ricky almost jumped with excitement; someone was listening to him! "Charlie Meninick. He's friends with the trees too. Can we go see him, Grampa? Please?"

Grampa Nystrom looked away and nodded absent-mindedly. "I have to—"

Ricky watched him rummage around in his bag. When he pulled out the plastic bags and shears, Ricky knew what was coming.

"Grampa, do you have to?"

"Do I have to what?" asked the old man, taking out a notepad and pen.

Ricky pointed at the shears.

"I'm sorry, Ricky, but yes." He jotted down notes and labeled the plastic bags. "I have to catalog these specimens. Then I can go back to the lab and see how they're different, you see?"

"But you can already see how they're different!"

Grampa Nystrom stopped and looked at him. "Ricky, your Grampa just realized he has a problem that he can't solve all by himself. I need your help, okay?"

Ricky nodded.

"I just need to do some tests to make sure the trees are healthy."

Ricky fidgeted. "But what if they're not? What if they're sick? Are you going to chop them down?"

His grandfather bent down to his height. "No, I'm not going hurt them. But there are some other people, bad people, who are trying to harm the special trees. That's why I need you to help me find them before the bad guys do. Can you do that?" Grampa Nystrom stuck out his hand for Ricky to shake.

"Yeah, Grampa!" said Ricky, shaking his grandfather's hand.

"Good! Now, we've got some work to do." He looked up into the branches of the oak from which Ricky had descended. "Why don't you climb up there again; distract it while I take the samples I need."

"Grampa, maybe Charlie can help us. Maybe you don't have to—"

"Ricky."

That was the grown-up tone Ricky knew he couldn't argue with.

The older man pulled a long, thin metal tube out of his bag and unscrewed the end. With a rustle and a blur of needles, a pine bough swept toward him and knocked the tube out of his hands. He yelped and pulled Ricky away from the tree.

"Grampa look!" Ricky pointed at the machine on the trunk, which displayed a new message: ONE HUNDRED SIXTY THREE YEARS

"What does that mean?" Ricky asked.

His grandfather's mouth hung open.

"Grampa?"

Grampa Nystrom jerked back to attention. "I, ah, I think I've got everything I need from this one." He extended a cautious arm to the tree and sidled up to it to retrieve his machine.

Ricky ran up to the pine and patted its bark. "Don't worry, tree. Grampa and me, we'll keep you safe."

CHAPTER 25

CHARLIE AND EDDIE sat in the living room staring at, but not really watching, the TV. The sound was down low. A sliver of late afternoon sun obscured the middle of the screen, but neither of them got up to close the gap in the curtains. Pots and pans clacked against the stovetop as Eddie's wife prepared dinner. The scent of baking salmon wafted out of the kitchen, along with her voice calmly directing the children to sit down and finish their homework.

"You know," said Eddie, "if you're tired of sleepin' on the couch, one of the guys at work is lookin' to rent out the space above his garage. It's cheap."

"How cheap? You know I'm tryin' to save up for another truck."

"Cheaper'n a truck. And it's close to your work."

"But I wasn't planning to keep that job too long," he said, though staying at the Cultural Center *would* make it more convenient to keep in touch with Liz. "Don't you want me back out at the cabin?"

Eddie stretched his arms upward and slung them around the back of his head. "Nah. That accident freaked people out. No one's headin' back to that part of the woods anytime soon."

Charlie looked over at Eddie's profile, surprised that he'd brought up the accident. "So, what ever happened with that kid who came by here, the Greyfox kid?"

"I told you not to worry about him."

"If you need help with anything . . ."

Eddie's eyes flicked in his direction. "Nothin' to help with." He reached for the remote and turned up the volume on the evening news.

The anchor's voice boomed into the room. "And tonight, we end with a story that hit local news outlets like a bombshell this week: the tale of the talking trees."

Charlie's eyes shot back to the TV.

"An astounding revelation from the office of Governor Palmer. According to a press release and video e-mailed from his office late last week, Washington scientist Barbara Block claims to have discovered a means of speaking with trees. The video has gone viral, popping up on websites and media outlets around the world. Where did this video come from, and could it possibly be true? News 4 science reporter Trish Evans went to check it out."

"What the hell?" snorted Eddie, raising the remote to change channels.

"Shhh!" Charlie held out his hand to stop Eddie.

A young, blonde reporter stood in a park, surrounded by trees. "Scientists and environmentalists around the world have been speculating about the authenticity of the by-now famous video released by the office of Governor Tad Palmer. The video features Dr. Barbara Block, Professor Emeritus of the University of Washington, demonstrating a device that she says allows people to communicate with trees." A snippet of the video showing words scrolling across the translator's screen accompanied the reporter's voiceover. "Governor Palmer's office has since published a retraction of the statement, but the video still remains on dozens of websites. And the question on everyone's minds is, could this be true? Could humans actually talk to the trees?"

The shot switched to a bemused-looking Forest Service official. "Well, this is an unprecedented phenomenon, and we currently don't have any data to support it. Bottom line, our main concern is the health of the forest, and if we see solid evidence of any biological changes occurring—which we haven't—we'll take appropriate action. But we also have to keep an eye out for unintended consequences, like increased numbers of people coming in and disrupting ecologically sensitive areas looking for these talking trees."

"No," said the next interviewee, a haughty blonde forestry specialist from the University of Washington. "Completely impossible. We can hear lots of things going on in the inner life of trees, such as the circulation of water and sap, and we can make inferences about what that tells us—indicates to us—about the health of the tree. But a conversation?" She shook her head vigorously in front of the reporter's microphone. "No. They simply don't have the intelligence to recognize speech, comprehend a message, and formulate a response."

"See?" muttered Eddie. "It's bullshit."

"Hang on," said Charlie, leaning over and snatching the remote away from him.

"Well, this is the first time we've heard anything like this," said a wide-eyed, frizzy-haired representative from the Sierra Club. "But wouldn't it be wonderful? It would completely transform the way we interact with our environment. We're going to keep watching this story."

A young Olympia resident holding her toddler was next. "Wow, that's kind of weird, but I'd be curious. I mean, if they can test for it, why not?"

The anchor in the studio appeared once again in a split screen with the reporter in the field. "Trish, that last person mentioned testing. What is that?"

"Chris, Dr. Block has created a blog with videos and contact information, and is offering free consultations for anyone who wants to test their trees' ability to repeat speech or even hold a conversation. It all happens through her machine, which she calls a 'circulatory translator.' She is the only person known to have this type of translator, which is making some experts skeptical. But it's getting a lot of attention, particularly from environmental circles."

"And what does the governor's office have to say about all this? This story originated from that office."

"Chris, in a written statement, the governor's spokesperson apologized to the recipients of this very unusual video, saying that the message was by no means an official communication from the office of the governor. They also assured recipients that their information has not been in any way hacked or compromised, but rather it was an unfortunate staff issue, which has since been dealt with."

"Did they have any comment on the content of this press release, about the concept of talking trees?"

"No, they are just advising people to stay calm, and if they have any concerns about the health of their trees, to contact their local horticulturist. Now, Dr. Block has been bombarded with requests for testing. News 4 spoke with her today, and we've arranged an interview on site tomorrow morning, so we'll be back with an update on this very interesting story. Chris?"

"Thank you, Trish. We're looking forward to more about this strange case. In other news—"

Charlie turned off the TV. "Eddie? You think maybe we should get our trees tested?"

"Are you kiddin' me?"

"No, I'm not." He looked down at the remote in his hands. "Look, Eddie, there's something I never told you. I saw some things in the forest."

"You saw the bottom of a few too many beers, Cuz."

Charlie's anger sparked. Why did it always come back to that? "I'm talkin' about the poachers."

"We're done talkin' about that accident." Eddie stared into the black screen. "It's done, investigation over, the Nation got the tree back. Everyone's happy."

"Not everyone," said Charlie. Eddie turned to meet his glare.

Eddie's wife's voice drifted in from the dining room. "Come on, kids, time to set the table. Dinner's almost ready."

"Let me help you with that," Eddie called out. He hoisted himself off his recliner and headed into the kitchen.

Charlie knitted his eyebrows and stared at the floor. Didn't they just watch the same report? It was like Eddie was intent on ignoring everything.

So what was he trying to hide?

CHAPTER 26

A FRESHLY-FIRED Tamia stood with Dr. Block and the latest TV crew in a section of forest less than five miles from the scientist's bungalow. A gust of wind ruffled the leaves overhead. They sounded brittle to Tamia's ears. A fair number of them had turned yellow and brown.

Dr. Block had been moving their testing area closer and closer to her bungalow over the past few days. The trees' speech ability was consistent no matter where they tried it. For Dr. Block this was an exciting scientific development, but for Tamia it was a cause for concern. Two nights ago, another fire had "mysteriously" broken out in one of the test plots. Tamia crunched a few fallen leaves under the toe of her boot, counting back the days since the last rainfall.

Crazy, a Seattle girl yearning for precipitation.

Her phone rang, and she stepped away from the crowd. It was her mother, no doubt calling to ask when she was going to move back in.

"Hey Mom."

"Tamia, I just heard about the fire."

"Yeah, Mom, it's out. It was miles away, anyway." She spared her mother the small detail that they'd seen and smelled the smoke.

"Baby, when are you going to come home?"

"Mama, I'm fine. I've got an internship with Dr. Block now."

"Internship, huh? So free labor."

Tamia was silent. They'd already had it out over how she'd lost her job, and she wasn't looking to get fussed at so soon again.

"I knew it," said her mother. "How are you going to make a living? Come home so we can figure this out. You can work for your father till you get on your feet."

She knew how bad things must look from her mother's perspective. Tamia couldn't blame her for being skeptical, after all the doubts she'd shared about Dr. Block. At any rate, she'd have to find a real job or another place to live by the end of the month. Her housemate was pissed about the short notice, and had already started screening new candidates. And who knew if she would ever get a job in government again. Or anywhere else, for that matter.

"Mom, if only you and Dad would come down here and take a look for yourselves. Dr. Block's finally making headway, and with serious people. UW sent folks out here to take samples. And the Forest Service too, although they were kind of dicks about it."

"Tamia."

"Sorry. But Mom, if you come down here, you'll see it. People are starting to take us seriously!"

Her mother sighed. "Baby, of course we support you. But you know, you've got your career to think about. And those loan payments."

"I'll take care of my loan payments."

"They're in our name too, remember." Tamia filled in the rest: *Don't squander our investment.*

"I hear you, Mom, I do, but I've got to help Dr. Block with this first."

"For how long?"

She knew her mother wouldn't leave her alone without a definitive answer. "I don't know, another couple of weeks? Just until the first wave of craziness calms down. Then . . ." She sighed. This was the last thing she wanted to think about right now. "Then I'll move back in and get a job. Any job."

"Not just any job," said her mother. "The right job, you'll see. They weren't treating you right at the last place anyway. You'll find another job where they appreciate you."

Tamia had to smile—Mama Bear all the way. "Okay, Mom. I have to go now. I have to keep Block on schedule. Call you this weekend. Love you."

"Love you too, Sweet T."

Tamia slipped the phone back into her pocket and returned to Dr. Block and the camera crew. The warm, protective glow she'd felt during her call faded with every step toward the reporters. Their shocked expressions told her Dr. Block was mid-demonstration.

"Where did you come from?" the scientist asked, facing the furrowed trunk of a Douglas fir. Her eyes darted between the machine strapped to it and another recording device. "How were you made?"

EARTH SUN WATER

"How did you learn to speak?"

WE SPEAK MACHINE

"Yes, but how did you learn to speak through the machine?"

TREES LEARN TREES

"How do trees learn from trees?"

ROOTS

Dr. Block looked over to Tamia, her eyes both excited and frightened. "They know what 'roots' are now. They're learning faster every day." She turned to the reporter. "Yesterday I was reviewing basic tree anatomy with that alder way over there, and they—there is no 'I' for them, by the way. Each tree refers to itself in the plural, always 'we' and 'us.' At any rate, they learned the difference between 'feet' and 'roots.' They're not just parroting words back; they really understand them. And that understanding spreads quickly from tree to tree."

"So trees teach trees through roots," said the doctor to the Douglas fir. "But who taught the first trees?"

TREES

"Did a human teach the trees?"

TREES HEAR HUMANS ALWAYS

"And that's exactly what a company like ArborTech might have had in mind," said Dr. Block.

The reporter's eyes brightened. "Tell me more about ArborTech, Dr. Block."

"ArborTech," she replied, "is one of the world's go-to companies for tree biotechnology. Their mission is to maximize the productivity of trees by engineering frost-resistant varieties; creating specimens that grow bigger, taller and straighter to produce more salable timber; and maximizing growth rates and production of pulpwood, cellulose, and biofuels. You know, bigger, faster, stronger, like the Bionic Man."

The TV crew smiled, but Tamia had heard this more than a few times by now. Dr. Block had been reluctant to mention ArborTech at first, but the closer the fires got to her home, the more she'd started talking about them. It was like she was in a race to tell as many people as possible about their involvement before the next blaze broke out. And here they were, just sitting around in a pile of kindling waiting for that match to drop.

The scientist went on. "Now, for some of these features they use traditional breeding methods, but their specialty is genetic modification. As you can imagine, they're eager to gain approval for field trials of genetically engineered products. In fact, they've actually been known to help defend the USDA in court for allowing certain field trials."

The reporter's eyes twinkled. "You're saying ArborTech colluded with the USDA to steamroll new products through the approval process?"

"Let's not sensationalize," said Dr. Block, raising her hand. "They merely interceded—proactively—to help the USDA prove that proper procedures had been followed. The takeaway is that companies like ArborTech don't have the adversarial relationship with the USDA people might assume. Most people think of the USDA as a 'watchdog' or 'gatekeeper,' but it can sometimes be more like a partner. And the USDA is not alone."

Dr. Block counted examples on her fingers. "There are private companies working with the Army Corps of Engineers on toxic waste cleanup, and the Department of Energy is investing in biofuel research. I suspect a company like ArborTech would need the support of a powerful government agency for an ambitious project like *this*," she said, patting the trunk of the Douglas fir she'd been interviewing.

Academics, thought Tamia. Dr. Block seemed to think she was tiptoeing around ArborTech and DARPA, but there was no way she could talk to so many reporters and expect that nuance to be preserved. She was like one of those guys with two flashlights at the airport, leading ArborTech right to her doorstep.

Tamia shepherded reporters around for the rest of the afternoon. Dark clouds smudged the sky as the last crew packed up to leave. Thunderstorms had been predicted for that evening. For the third night in a row, Dr. Block invited Tamia to stay for dinner. Her housemate hated her anyway, so why not?

As they ate, the clouds thickened and the wind picked up. After dinner, they read the press from the previous day and reviewed the schedule for the next. Neither of them cared how late it was; their shared conviction carried them through the hours. It reminded Tamia of working on an election campaign—something she would probably never get to do again.

Dr. Block put her fists on her hips and looked at a map they'd pinned to the wall. "I want to bring the press here tomorrow." She pointed to an area even closer to the bungalow than they'd been that afternoon.

"Don't you think that's too close? Why can't we go over here, or here?" asked Tamia, picking spots farther away.

"We already know about those areas. I'm trying to document the spread."

"And you think ArborTech's just going to sit still while you implicate them?"

"They've already come right through my door and ransacked the place. I'd say I'm already on their radar."

Tamia scowled and pointed to the map again. "Okay, but why not here, or here? We haven't brought anyone in there yet."

"No, those are protected areas."

"Yeah, well—"

"What does that mean, 'yeah well'?" snapped Dr. Block. "That's the whole problem. If something threatens a person, it gets attention, but if it's just a few hundred animals and old growth trees, well, that's no problem?"

"Okay, I get it. But why guide the fires toward you?" asked Tamia. "Aren't there other homes around here? Other people?"

"I'm not the one setting the fires. I'm just making sure the focus stays on Arbortech so they can't keep on burning with impunity." She sat down at the table and folded her hands. "I don't have a death wish, Tamia. Even ArborTech has to blink at some point. Burning down trees is one thing—they could simply say they were destroying materials that got beyond their testing area. But burning down homes, putting people in danger? There would be no excuse for that. I can't believe they would take that risk."

Tamia leaned against the map on the wall. "You're putting a lot of trust in a company that's trying to take you down."

"Perhaps," mused Dr. Block.

"You're not exactly being coy about the government's involvement either."

"You noticed?" she replied with a fleeting grin.

"Do you think . . .?" Tamia sat down across from Dr. Block. "Do you think the government might come after you? Like, arrest you for possession of unauthorized material or releasing secret information?"

Dr. Block nodded thoughtfully. "I'm sure they could try. But that would mean admitting their involvement."

Tamia clenched her hands together. "Could they come after me too?" It wasn't the first time she'd thought about it, but it had all seemed too unreal to mention until now.

Dr. Block shook her head. "Even if they tried, I don't think it would stick. They can't prove you have access to any government documents or secrets. The video you disseminated was our own. They can't arrest you for suspecting something."

"I guess not," said Tamia. *I hope not.* She tried to ignore the feeling of dread pressing down on her chest. The wind whipped around outside the cabin.

"Sounds like quite a storm brewing out there," said Dr. Block. "Why don't you stay here tonight?" With the long days of testing and interviews, this had become part of the drill too.

Tamia smelled rain in the air when she went out to the car for her bag. Leaves tumbled along a patch of ground illuminated through the window. Hopefully it would rain hard enough to put out any fires ArborTech planned on setting.

After Dr. Block went to bed, Tamia settled on to the couch and listened to the wind gathering strength. Trees clicked and creaked against one another like a giant gnashing its teeth. Far away thunder rumbled soft and low. Normally Tamia liked thunderstorms, but their conversation about ArborTech and potential prosecution had left her feeling exposed.

She dozed off a couple of times before finally standing up to get ready for bed. She felt silly for being spooked, but still took twice as long to brush her teeth, stopping to listen for any strange noises coming from outside. Heading back into the living room, she grabbed the blanket and pillow Dr. Block had left for her and flopped back onto the couch. She stretched out and stared at the ceiling, now annoyingly awake.

Something gnawed at her. She dug out her phone and did a search, but couldn't find any updates about the dead timber poachers in Palalla. She wasn't sure why she was so obsessed with them. Perhaps the "random" fires breaking out around Dr. Block's cabin were causing her brain to churn out murky conspiracy theories. If only there were some way to reach that guy, Meninick, who was supposed to have seen the accident go down.

A flash of light sliced into the room around the edges of the blinds. Tamia counted the seconds until the thunder rolled to her ears. It was still far away. She closed her eyes, telling herself to breathe deeply and relax. The first drops of rain pattered on the windowsill, fat and heavy. She'd always loved that sound. Her breathing grew deeper and her muscles relaxed as she listened to the pat pat pat of raindrops.

Crack!

Tamia awoke with a start, and it took her a moment to remember where she was. Something had—

Crack!

She sat up and strained to listen. It was raining hard. Light flashed in around the window blinds, quickly followed by booming thunder.

Crack!

There was something more than thunder in that sound, something big and close. It sounded like wood breaking, but the wind wasn't strong enough to snap limbs, was it?

Crack!

That was it! She had to go check it out.

Tamia found the flashlight and checked the batteries. She looped the bag holding the translator across her chest, zipped her hooded coat up over it and stepped outside. After a moment's thought, she stepped back inside and grabbed a meat cleaver. Irrational, yes, but somehow it made her feel a little more secure.

She stood on the porch, sweeping the flashlight beam from side to side. She listened for something through the syncopated rhythms of raindrops hitting the roof, the leaves and the ground. Lightning illuminated the whole clearing for a second. Thunder popped, quick and fierce. Tamia listened, waggling the weight of the meat cleaver in her hand and breathing in the peaty odor of wet earth. She heard more creaking and cracking, but couldn't figure out where it was coming from.

Then she heard a cry for help.

Tamia leapt off the porch and ran around the side of the house, toward the yelling. She spun like a top in the wind and rain, trying to see whoever was crying out. It sounded like a man, and he sounded hurt—and high above her.

She pointed the beam of her flashlight straight up the nearest tree, catching a glimpse of thrashing branches and black clothing. Water and leaves fell into her eyes, forcing her to back away. As she looked up again, a flash of lightning revealed a screaming man writhing fifty feet up the tree. He was horizontal, twisting, fighting tangles of twigs and branches around his head and feet. Thunder cracked and the lightning died out.

"Hey!" called Tamia, directing the beam of her flashlight at him. "Hold on, I'll get—"

The man's body rose sharply. The branches holding him swooped down, striking him against another tree limb below. The man's screams turned from panic to pain. The meat cleaver slipped out of Tamia's hand. The tree limbs holding the man jerked up and whipped down again, battering his body against the branch below.

Tamia backed away, unable to breathe. Lightning illuminated another thrash of the man's body against the sturdy branch beneath him. Thunder boomed and the sky went dark. Next came the cascading crash of something falling through layers of branches, followed by a sickening dull thump.

Tamia's breath came back in gasps. Fat, cold raindrops pelted her and she began to shake. She trained her trembling flashlight on the ground below the tree. A twisted lump lay motionless on the wet earth. Steeling herself, she swooped the light upward to check for any more movement, then stumbled over to the body. It was a white man with blue eyes—they were still wide open. His black windbreaker was slick with rain and blood. She knelt down next to the body and tried to check for breathing or a pulse. His neck felt loose in her hand.

A fresh wave of shivers overtook her. She stood and turned to run inside, but a blinding light stopped her. The beam of light descended from her face to the body at her feet.

"It's me," said Dr. Block. Her voice floated out of the shadow cast by the porchlight behind her. A long, dark shape resembling a shotgun hung by her side.

"Dr. Block, I think he's dead!"

"Who is that? What's going on out here?" She walked toward Tamia and the body, her voice harsh with fear.

"We need an ambulance!" Tamia yelled. She ran past Dr. Block to get to a phone inside. But even as she dialed 9-1-1, she knew it was too late.

CHAPTER 27

RICKY HUNG BY his knees from an oak, but despite his best efforts, it wasn't moving.

He was tired. Excited, but tired. He'd been leading Grampa Nystrom around the woods all day, showing him the trees he'd become friends with. Grampa had brought little colored ribbons this time, which he attached to the trees depending on what they could do. Bright blue if they could move, yellow if they could talk, or day-glo green if they did both. He'd even let Ricky see what a couple of them were saying through his machine. Grampa told him he'd invented it but the bad people wanted to take it away from him, so Ricky couldn't tell anyone he had it, not even his mom and dad.

"How about a lunch break?" asked Grampa. Ricky watched him attach a yellow ribbon to the oak, then dig around in his backpack and produce a couple of sandwiches. They sat down on a fallen tree trunk and unwrapped their lunches. It was just peanut butter and jelly, but Ricky was so hungry it tasted like the best thing he'd ever eaten. The old man smiled at him and ruffled his hair. Grampa wasn't so bad after all.

Ricky heard a tiny mariachi band, and Grampa felt around his vest pockets before pulling out his phone. He frowned at it before he answered.

"Hello, Barbara," he said.

Who's that? wondered Ricky.

"Yes, I'm all right. I'm sorry I haven't answered your calls." Grampa Nystrom wrapped up the rest of his sandwich and stood. "I didn't think it would be wise at the time. But things have changed." He looked at Ricky. "Just a moment," he said, and put his hand over the phone. "I'll be right back," he told Ricky. Then he walked away, murmuring seriously into the phone.

Does Grampa have a girlfriend? Ricky wondered. *Is that why he's so nice now?* No, he knew it wasn't just that. It was also about the trees. Grampa was really excited about them, and he didn't prod and scrape at them as much as he used to, which made Ricky happy too.

Ricky shoved the rest of his sandwich into his mouth and walked up to the machine left strapped to the tree. Yellow ribbon: it could talk. He swallowed his mouthful and took a drink from the bottle his mother had insisted he attach to his belt loop.

"Hello tree?"

HELLO RICKEE

Ricky was surprised. He hadn't talked to this one yet. "How did you know my name?"

TREES LEARN TOGETHER

"Really? So if I tell one of you something, you tell everyone else?"

WE NOT TELL WE ALL KNOW

"Like the Borg!" said Ricky. A little scary, but cool.

WHAT BORG

"The Borg, it's this thing in Star Trek, this creature," said Ricky. "If one Borg sees or hears something, it's like all of them see and hear it. They're, like, one monster with a bunch of separate parts."

ARE WE MONSTER

"No, of course not. Trees are good. Monsters are bad."

WHAT GOOD WHAT BAD

Ricky looked over at his grandfather, who was still in the middle of his call. He faced the machine again. "Well, if someone is good, they do good things. They try to help people, like, I don't know, give them food if they're hungry, or help them if they're sick, or protect them from the bad people. Bad people try to hurt you or take away your stuff. They're mean."

RAIN GOOD AXE BAD

"Yeah!"

180

HUMANS GOOD OR BAD

Ricky twisted his lips. Had the tree just asked a question or stated its opinion? Either way, he felt like he should answer. "Well, some of us are good and some are bad. It depends. But Mom says sometimes good people do bad things. Like when I get in trouble she says 'I love you, but I don't like what you did.'" Ricky twisted his lips the opposite way and thought about it some more. "It's all mixed up, I guess, but some people are mostly good, and some are mostly bad. What about you? Are there good trees and bad trees?"

TREES NOT GOOD NOT BAD TREES ONLY LIVE

"Well, you're good for us."

TREES GOOD FOR HUMANS

Once again, Ricky wasn't quite sure if this was a statement or a question. "Yes. You're very important. You make our air better, and we make lots of things out of wood—" Ricky clamped a hand over his mouth. "Would you like some water?" he asked quickly, unscrewing his bottle and dumping the rest of his water out at the foot of the tree.

HUMANS BAD FOR TREES

"No, not all of us!" insisted Ricky. "I just gave you the rest of my water, didn't I? And my Grampa, he's trying to help you."

SOME GOOD SOME BAD

"Yes, some people are good and some are bad."

SOME MONSTERS

"Monsters?" Sure, some people did bad things to trees, like cut them down and burn them. Even he had sliced his initials into one with a penknife he found. But that was before he was friends with any of them. If people knew they could talk to trees, they wouldn't hurt them. But on the other hand, people still needed wood for houses, paper, books, tables, and chairs—everything. How were you supposed to get all those things without hurting a tree?

"Well, maybe some bad people hurt you," he admitted. "But there are other good people who are trying to protect you. Like park rangers and forest service people, the ones who make up the rules about campfires and stuff. And scientists like my grampa."

HOW GRAMPA HELP

Ricky looked in his grandfather's direction just in time to see him tuck his phone back into his pocket. He didn't think Grampa Nystrom would like what he and the tree had been talking about. Ricky fumbled around the buttons of the machine. He didn't know what he was pressing, exactly, but somehow managed to turn the translator off before Grampa Nystrom reached him.

His grandfather was wearing his usual serious expression even before he noticed the machine was off. "What were you doing here?" he asked. "This isn't a toy." He flicked a switch and turned the machine on again. Ricky breathed out with relief when he saw that the screen was blank.

Grampa Nystrom looked at him closely. Ricky swallowed, wishing he had some water left. Grampa turned the machine off and unstrapped it. "Time to go, Ricky."

"Why? You haven't met everyone yet," said Ricky, spreading his arms out.

"We're going to have some visitors tomorrow, and we need to talk to your dad and mom first. They need to come out here and see this before anyone else."

"Who? What visitors?" Ricky still felt uneasy from his conversation with the tree—or *trees*. Whatever you said to one of them, they all found out. That meant you had to be careful. You couldn't take anything back.

"My colleague Barbara Block, the woman who just called, will be coming. She's a botanist like me. And there will be some reporters."

"But you said I couldn't tell anyone." This morning he couldn't tell his parents, and now they had to see it right away? And who were all these other people coming out tomorrow? What did they want?

"Well," said Grampa Nystrom, "sometimes things have to go more quickly than you want them to."

But it wasn't fair! He was just getting to know his tree friends, and now he had to share them with a bunch of strangers who would probably hog the machine all day. That's what grownups did when they thought something was important. He needed another grownup on *his* side.

And he knew just the man.

"Grampa," he asked. "Can I invite someone too?"

CHAPTER 28

CHARLIE SAT IN front of a computer at the Palalla library, looking through the burgeoning supply of news stories about the talking trees. He'd like to get that woman professor out here, figure out if their trees could talk. Maybe he'd finally be able to prove he hadn't been crazy for thinking there was something going on out in the forest. But what he had to do first was come up with some kind of presentation for those kids in Tacoma, so he could connect with Ricky—it seemed like that boy could get the trees to move on demand—and see Liz again.

He opened a fresh browser window to look up—what? What was he actually going to say? He couldn't just get up there and talk about his own life. Was he supposed to tell the kids about struggling through high school and discovering pot? About dropping out of college and working odd jobs and winding up in construction? About how he could fix anything, except his strung out girlfriend and his cravings for booze? No, this couldn't be about him. He was a walking *Just Say No* billboard.

He rubbed his eyes and stretched his back, then looked around the library. At one table, kids pointed at pictures while their grandfather read the paper, just like he and his sister used to do with their mother. Things had been good once. He looked away.

On the other side of the room, a guy in an "NDN Power" cap leaned against the circulation desk chatting up one of the librarians. There was some kind of community here. Probably would have been similar at the Seattle Indian Center, if he'd ever bothered to go. If he hadn't been so busy congratulating himself on "advancing" out of Palalla. Turns out he'd "advanced" into a man who didn't have his shit together at all.

Charlie froze. He was looking right at Louis Greyfox. The kid was sitting at a table across the room, wearing the same tattered jean jacket, headphones in his ears, magazine open on the table in front of him. Glaring right at Charlie.

The Greyfox boy slapped the magazine shut and stood up. Charlie stood as well, and when Louis stalked out of the library, Charlie grabbed his coat and followed. Out of the corner of his eye, he saw other library visitors raising their heads.

Charlie tugged his coat on as he pursued Louis out the front doors into the street. He wasn't even sure what he wanted with him, but he stuck to his trail by instinct, like a fox after a rabbit.

"Hey," called Charlie.

Louis kept walking, turning his head briefly to shoot back a nasty glance.

"Hey!" called Charlie again. He jogged up to Louis and put a hand on his arm.

"Get off me," snarled the boy, tearing his arm away and storming off.

Charlie grabbed his arm, this time firmly. "Stop."

Louis stopped, casting a contemptuous glance at Charlie's hand before glaring into his face.

"Don't run away, okay?" Charlie slowly released the boy's arm.

"What do you want?" he asked through clenched teeth.

Now Charlie felt like the one who had been caught. "What's goin' on between you and Eddie?"

The boy's eyes seared into him, calculating. "Why don't you ask him."

"I'm askin' you," said Charlie. He felt the presence of bystanders pretending not to be watching and listening.

Louis took a step back and shook his head. "Nope. Can't. Eddie's keepin' up his part of the bargain."

"What the hell does that mean?"

"Why should I tell you? You didn't do me no favors." Louis stalked away, boldly turning his back on Charlie.

Charlie's hands balled themselves into fists. He kept his eyes on the boy's back, waiting until all the other curious glances shifted away. The few people on the street still watching avoided looking at him when he turned around and walked back toward the library.

What was this bargain with Eddie? And what were the chances the boy would just happen to be in the library at the same time he was?

Charlie thought for a moment about the windows he'd left open on the computer. He didn't care. He couldn't concentrate on that anymore. He could go back to Eddie's, but it was Saturday and everyone would be home. He didn't feel like facing them again, especially Eddie, who would talk about everything in the world except the real problem between the two of them.

Charlie wandered around for a bit, hands stuffed into his pockets, not wanting to stop any place in particular. The late afternoon sun slid down toward the horizon. It was getting cold, but maybe if he walked long enough he'd figure something out. He roamed aimlessly for a while, then turned in to a café and nursed a cup of coffee until the sun went down. Eventually there was nothing to do but go home.

As he walked through the front door, Eddie's wife Norma looked up from the shawl she was fringing and smiled. "Hey, Charlie."

"Hey." The TV was on, but the sound was down and she was more preoccupied with the fabric on her lap. Even when she wasn't at the gift shop she managed, she was always doing something productive.

"Eddie's out with the kids."

Charlie nodded. He felt big and dumb, standing in his cousin's living room not doing anything of use.

"You got a call while you were out," she said.

His shoulders slumped.

"Not your ex. Some teacher in Tacoma. The message is by the phone."

"Thanks, Norma," he said, trying not to look too excited. He headed for the phone with a measured pace and picked up the note. "I'll get this in the other room."

"Okay, Charlie." He could hear the smile in her voice. Let the gossiping begin.

He carried the piece of paper into the small room that Eddie called his office. The papers that usually littered the desk were gone. Had his cousin been clearing documents away on purpose?

Charlie dialed and waited for Liz to answer, realizing with a pang that he hadn't come up with anything for his presentation. Maybe it would go to voicemail.

"Hello?" Even with one word, her voice was distractingly soft and sweet.

"Uh, hi Liz. It's Charlie."

"Oh, hi Charlie," she said. "Thanks for calling back." She sounded glad to hear from him, but businesslike. "I got an interesting call today, regarding you."

"Regarding me?" Charlie's mind raced. Which of his various demons could be coming back now?

"Yes. You know Ricky Nystrom, the boy with the tree friends? Well, somehow he's involved in all this news about talking trees. You've heard about them, haven't you?"

"Yeah, but how . . ." He didn't even know where to start.

"Ricky called me to see if I could get in touch with you. This wasn't his parents calling, this was him directly. He got my number from the field trip emergency list. Smart kid. Anyway, he said there were some people coming over to ask him about the trees tomorrow, and he really wanted you to be there."

"Where is it? When?"

"Hold on," she said. "That's not why I'm calling. I just—have you spoken with him since the field trip?"

"No," said Charlie. "But I can come tomorrow." He'd be able to scare up a vehicle for the day, somehow.

She paused. "I'm not sure that's such a great idea," she said. "And I don't think his parents would like it either." Her voice turned stern. Protective.

"Is that what they said?"

"I didn't ask them," she said. "But I think they would be curious to know why you're so eager to come."

Charlie held his breath. He could either tell her that he'd seen the trees move, and come across as a maniac, or he could try to come up with some other story and risk sounding like a creepy stalker. There didn't seem to be a good answer here.

"I don't know," he said. "I was just tryin' to help."

Liz sighed. "I'm sorry. I don't mean to accuse you of anything. But this is just so strange. Ricky sounded really agitated, so I need to follow up with his parents. I wanted to get all the information I could before I called them."

"I understand," he said. "Look, Ricky seems like a nice kid, and if I can help him—and if his parents are okay with it—I can come up there. So maybe, if you think it's all right, you could just offer."

"I don't know, Charlie," she said. "I'll see. It's getting late, I'd better get in and call them."

"Okay," he said. "I hope it goes all right."

"Yeah, Charlie, me too."

"Liz?" He didn't want her to hang up just yet. "Can I call you tomorrow, see how it went?"

She paused. "Yes," she said, her voice softer. "That would be nice."

Charlie hung up, glad for at least one thing to look forward to.

CHAPTER 29

TAMIA STOOD JUST outside the yellow police tape as the first signs of daylight crept across the sky. She stared at the tagged stakes marking where the body had landed two nights before, an area now covered by a mottled carpet of brown and yellow leaves. The forest landscape changed almost daily as fall approached, with different varieties of leaves dropping off to expose the crooked, winding branches behind them.

Two nights ago, in the rain and darkness, the troopers had come. The ambulance had arrived, lights flashing. Radios barked out garbled commands while paramedics bent down around the body. More cars and trucks had rolled in, bringing investigators wearing plastic gloves. She'd felt like she was on a movie set, watching an army of actors swarm around her. Suddenly, she'd found herself inside Dr. Block's bungalow, a change of dry clothes being pressed into her hands. Then, just as suddenly, holding a mug of tea, answering questions while an officer scratched out notes: *"I heard a noise and went outside . . ."*

"Tamia."

She snapped back to the present and looked at Dr. Block.

"Are you okay?" asked the older woman.

Tamia took a deep breath and nodded. "I'm sorry I didn't stay out here with you the past couple of nights."

Dr. Block waved away her apology. "I didn't sleep here either, thanks to my neighbors."

"Have you heard anything else from the troopers?" The investigators had already told them about the scorch marks on the tree, as well as the lighter and accelerant

191

found near the body. They would just have to check fingerprints to make the case. The troopers suspected that he had been involved in the recent spate of fires in the area. But they didn't have a motive yet, and they still couldn't say with certainty if he'd been acting alone.

Dr. Block shook her head. "No, nothing new. All they're saying is to keep my eyes open and report anything suspicious. But then, you reported something pretty damn suspicious and they didn't want to hear it, did they?"

"Can you blame them?" Tamia didn't want to believe it herself. She knew she sounded like a crazy person, describing what she'd seen the tree do to that man. The officer had asked her a bunch of questions and told her he wanted to talk to her again later—presumably when she wasn't still in shock and babbling nonsense.

"And when you talk to them again," asked Dr. Block, "what will you say?"

"What do you mean?"

"Will you tell them the truth?"

"All I can say is what I saw," said Tamia.

"Good. They'll try to tell you that you were just seeing things, you know, that the victim simply fell out of that tree, and what you saw—what you thought you saw—was just a trick of the light. They won't be able to explain why the hell anyone would climb up a tree in the middle of a thunderstorm, but that won't stop them from saying that's what happened. And the truth is—" Dr. Block stopped, glancing over to the crime scene. "Come with me."

She led Tamia inside the bungalow and closed the door. "The truth is," said Dr. Block, "the trees are mutating. They're watching and listening, and their capabilities are changing much more rapidly than I ever thought possible. Their language abilities are growing more sophisticated, and now they've learned to physically defend themselves."

"Dr. Block, someone just tried to set fire to your house in the middle of the night. Shouldn't we be glad the tree kept that from happening? I mean, who's the bigger threat here?"

"Ah, but was it defending us, or itself?" Dr. Block asked. "The tree had the burn marks, not the house."

"What does it matter? Everything would have gone up in flames if it hadn't acted."

"Yes, but we can't make the mistake of thinking it's on our side just because its actions benefitted us."

Tamia blinked. The trees knew her and Dr. Block. Why wouldn't they be on their side?

"We have to look at this objectively," cautioned Dr. Block. "It may appear they think like us, because we've given them a tool to communicate with us. But they're not human. We can't assume they have the same instincts or reasoning we do."

Tamia detected an unfamiliar edge to the scientist's voice. "Dr. Block, do you want to, maybe, come up to Seattle for a couple of days? Get some rest? My parents have a guest room." Tamia had brought her overnight bag, but would be glad not to use it.

The older woman exhaled and rubbed her eyes. "I'm fine. I just haven't had much sleep. I must have sat up all night listening for—I don't know what." Dr. Block let out a terse laugh. "I never thought I'd hear someone advise me to get out of the woods and head into town to get away from it all."

The sound of an engine and tires on gravel outside turned their heads. "Must be Channel Eleven," said Tamia. "They're early."

"Let 'em wait," muttered Dr. Block.

Tamia smiled. That was more like the Dr. Block she knew. "Let's cancel the last appointment today," she said. "Get on the road before too late. I'll call my folks and let them know we're coming."

"Hmm, apparently I missed the part where I said 'yes.'"

"Come on, why sit around here and wait for them to try it again?"

"ArborTech? Something tells me they aren't going to be so quick with their matches now, not with this death and the investigation."

Tamia's thoughts flashed back to the rain and thunder and screams, lightning on thrashing branches, the mangled body lying on rain-soaked ground. The tree's movements had been so deliberate and precise—it was no accident. "Do you still feel safe out here?" she asked quietly.

Dr. Block examined her face. "You're not referring to ArborTech, are you?"

Tamia looked down at her feet. The muffled sounds of the news crew unloading equipment outside filled the silence. "I'm talking about them," she admitted, gesturing toward the window. "The trees. Like you said, how do we know what they're really thinking?"

The scientist shrugged. "We don't, not yet."

"How do we know what sets them off? I mean, animals defend their young, so what will they do if you happen to step on a sapling or crush a seed?"

"Hey, weren't *you* supposed to be getting *me* to relax?" asked Dr. Block, annoyed. "Yes, some animals fight for their young, but others just lay their eggs and leave. In any case, these aren't animals." She looked out the window. "We'll just have to watch them closely, and make sure they know we mean them no harm."

The news crew's voices grew louder and there was a knock at the front door. Dr. Block put a hand on Tamia's arm. "The more we learn about the trees, the better. Let's go." Tamia nodded and followed Dr. Block to the door.

Dr. Block stopped abruptly and turned to face her. "Tamia, I almost forgot to tell you, Dr. Nystrom finally called me back." She shook her head irritably. "He seems to feel safe enough to come out of his hole now. He's been making observations as well, and wants to compare data." She pursed her lips. "I suppose a meeting in Seattle would be convenient enough for both of us. That is, if I'm still invited."

Tamia smiled. "I'll drive."

CHAPTER 30

CHARLIE FLIPPED THROUGH the paper at the library, scanning articles and trying not to think about why Liz hadn't returned his call. A headline fluttered by and pried his eyes open.

"Timber Poacher Felled by Trees?"

Charlie sucked in a breath and spread the paper out on the table. Another poacher had been injured while trying to take a tree out of Palalla land. It was miles away from where he'd been patrolling, but the scenario was eerily similar. The poacher claimed to have been attacked by the tree he'd attempted to cut down.

Memories of the battered bodies in the woods came flooding back. He wanted to go see the guy in the article, ask him what happened. But with his injuries, they'd had to send him up to Seattle. And without a vehicle, Charlie had no way of getting up there.

Dammit, he was tired as hell of this. Starting over like a child. No truck, no place to live, earning nowhere near what he used to pull down on construction jobs. There was more work up in Seattle, but too much risk. It'd be too easy to get back in with his old friends and his old life, strung out all the time, spending every day regretting what he'd done the day before.

And it was where he lost his daughter.

He ran his hands over his face and stood up. Even he had a limit to how much time he could spend at the library. He'd have his own space soon enough. He was set to move next week into that place above the garage Eddie'd told him about. But for now he'd just have to pull on his coat and step outside.

It was Saturday afternoon, still light outside, but a distinct chill had crept into the air. He zipped up his coat and shoved his hands into his pockets. With no particular destination in mind, he headed off in the direction with the fewest people. He didn't look at anything really, just stared off into the distance and tried to clear his mind. Tried to stop wondering what was up with Liz, stop thinking about the Greyfox kid and how Eddie stonewalled when he asked questions about the Greyfoxes or trees. Could Eddie be protecting a family of tree poachers? He hated that his thoughts went straight to shady dealings, but what was he supposed to think with Eddie being so tight-lipped?

People aren't always who you think they are, his mother used to tell him, *but try and forgive 'em anyway.* Another one of her favorites: *People have their reasons, and you shouldn't always assume they're bad ones.* He'd be curious to know what her reasons were for this current disappearing act of hers. He hadn't heard from her for a couple of years now.

An eagle cried overhead. Charlie watched it soar above him, coasting on the brisk wind. Such a beautiful creature, heading off to some filthy dump to scavenge for food. That's how it was in Seattle, at least. But somehow, he had higher hopes for the eagle out here. He imagined it flying over to some tiny apartment above a garage. The big time. He let out a bitter little laugh, then looked down. The toes of his boots were wet. He'd already reached the river's edge without realizing it.

He was about to turn around and head back home when he heard someone speaking over the rushing water. It sounded like an old woman. He spotted her under a wisp of smoke downstream, on the opposite side of the river. What was she doing out here in the cold? Her back was to him, but he could see that she was burning something near the trees.

How did she even get there? He scanned up and down the river for a dry path to the other side. He stepped half on rocks, half through the water to cross over to her. What the hell, his feet were already wet. Her chanting softened and stopped as he grew near, but she didn't turn around. He watched her back for a moment, frigid water seeping through his socks.

"Excuse me, Grandmother," he said quietly, so as not to startle her.

She turned, head and shoulders moving in tandem, to look at him. It was the same old woman who had almost been knocked over by the Greyfox boy. Coals smoldered in a shallow stone bowl she'd placed on a boulder in front of her. She pulled a sprig of sage from a pouch she wore around her neck and sprinkled it into the bowl. A plume of smoke rose into the air and she waved it with her hands in the direction of the trees, murmuring quiet words of prayer. When the smoke died down the old woman waved Charlie toward her.

"The trees are restless," she said as he approached.

"Restless?" He ignored the cold pricking his toes. "Why are they restless?"

"We give them many reasons." She sprinkled more sage into the bowl. The flames licked at the sage, and she waved the pungent smoke toward him. "You seem restless too," she said, and offered up a few words of prayer for him.

Somehow, he thought, *these old Palalla ladies always know the score.*

The elder cinched up the first pouch and opened another one, from which she pulled a braided bunch of sweetgrass. She lit one end of the braid against the coals, and it smoked without flame. Then she approached the edge of the woods and walked a line in front of the trees, waving the fragrant plume of smoke along the edge of the woods. Charlie could still hear her speaking, but only recognized a few words here and there, mostly from context: *kw'ałanuúsha* (thank you), *tiichám* (earth), *chiish* (water). All the things his mother and grandfather and uncles had tried to get him to pay attention to.

The old woman returned to her stone bowl and used it to extinguish the braid of sweetgrass. Once she'd returned the herbs to their pouch, she picked up the bowl with a small grunt. Charlie hurried over to help her.

"Thank you," she said, handing the bowl to him and heading toward the riverbank. He wriggled his clammy toes and looked back across the river, instantly spotting a dry path to the other side. Of course she'd known exactly where to pass.

The old woman started out across a trail of dry rocks jutting above the water. Her balance was pretty good, better than his cold, clumsy feet would allow at this point. Charlie followed her footsteps, lopsided with the heavy bowl on one arm.

He had just stepped halfway across the river when he heard the too-familiar creak of wood. He looked up at the older woman standing on the opposite shore, her face a mixture of fear and awe. The popping and cracking behind him intensified as he hopped the last couple of rocks to join her. He looked back across to the other side, where the woman had just made her offering.

Amidst a plume of dust and twigs and yellowed leaves, an alder was bending over. It wasn't slumping over like an old tree hollowed out by disease, or crashing down like a dry stick of a tree toppling in the wind. Slowly and deliberately, booming and popping, the alder lay down like a giant preparing to sleep.

Charlie put a protective arm around the grandmother's shoulders. His heart galloped. He should be leading her away to safety, but they were both grounded by wonder. As the dust settled, a new round of creaking and popping rang out of the forest. He scanned the stand of trees and spied another alder stirring. The old woman clutched at his coat, and he gripped her shoulders tighter. They steadied each other as a second tree made a graceful, deliberate descent to the earth. As soon as the second tree settled, a third tree felled itself, carefully lowering its trunk to the ground between its neighbors. The trees creaked and groaned into place until the only sounds left were the rush of the river and the periodic snap of a limb settling into its new position against the ground.

Charlie and the grandmother stared into the forest as the cloud of dirt and leaves subsided.

"Well, would you look at that?" the grandmother murmured.

"What *was* that?" He turned the old woman's shoulders until she faced him. "Did you do that?"

Her face was flushed. "I asked them for guidance. I asked them how we can live together in peace."

Charlie looked back across the river in disbelief, just then noticing how much the afternoon light had faded. A shiver passed through the old woman. It was too cold for her here, and he had wet feet and frozen hands. "Come on," he said. "We should get out of the cold."

But neither one of them moved. They both stared at the fallen trees until the old woman shivered again. Charlie gently guided her away from the river toward the warmth of town, wondering what this message could possibly mean.

CHAPTER 31

TAMIA PULLED BACK her slumping shoulders, willing herself to understand the jargon spilling out of Dr. Block's and Dr. Nystrom's mouths. She watched them lean over a pile of maps and binders, debating across the dining room table at Nystrom's son's house. His grandson, Ricky, had made a brief appearance, pointing out a couple of places on the map before wandering out to play. Meanwhile, the two botanists, who were supposed to love being around trees, insisted on working inside with the doors and windows shut tight.

Tamia looked at the map. With Dr. Nystrom's observations added to Dr. Block's charts, they could finally trace the full extent of the phenomenon. The anomalies—Tamia still wasn't comfortable with their use of the word "outbreak"—had started in several isolated swaths of State-owned forest. Now the affected area stretched over the western half of Washington State and was creeping up into British Columbia.

She couldn't help but note that the Palalla reservation marked the eastern edge of the disturbances, and there was still a suspicious silence hanging over the tree poachers who had died there. There were three now, the two Charlie Meninick had witnessed, and a second alleged attack on a lone poacher, who subsequently died in the hospital. And now *she* had seen it; she'd seen trees kill. She wanted to talk to Charlie. She had to speak with someone else who had seen the same thing.

"Richard, you can't stay silent about this any longer," said Dr. Block. "You don't have anything to worry about. You won't be releasing any classified material."

"Nothing to worry about?" scoffed Dr. Nystrom. "I violated the nondisclosure agreement, Barbara. And you and I both held on to translators."

"I doubt ArborTech will want to draw attention to their role in this, or to their porous security, for that matter. Our translators didn't start the outbreak."

"Actually," interjected Tamia, "I still don't understand exactly what 'broke out'. I mean, in non-scientist, regular-person speak."

Dr. Nystrom turned to her. "You know that Barbara and I both worked with ArborTech on mapping the circulatory acoustics of pine and fir trees. That's about all our confidentiality agreements would allow us to say. But Dr. Block is an extremely intelligent person," he said, glancing again in her direction, "so I'm not surprised she figured out what was going on behind the scenes."

"And the important thing is, you didn't cause the problem," said the older woman. "Not directly."

"But I'm still liable under their non-disclosure agreement," he answered. "They had to cover themselves just to discuss the project outline with me. They didn't share specifics, but the goals and parameters, the compartmentalization required, the amount of money they would have needed for such an ambitious project—it all points in one direction."

"Still, no one ever told you outright it was a secret government project," said Tamia.

"Exactly," Dr. Block chimed in. "And the government can't come after you without implicating themselves. They'll rely on plausible deniability and let ArborTech deal with it, which we can fight. This is a public safety issue now, clearly a whistleblower situation. You have to come forward, Richard."

"It's not that simple." He stood and ran a hand over thinning hair. "The government may want to keep a low profile now, but what's to keep them from hauling me in on some fabricated charge? What's to say an FBI hacker isn't going through my files right now, looking for some shred of evidence to hold against me?"

"Richard—"

"Look at who we're dealing with. They wanted ArborTech to engineer a forest full of spies." He placed both hands on the table, leaning in over the maps. "They want millions of invisible microphones picking up our every word, out where we least expect to be heard. We've already got cameras on every city street, people hijacking our laptops and appliances. Now this? Privacy would no longer exist."

"What if it was just ArborTech acting alone?" asked Dr. Block. "You know what they're like, ambitious to the point of being reckless." She put a hand on Dr. Nystrom's. "They could have dreamt this up all on their own, without the DoD. Coming forward would be a public service."

Dr. Nystrom put his free hand over hers. "I appreciate that, Barbara, but we both know they wouldn't have been able to get this far without significant capital. And without my advice." He stepped away from the table and folded his arms. "I told them it was impossible, but that if I were going to try . . ." He shook his head. "It shouldn't have actually worked. No one with a thorough understanding of botany would have launched a project that relies on plants having a central nervous system and language processing centers. ArborTech's response to this dilemma was, naturally, to attempt to genetically engineer them." He clenched his teeth and stared at the floor. "But you can't just mash up genetic material, toss it into an organism and wait for magic to happen. Speech-related genes are found in other animals—mice, birds, primates—but you don't hear them speaking."

"Then how did it happen?" Tamia asked. *And what's keeping the mice, birds, and primates from chiming in now?*

"I wish I could tell you," answered Dr. Nystrom. "They didn't share that part of the project with me."

Dr. Block studied Dr. Nystrom. "You only told me the project was about encoding."

"Because they told me they'd decided not to pursue the rest. Our sole object was supposed to be analyzing and encoding cavitation patterns under different environmental stressors."

"Which means," Dr. Block explained to Tamia, "we were listening to how the trees sounded with various types and amounts of nutrients, different temperatures, exposure to various pathogens or pests. The hope was that we could associate specific patterns with specific stressors and create a codex of sorts."

Tamia nodded. "So, figuring out how 'low water' or 'need fertilizer' or 'birch bark beetles' sounds and making that appear on the translator?"

"Exactly," said Dr. Nystrom. He looked at Dr. Block. "You understand why I wanted us to take this on, don't you? Just think, what if we could translate environmental stressors into signals, language, that everyone could understand? Not just experts, but *everyone*." His face brightened. "We could diagnose pathogens before their first visible effects and stop them before they destroyed acres of trees. Urban canopies would flourish, because everyone could pinpoint exactly what their trees needed."

He paused, his excitement fading. "If people could hear for themselves what our trees are trying to tell us, just imagine how much more we could do for them."

"When did they shut down your work?" asked Tamia.

"About five years ago," said Dr. Block.

"Between the impossible science and all the government surveillance scandals," said Dr. Nystrom, "I assumed the whole thing had been mothballed. But they must have been testing it the entire time."

"And quite aggressively," said Dr. Block, her fingers tracing the vectors of outbreak on the map. "Imagine how much *Agrobacterium* it would take to insert their genetic modifications into so many full-grown trees, this quickly."

"*Agrobacterium*?" asked Tamia.

"*Agrobacterium tumefaciens*," said Dr. Nystrom. "The most common bacterial agent researchers use to insert genetic material into plants. But they would have had to drench the forest in it. No, I believe they were testing a new bacterial or viral agent."

"I guess, with Governor Palmer's protection, they weren't worried about getting caught," said Tamia.

Dr. Block's face twisted in disgust. "Must have been one hell of a donation."

"Oh, I doubt he knew the full scope of the project," said Nystrom. "They probably only told him about the modifications that would actually *benefit* the trees. You see," he explained to Tamia, "those embolisms we've been listening in on are actually quite harmful to the tree."

Tamia nodded. She knew that when the air bubbles pop, they usually rip the xylem they're traveling through. "Dr. Block said the trees must have developed a way to repair themselves more quickly to counteract the damage."

"Yes," said Dr. Nystrom, "that's one aspect I'd hoped ArborTech would actually accomplish. If they wanted to encourage cavitation, they'd have to figure out a way of controlling or repairing the damage."

"Or keep it from happening in the first place," added Dr. Block. "If they introduced more plasticity into the tissues, they could maintain the integrity of the xylem despite increased pressures."

"Bend rather than break," Tamia summed up. "Looks like they overshot on that part."

"And now they're trying to clean up their mess," said Dr. Block darkly.

"Well, they can't burn down the whole damn state," Nystrom said.

The older woman frowned. "Who's to stop them from trying?"

"Us." Dr. Nystrom rubbed his cheek in thought. "But even if we figure out which transmission agent they're using, and its potential side effects, that still won't explain the language acquisition process."

"Well, then we revisit our theory that the trees are spreading it themselves," said Dr. Block.

Dr. Nystrom sighed.

"How else would you explain these vectors?" she argued. "We need to consider the possibility that the trees are playing an active role here. Perhaps they've always been sentient, watching and listening to us, possibly for centuries, and now we've finally given them a means of interaction that we can comprehend. Maybe the modifications are spreading so quickly because the trees are purposely sharing them. And maybe they're teaching each other how to use the modifications because they want to communicate with us."

Dr. Nystrom shook his head. "I can't say which frightens me more, the idea that ArborTech designed this, or the thought that it's completely out of their control."

"Hey, Dad."

They all turned toward the voice. Dr. Nystrom's son stood, holding a laptop, at the entrance to the dining room. "You need to see this."

CHAPTER 32

DR. NYSTROM'S SON brought his laptop to the table and turned up the volume on a newscast filling the screen.

"Three timber industry employees were killed yesterday, and four others seriously injured, in what the survivors claim was an attack by trees. The loggers were working near Lake Lawrence in Thurston County for Weyerhaeuser Wood Products when disaster struck. We have exclusive footage captured by a tourist, in which a sightseeing flight turned into an unnatural nightmare."

The video started with an aerial shot of lush, tree-covered hills surrounding a lake. The camera zoomed in on a clear-cut area, and the pilot explained over the noise of the helicopter that logging was taking place. Despite the shaky footage, it soon became obvious that something was wrong. The treetops in the immediate area began to flail back and forth, and as the pilot announced he was going in for a closer look, the camera picked up something falling out of a tree. The shot stabilized and zoomed in on a body lying on the ground, its limbs splayed at unnatural angles. As the trees continued to bend and flail, another body dropped to the ground. The panicked tourists' yelling drowned out the noise of the rotors.

The announcer's voice cut into the eyewitness video. "The survivors were airlifted to area hospitals. Two were treated and released and another two are still in critical condition. This escalation of tree violence and a spate of unexplained forest fires have set communities throughout the region on edge. Washingtonians have been on alert since the appearance of Dr. Barbara Block's video documenting speech capabilities in area trees."

211

Dr. Block winced as a wide-eyed still from her video flashed on the screen.

"In the wake of this recent tragic incident," continued the reporter, "some residents are taking matters into their own hands. Tree removal services are seeing increased demand for their services. Retail outlets throughout Western Washington have reported a rush on chainsaws, axes and woodchippers."

The shot switched to a man in a baseball cap carrying a chainsaw out of an Ace Hardware store, then to a close-up of another man holding an axe over his shoulder in the parking lot. "Yeah, you know," he said into the reporter's microphone, "just in case. I have two boys, you know, so you want to be prepared."

"Well, I have to worry about my dogs," said another interviewee standing in front of a thinned-out display of axes. "They don't know any better. You can't tell 'em to stay away from trees, can you?"

The segment closed with a shot of the reporter in the hardware store parking lot. "Local authorities are still looking for answers," she said, "leaving citizens few options but to stock up and wonder what will happen next."

Dr. Block's phone rang even before the news clip finished. As soon as she rejected one call, another one lit up her phone. She turned the phone off and stuffed it away in her bag.

"This proves it," said Tamia. "What I saw, what happened to those poachers in Palalla, they can't keep saying these are just accidents." Not that she was excited about someone else dying, but this was the proof she needed. She'd try to reach Charlie again tomorrow, assuming ArborTech hadn't gotten to him first.

"Well, I'm heading out to the Palalla Nation tomorrow," said Dr. Nystrom. "I'm meeting with Charlie Meninick. He's the—"

"I know who he is," she replied, perhaps a little too quickly. *But how did Nystrom know him?*

Dr. Block broke in with a barrage of plans: people to be called, appointments to be scheduled, a press release to calm citizens down. *She's right,* Tamia told herself. There was no time to be jealous over which of them got to talk to Charlie. People needed answers, and they didn't have any answers for anyone yet. What they needed most was time to think—if the trees would allow it.

CHAPTER 33

CHARLIE WAITED FOR Dr. Nystrom at the edge of the river where the three alders had fallen. He'd taken a chance and told Liz about the old woman's ceremony and how the trees had sacrificed themselves. Thankfully, not only did she believe him, but she'd also thought to contact Ricky's grandfather. Charlie had returned to the site twice since then to take pictures, worried that some kind of reverse magic would set the three trees upright again before Dr. Nystrom could get there.

Many townspeople avoided the fallen trees, thinking they were haunted. But according to whispers going around, others were tempted to come and cut them up for firewood before the Palalla mill claimed them. In the meantime, a group of elders had held a welcoming ceremony for the trees, and people of various faiths had left flowers, tobacco, rosaries, votives, dreamcatchers, and incense. The area had turned into a pop-up temple of every religion in Nakalish. A couple of folks were there paying their respects that morning, breathing prayers into the woods or merely staring at the trees while Charlie waited for Dr. Nystrom.

Charlie cocked his head as a maroon SUV rolled up to the riverbank. It was the same vehicle he'd seen creeping around the woods when he was living up at the cabin. Ricky's grandfather, Dr. Nystrom, stepped out. Charlie masked his surprise before shaking Nystrom's hand and leading him over the sturdy planks that had been placed across the river.

"Very interesting," said Dr. Nystrom, bending over the three alders. "The breakage at the base is consistent with the collapse of a compromised tree, but the core is still healthy. No sign of deterioration or disease. But there are indications of torsional stress at the base." He glanced briefly at Charlie before turning back to the trunks. "This definitely appears to be intentional."

He unzipped his backpack and took out the boxy translator. A murmur went up from the small crowd as he began strapping it around the closest upright tree.

"You know what this is?" he asked Charlie, flipping the machine on.

"I've seen the videos," said Charlie. "But this one looks different."

Dr. Nystrom smiled, and his chest puffed up a little. "I made a few upgrades. It has enhanced voice recognition, ten gigs of memory, active battery life of sixteen hours, stores up to two hundred hours of speech." He went through the customary formalities of recording date, time and location before introducing himself to the alder. Charlie didn't know what to think about a grown man saying, "Hello, my name is," to a tree.

HELLO RICHARD NYSTROM, read the display strapped to the trunk. HELLO CHARLIE MENINICK

"How did it already know my name?" asked Charlie.

"Not 'it'," said Dr. Nystrom. "'They.' And they've been listening."

THANK YOU CHARLIE MENINICK AND MINNIE LITTLEDEER.

"Minnie Littledeer?" asked the scientist.

"The elder I was with when it happened," Charlie explained.

THANK YOU FOR ASK

Dr. Nystrom raised his eyebrows. "What does that mean? What did you ask?"

"Well, she asked 'em what they wanted and how we could live together in peace."

The scientist frowned. "You had a conversation with them? How? Do you have one of these?" he asked, pointing at the machine.

"No, I don't, I—"

The letters scrolling onto the display drew both men's attention: NYSTROM ASK TO TREE

"Yes," said Dr. Nystrom quickly. "Yes." He thought for a moment. "Why did those trees fall down? Were they sick?"

NO TREES OFFERING

The two men looked at each other.

"An offering?" asked the botanist.

YES OFFERING TO YOU

"To whom, to the tribe?"

TO PALALLA PEOPLE FOR PEACE

Dr. Nystrom turned to Charlie. "Have the Palalla been in some kind of negotiations with them?"

"No, I don't think so." *And what made it this guy's business anyway?*

PEOPLE WANT TREES

The men stood in stunned silence. "But these were perfectly healthy trees," Dr. Nystrom said softly. "It doesn't make biological sense. Why wouldn't they have eliminated the weak ones?"

Charlie shook his head. "That's not how an offering works."

HUMANS WANT GOOD TREES . . . WE GIVE IF NO HARM TO COMMUNITY

"What community?" asked Dr. Nystrom.

TREE COMMUNITY

"What's a tree community?" asked Charlie.

TREES HELP TREES GROW . . . SHARE SUN, WIND, RAIN, EARTH

"The trees are linked by an underground network of roots and fungus," Nystrom explained. "They use it to share nutrients and information. Some scientists have observed a system by which mature 'mother trees' appear to feed younger trees of their own type." He addressed the tree. "How large is your community?" asked Dr. Nystrom.

THOUSANDS

"How far does your community extend?"

FROM HERE TO END . . . UNTIL PATH IS BROKEN

"What does that mean?" Charlie asked.

"They must be referring to breaks in the network," said Dr. Nystrom. "Maybe construction or mountains, perhaps a river. We have no way of knowing where their borders are." He addressed the tree in a louder voice. "Who makes the decisions in your community?"

WE DECIDE TOGETHER

"But what if you don't agree? Who makes the final decision?"

WE AGREE . . . WE DECIDE TOGETHER ACT TOGETHER

"And why did you decide to make your offering here, now?"

MINNIE LITTLEDEER ASK FOR PEACE

"So, peace, that means no chopping down, no burning, nothin' like that?" asked Charlie.

MEANS NO HARM . . . WE GIVE YOU . . . YOU NOT TAKE

"But what if we need more than you can give?" asked Charlie.

HOW MUCH NEED

Dr. Nystrom broke in. "Just a moment, Charlie, we're not in a position to negotiate. I don't have the authority. Do you?"

"Well, shouldn't we at least try to figure out how to work with them?"

"Yes, but it has to be coordinated. We'll be providing inconsistent inputs if we make an agreement and then someone else comes and takes an axe to them. It will confuse them. And you," said Dr. Nystrom, looking the smooth, mottled trunk. "I can't believe I'm saying this to a tree—we need to teach you to negotiate. You can't just offer people whatever they want. You have to offer less than you would be willing to give and leave yourself room to go up."

NOT UNDERSTAND

"I know," said Dr. Nystrom, "but that's the way it is with us humans. Charlie, we need to find out who's in charge on your side, someone who could tell us how much your people want, and the minimum they'd be willing to take."

"So, *you're* gonna help them negotiate?" asked Charlie. Like hell this old man was going to insert himself into tribal matters.

"I don't think we have a choice," said Nystrom, oblivious. "Do you know what it's like out there right now? People are nervous, they feel threatened. They're surrounded by an emerging form of life they don't understand, and I'm afraid that this fear will lead to terrible things." The scientist gritted his teeth. "At this very moment the state legislature is trying to convince the Forest Service to accelerate their controlled burns. Those burns are carefully scheduled according to weather, environmental conditions, personnel capacity. You can't just go around burning whatever patch of land happens to give you the willies. But now, fear-based decision-making is taking hold and that can only lead to disastrous consequences." He looked into the woods beyond the river. "And it's only going to get worse as we uncover more of their capabilities."

He turned to face Charlie. "This is a real opportunity, Mr. Meninick. If we can come up with a system here, we may be able to apply it on a wider scale. We could prevent a lot of harm on both sides."

Charlie glanced over at the knot of people nearby. As much as he didn't like the old man trying to take over, he was right that they would have to act carefully. They could probably save lives by striking some kind of bargain with the trees.

But if this town couldn't even agree on what to do with three downed trees, how were they going to deal with a whole forest full of change?

CHAPTER 34

RICKY SAT ON the couch with the controller in his hand, slaying zombies for what seemed like forever. His dad had come in once to check on him, but he hadn't tried to get him to play outside. Mom and Dad used to practically shove him out to the yard to play, even on the coldest days, but now they hardly let him set foot out the door.

They were nervous about the trees. Everybody was, even Grampa Nystrom, who was supposed to know everything about them. He was trying really hard not to be mad at Grampa anymore, even though it still wasn't fair that he got to go out to the Palalla Reservation without him.

He threw down the remote. He was sick of this game, and sick of all these grownups telling him what to do. They said the trees had started hurting people, but really they only hurt people who were hurting them. He never got to use the machine to talk to them anymore, because Grampa was too busy with that other scientist lady and everybody else. Well, the trees were his friends first, and he was going to see them whenever he wanted.

Ricky put the game on demo mode so it would keep making noise. He looked around for a sweater and some shoes to put on, but unfortunately someone had cleaned up. He'd have to sneak by his parents to get the coat and boots he'd left by the front door. He tiptoed down the hall, avoiding the creaky spots in the floor, until he finally reached the entrance to the kitchen. His parents were talking over the drone of the news.

"The NSA?" he heard his mother say. "They're being called to testify on this?"

"Holy shit," said his dad.

Ricky clamped his hand over his grin. He went down on his hands and knees and peeked around the corner.

"What's ArborTech?" his father asked. "One of those GMO companies?"

"Yeah," said his mom. "They're like Monsanto, but they specialize in trees."

His parents had their backs to the hallway, watching the news on a laptop. They said no to getting a TV for the kitchen, but they were always watching something on their laptops. Grownups.

"Really? Frankentrees?" said his father. "How is it we're just now hearing about this?"

"Apparently, it's been going on for quite a while now," answered his mother.

"Hmm. Well, they're in front of Congress now. Some senator's gonna rip 'em a new one."

A new what? wondered Ricky, crawling by the kitchen.

"Wait, did you hear something?" asked his mother. Ricky froze and held his breath. The newscast floated out of the kitchen, mingling with the sounds of his game on demo mode. His parents were quiet, and Ricky wondered how long it would take before his lungs burst.

"I don't think it was anything," said his dad finally. "Maybe you're just feeling a little jumpy."

"Me? Who just bought a chain saw?"

"I had to, Marla. It was the last one on the shelf."

"But have you ever used one?" she asked. "And what if Ricky finds it? He'll cut his fingers off."

"No, he won't. He doesn't even know where it is."

Ricky listened in a little longer, to see if his father would mention where it was. He'd always thought chainsaws were pretty cool. He wasn't quite as excited about them now that he'd met the trees, but still, he'd kind of like to see one up close.

His parents moved on to other topics, however, so he crept toward the front door. He slipped into his boots and stood on tiptoe to reach the extra house key on its hook. Once outside, he eased the door shut, wincing at the soft click of the latch. Only then did he dare put an arm into the sleeve of his jacket. His mom seemed to be able to hear him putting his coat on from anywhere in the house.

Now that he was outside, he wished he had gone to the bathroom first. He'd never had to think about it before, really. Even if he were too far from home and desperate, well, it didn't matter because he was a boy. But now that he actually knew the trees, and they knew him, and especially now that they could talk, he wasn't comfortable with the idea of peeing all over his friends, or even *between* his friends. But maybe it was just like the school bathrooms. Except the trees weren't going there to pee too, so it would be more like peeing between the desks in class, or like peeing at the edge of the playground at recess. And the more he thought about it, the more he had to pee.

Grampa had the machine with him, so he couldn't even ask the trees what *they* thought about it. This must happen all the time in the forest, so why hadn't anyone thought to ask them yet? That was the whole problem with grownups, he thought, storming around the side of the house and into the woods. They made all these rules about you, for you, without even asking you what you really wanted in the first place.

CHAPTER 35

TAMIA'S EYES WERE closed. The radio was on, and as always in her parent's house, tuned to the public radio station. She sat on a bar stool in the kitchen wearing one of her father's old shirts. Her hair was divided into sections, like a landscape of tiny farm plots, and her hairline and ears were slathered with Vaseline. The fragrant, slightly acidic smell of the relaxer always seemed to trigger a sense of relief in her, like she was finally dealing with a problem that needed to be resolved. This was far from the biggest problem on her plate, but she was grateful for small, attainable goals like this.

She heard the snap of latex gloves and felt her mother pull the clip out of the first section of hair. "I'm going to start in the middle, then go up front, then end at the base."

"Okay," said Tamia. Her mom did it like this every time, but it had become part of the ritual to say it. Ignoring the *Economist* on her lap, she kept her eyes closed and listened to pundits debating key congressional races while her mother smoothed relaxer onto section after section of her hair. She knew it didn't make any sense, but somehow her head always felt lighter after getting her hair relaxed. *She* felt lighter, calmer, more in control of her hair and everything, which was just what she needed right now. She shouldn't feel guilty for leaving Dr. Block. They had both agreed they needed a break from the relentless round of reporters and agencies. But what did it say about her that her idea of taking a break was running home for a beauty ritual, while Dr. Block's version was teaming up with a molecular biologist to write a report?

"Tamia, baby, you're going to set this when we're done, aren't you?"

"Eh, that takes too long. I'll just blow it dry."

"You know it would look better—"

"Nope, no curlers." Her mom knew this already, but asking seemed to be part of the ritual too. Tamia hadn't put a single curler in her head since the freshman year fire alarm prank that had sent everyone running outside at three o'clock in the morning. Of course, she'd been the only one in the dorm who used rollers. And since that night, never again.

"Put your head down," her mother said.

Tamia tipped her head forward. She was always sleepy by this point in the process, another reason not to mess with curlers. Better to just blow it dry.

A news announcer's voice derailed her drowsy train of thought. "A neighborhood in western Washington State was engulfed in flames after an incident with a tree removal company spiraled out of control."

Tamia's eyes popped open.

"Don't move," warned her mother.

"Sorry," said Tamia. "But listen."

"Three homes were damaged and one person killed when an attempt to remove a tree from a Puyallup resident's property was thwarted by," the announcer paused dramatically, "the tree itself. According to witnesses, the cottonwood fought back when the tree removal procedure began, killing the employee. Authorities believe that power lines damaged during the altercation ignited a fire on the roof of one of the houses, and the blaze quickly spread to neighboring houses in the windy conditions."

Her mother stopped smoothing relaxer into her hair. "Oh my god, Tamia. You're not going back out to that cabin."

"Mama, we're not chopping them down," said Tamia. "They won't hurt us." But she wished she felt as sure as she sounded.

"How do you know?" asked her mother, taking up her hair again. "We don't know anything about them."

"Aside from the one fatality," continued the announcer, "there were no additional injuries. Two of the three families have already moved back into their homes, and the third residence is undergoing repair for extensive damage to the roof. The tree in question remains in place as authorities determine how to remove it with no additional loss of life or property."

"That's it, you're done," said her mother.

"But Mama, this is exactly why Dr. Block and I—"

"I mean your hair. It's done." Her mother stripped off her gloves and handed her the bottle of neutralizing shampoo. "Go wash it out before it starts to burn."

Tamia padded into the bathroom and stepped into the shower. She tipped her head back and rinsed the thick helmet of cream out of her hair before lathering up, then breathed in the pungent, slightly tangy smell of neutralizing shampoo hitting the remaining relaxer. How much time had she spent on this routine, on her hair, straightening, prodding and poking her way into someone else's image of what she should look like? Only, by now she couldn't exactly call it someone else's image: she'd internalized it. Walking around with unrelaxed hair was like leaving the house without a bra. Sure, other folks did it all the time. But that was other folks, not her.

Whatever, she shouldn't waste any more time obsessing about her hair when she had more important things to think about. One more person killed just now and another up in Olympic National Forest last week, plus those Weyerhaeuser loggers. Things were just going to get worse. Dr. Block was afraid people would start setting more fires, but Tamia hadn't believed it until now. If people couldn't cut the trees down, what would they try next?

She stepped out of the shower and wrapped herself up in one of her mother's fluffy, luxurious towels. *Enjoy this now,* she told herself. *You're going back down to Dr. Block's tomorrow.*

Tamia got dressed and went into the kitchen to show off her new hair.

"You like it?" asked her mother.

"You're my favorite stylist," she replied, kissing her on the cheek.

Her mother smiled. "Your phone went off while you were in the shower."

Tamia picked her phone up off the kitchen table and checked the number. *Restricted.* Could it be Charlie Meninick finally calling back? She dialed into voicemail and punched in her code.

"Tamia, this is Rima from Governor Palmer's office. Please call me back."

She'd never had a good poker face. As soon as she hung up, her mother frowned and asked who it was.

"They didn't say." She didn't want to get her mom's hopes up. It wasn't likely they were calling to hire her back. "Guess I'll find out," she said, heading up to her room before her mother could ask any more questions.

She closed the door behind her and dialed the number Rima had left. What other shoe was about to drop? It had likely been naïve to think firing was all they had in store for her.

Rima answered, her voice crisp and efficient.

"It's Tamia. You called me?"

Rima's voice instantly melted into a friendlier tone. "Ah, Tamia, yes. How are you?"

"I'm fine. How are you?" *Play it cool, play it cool.*

"Well, we've been very busy responding to this whole business of the trees. I suppose you know as well as anyone the kind of calls we're getting."

Word must have gotten back to them that she was working with Dr. Block. "Yes," she said, "we've been busy."

"Well, Tamia, I know you didn't expect to hear from us, given the situation when you left. But things with the trees have gotten serious. The governor is putting together a task force, and he'd like to get Dr. Block and Dr. Nystrom on board."

Tamia held her breath, trying to predict what was about to bite her. Lawsuit? Prison? Visit from ArborTech goons? "What do you need from me?"

"We've tried contacting them, but we haven't been able to reach them yet. We were hoping you could help move this along."

They needed her help? Did this mean she was safe? "Who's going to be on the task force?" Rima didn't respond right away, so Tamia coaxed her. "I'm only asking you because I know they'll ask me."

"Forest Service," said Rima reluctantly. "Natural Resources, State Troopers, the Guard."

"The National Guard?"

"Absolutely. We're bracing for more fires, search and rescue, patrols, crowd control."

Tamia felt like she'd walked into a disaster movie. "Right. I'm sure Dr. Block and Dr. Nystrom will want to be there."

"Good," said Rima. "Can you get them over here tomorrow afternoon? We have to get on this before the weekend."

"I'll call them right now," she said. "So there won't be anyone else there?" Everyone knew ArborTech and the NSA were testifying before Congress about genetically modified trees right now.

"No, Tamia, not that I'm aware of. Is there anyone else you recommend?" There was a stern note beneath her friendly tone.

"I don't know," she answered, "I'll ask Block and Nystrom what they think."

"All right," said Rima. "Two o'clock in the large conference room. We'll add them to the security list."

"The three of us."

Rima was silent.

"Dr. Block relies on me to take notes. I'm not sure she'll have time to—"

"Fine. I'll have Greg put all three of you on the list. Please just make sure Block and Nystrom get there."

Greg. A few weeks ago, she would have found it immensely gratifying to see Greg do the scutwork for a meeting she'd be attending. But now she had more pressing matters on her mind, like how it could be that things were serious enough to consult with the National

Guard, yet Palmer and Jones were still trying to hide ArborTech's role in the whole thing. Lives were at stake now, so wasn't it about time for them to come clean?

Maybe they knew something she didn't. What if the scrutiny of ArborTech had fizzled? What if they found a way to deny everything, or the government kept it classified? If public outrage didn't save her and Dr. Block like they'd hoped, she might need a lawyer, perhaps even a bodyguard, or both. And those things cost a lot of money, which she didn't have.

"Tamia? Are you still there?" asked Rima.

"Yes," she said, blinking. "I am. And I'll make sure we're all there tomorrow."

Tamia braced herself for a barrage of questions as she went back downstairs. "Dad's not cooking?" she asked, by way of distraction.

"He's buried with work," said her mother, handing her peppers to chop. Tamia could feel maternal eyes on her as she washed and sliced the vegetables. "You know," she said casually, "while you're here, your father could use some help in the office."

"Mama, I can't keep working for him forever."

"Don't get all touchy," said her mother, hand on hip. "No one's asking you to work there forever. Just until you find another job." She turned back to rinsing her colander of lettuce.

"Well . . ." Tamia was out of the houseshare now, so she didn't have rent to worry about. But those student loan payments weren't going to make themselves. "Okay, you're right. I'll start tomorrow." She could put in a couple of hours in the morning and still get to the meeting in the afternoon.

Tamia moved around the kitchen through a fog of lies and omissions. Not too long ago she would have told her mother everything. She wasn't used to holding stuff back. She hated it, actually, the weight of it. She wondered if Dr. Block felt like that. Had she been holding something back the whole time they'd been working together? She must have suspected her research had something to do with the trees' transformation. Maybe she even knew it was coming. That might explain why she was hanging out in the forest with her translator in the first place. A guilty conscience masquerading as ongoing research, perhaps?

She had no way of knowing how much of the project Dr. Block was aware of and whether, or how easily, the scientist carried around the weight of deception. But then again, who was she to judge? She had lied about her work with the Governor's office to get involved in the first place.

Tamia wasn't really hungry by the time dinner was ready, but she played her part at the table, eating and chatting about her mom's work and DeShaun's day at school and what she would be helping her dad with the following day. Acting in front of family was a strain, but she had to figure all this out on her own, without getting them wrapped up in it. Sometimes deception was required to protect the people you loved.

CHAPTER 36

RICKY SAT IN the fading light, in the highest branches of an old oak. He hung on loosely as he looked downhill over the rest of the forest, knowing the tall oak wouldn't let him fall. The woods felt a little dry and sad now that most of the trees were missing their leaves, but the evergreens added spots of color among all the brown and grey tree skeletons. Ricky caught a whiff of someone burning leaves nearby. He turned in one direction and saw treetops mingling with rooftops and streets. In the other direction, there were evergreens mixed with crooked, leafless limbs as far as he could see.

The sun began to duck behind clouds on the horizon, and block by block, the streetlights in his neighborhood winked on. He'd stayed out too late. His parents must have discovered he was gone by now. His stomach tightened when he thought about how they would yell at him. He looked down the trunk. It was even darker below. He should go home. Soon the woods would be nothing but a blur of greys and blacks.

He took a last look out over the layer of treetops sloping away from town. A twinkling light in the distance caught his eye. He squinted, but it was hard to see through the clouds. He watched the light flicker and swell as the smoky smell grew stronger. He felt a twist in the pit of his stomach. Those weren't clouds. That was smoke. He clutched the tree, frozen in place from the moment he recognized flames in the distance. The woods were on fire! He had to tell somebody! But his body wasn't listening to him. His legs didn't move, and his hands couldn't let go of the tree.

Ricky's heart thumped. He watched tiny flames leap higher under darkening billows of smoke. The fire was getting bigger, brighter—closer. In the growing light, he could make out a rippling motion in the forest. The trees seemed to bend in toward the flickering light, as if they wanted to get burned. Once they were burning, though, it looked like they were flexing back out in the other direction. It was almost like watching a relay, or the Olympic torch on TV. He gasped. *Were they doing it on purpose?*

A plume of smoke made Ricky cough, shocking him into motion. He scrambled to the ground, scraping his hands and legs on craggy bark and bristly twigs all the way down. He had to get back home and tell everybody!

Ricky spun around in the darkness below, too scared to remember which direction he'd come from. *Why would the trees be setting themselves on fire? Maybe they were trying to stop it. But*—

He felt a current of heat on his cheek and ran in the opposite direction. The fire was moving too fast! He sucked in a breath full of smoke and coughed. The hot air tasted like ashes. His eyes began to water, but he kept on running, wheezing and stumbling over rocks and roots. A wave of relief rushed through him when he saw familiar ground, but a moment later he stubbed his toe and crashed to the ground.

Ricky rolled over and sat up, choking on a cloud of dust. His knee throbbed with pain. He held it and rocked until a pop and crackle echoed through the woods. *It's burning!*

He got up and ran, but the smoky smell intensified. Sparks drifted overhead like fireflies over a field at dusk. His knee hurt, but the wall of heat at his back kept him moving. At last, he heard the wail of a firetruck and followed the sound.

Ricky kept running, breaking out of the tree line into a park he recognized. He was close to his house. He cut a diagonal path across the grass and ran out onto the street. Almost home!

Tires screeched and a horn blared. Ricky froze in the middle of the street, shivering. He turned toward the car, and beyond the glare of the headlights he saw the shape of the driver standing behind an open door.

"Jesus, kid!" yelled the driver. "You okay?"

Ricky nodded and backed out of the street, breathing hard.

"Where's your parents?"

He pointed toward his house.

"Get home now," said the driver. "They're prob'ly waiting for you."

Ricky watched the car roll by, then saw a door open across the street. A couple emerged carrying bags and suitcases. Another door down the street opened, and a woman rushed over to her neighbor's house and pounded on the door.

Ricky blinked back tears and ran around the corner. *Almost home.* More people came out of their houses; garage doors opened and cars rolled down driveways. A baby's howl pierced the air. He ran even faster, his heart hammering in his chest. *Almost home!*

In the porchlight, Ricky saw his mother standing at the front door, looking up and down the street.

"Mom!" he yelled, running toward her. "Mom!"

"Oh my god, Ricky!" She ran toward him as fast as the Flash, practically colliding with him on the lawn. She squeezed so tight he couldn't breathe, then pulled him away from her and looked him over. "Are you okay, Ricky, are you hurt?"

"I'm okay, Mom. I'm sorry," he said. He was relieved, but frightened at the same time, watching his mother's face turn from furious, to scared, to happy, and back to angry.

She hugged him again, then stood up and dragged him toward their car. It was sitting in the driveway, already packed. "Get in, sweetie," she said, "we have to leave. There's a fire."

"Where's Dad?" he asked.

"I don't know, baby," she said. She pulled her phone out of her pocket with shaking hands. "He went out looking for you."

CHAPTER 37

CHARLIE CLUTCHED THE phone. "You're comin' out this weekend?" he asked, sitting up straighter behind his desk at the Cultural Center.

"Yeah," said Liz. "Unless they've canceled the powwow. Auntie would kill me if I didn't help her and Mom prepare. We've got family coming in, you know."

"Is it safe to drive?" he asked. The fire in Tacoma had been all over the news that morning. Every summer there were fires in parts of Washington he didn't pay much attention to. Didn't have to, state was so huge. Sure, he'd check in with folks in Nakalish, but they were always okay. Otherwise, up in Seattle he'd maybe see haze and smell a little smoke for a few days, but even that was pretty rare.

This summer, however, was a little different.

"Should be clear by tonight, or tomorrow morning at the latest." She paused. "Did you hear? Some people are saying the trees are spreading it."

Charlie shook his head. "Yeah, I heard that, but there's no way they'd go and burn themselves up." It didn't make sense to him at all. One minute the trees were bending down, killing themselves for peace, and now they're killing themselves for war?

"Well," said Liz, "I guess we just have to see what happens." She broke the silence with a change of subject. "So, is everyone out there ready for the powwow?"

"Oh, yeah, folks are lookin' forward to it."

"Auntie's been complaining that people are trying to mess around too much with our traditions because of all this stuff with the trees," she said. "You know, she's

237

traditional, wants to stick to the old way as much as possible. Then I talk to Mom and she says, 'Things are changing all around us, and we're just supposed to act like nothing is happening?'"

"Hmmm." He'd been there when the trees had made their offering, and they thanked him by name. Didn't that mean that he, of all people, should have answers? He hated that he didn't.

"Well, I don't know, but I'm curious," said Liz. "Maybe I'll sneak off and learn a new tree dance while Auntie's not looking."

"Well, if you want to do that, I know who you should talk to," he offered.

"Minnie Littledeer?"

"How did you know?"

"Come on," she said. "She's been making quite a name for herself, the famous 'Tree Whisperer' of Nakalish."

"She's not doin' it for that."

"Maybe not. Auntie just felt she should have consulted the Council first before going out there to negotiate."

"Oh, I don't think that's what she set out to do. But I guess nobody's really sure what to do about all this." Eddie seemed to have a plan, though. He'd called that morning to set up lunch, and Charlie was curious to hear what he was cooking up.

"Well, anyway," said Liz, "I just called to tell Ruth I'd be in town this weekend, in case she needs anything. And . . . to see if you'd be around."

He smiled. "Yeah, I'm around. It'd be great to see you. I just got a new phone." He gave her the number to call when Auntie relieved her from duty.

He hung up, still smiling. It almost wasn't right, to be this caught up in a girl with everything else going on. He wondered again if it would be safe for Liz to drive to Nakalish with fires smoldering across the state. But he didn't have time to call her back right now. He had to hustle to meet Eddie.

A cup of coffee was already steaming in front of Eddie when Charlie walked up to his table at the diner. He recognized Eddie's special smile as soon as he sat down. It was the look he gave you when he had an offer too good to refuse.

"Know what, Cuz?" Eddie asked, sliding the menu toward him. "I'm in the mood for a treat today. What do you say we get steaks, on me?"

"That's okay, Cuz, I'm a workin' man now. Thanks though." Charlie studied the menu, wishing his cousin would wipe that stupid grin off his face. After everything Eddie'd done for him, he'd help him with whatever he needed. He just wanted Eddie to be straight with him, not sell to him like a stranger.

They placed their orders and Eddie leaned back in his chair. "You know," he said thoughtfully. "This whole talking tree thing is big. Huge! It's gonna change a lot of things."

"Yeah," said Charlie, watching him carefully. "I guess you got a lot of adjustments to make at work."

Eddie nodded. "Oh yeah. I got guys who don't want to come in anymore, and other guys askin' for hazard pay. But in a way, it's okay. Demand's gone down a bit. Folks are kinda funny about buyin' wood that's killed people."

"Shit, I didn't think about that. How bad is it?"

"Oh, not too bad. Yet. We got existing contracts to fulfill, but it's down the road I'm thinkin' about." He smiled at Charlie. "We got to position ourselves."

Charlie cocked an eyebrow.

"Eco-wood," said Eddie.

"Eco-wood?" echoed Charlie.

"Think about it. Everyone's talkin' sustainability these days. It's practically all they ask about. Well, these trees are ready to give themselves up. What could be more sustainable than that? It's like wool from a lamb, only better. It's like the lamb up and shaved itself. People'll love it."

"So you're gonna market Palalla wood as 'Eco-wood'?" Charlie asked.

Eddie spread his hands out in anticipation of a standing ovation.

Charlie couldn't help but smile at Eddie's conviction. "Not a bad idea."

"You kiddin' me, it's a frickin' amazing idea. But we got to move fast before someone else takes it."

"We?" he asked.

"Yeah, you didn't think I'd leave you out of this, did you, Cuz? Besides, who else is gonna call in the trees?" His hand mimicked the motion of a tree falling down.

"Call in? You mean, you want *me* to ask 'em?" As much as he wanted to help his people, he had a weird feeling about personally leading trees to slaughter.

"Come on, Charlie, think about it. Most of our guys ain't exactly spiritual experts, you know?"

"But it was Minnie Littledeer who got 'em to respond. What makes you think I can do it?"

"You got a history with 'em. You always believed in 'em."

"Sounds like you're a believer now too."

Eddie shrugged. "I could be. I mean, yeah. But turns out they don't respond to just anybody. If anyone can get it to work, though, it's you."

Charlie smirked. "Minnie shot you down, huh?"

"She ain't much of a businesswoman," chuckled Eddie.

Their orders came to the table. Eddie tucked in to his steak right away, but Charlie just stared at his burger.

"Eddie, I don't know if I can." Not too long ago he was protecting trees from poachers. The idea that he would now be culling them for profit didn't sit right. "All kinds of people are prayin' to the forest now, why don't you get one of them?"

Eddie's cheek bulged with a bite of sirloin. "I don't understand. All this time you've been tryin' to prove something is going on with the trees, and now that it's out there you're just—backin' away. What's wrong?"

Charlie picked up his burger and thought back to his conversation with Dr. Nystrom and the trees. "Eddie, how much do we need?"

"How much wood? We do about a hundred forty million board feet per year now. But think how much more we could do with Eco-wood!"

Charlie shook his head. "But how much do we *need*?"

Eddie looked impatient. "This is a business. We're not in it just to break even." He cut off another piece of meat. "We need to be more ambitious. Don't you want to get ahead?"

Charlie watched oily, bloody juice spread out over Eddie's plate. He took a bite of his own burger.

"When Palalla businesses do better, all our people do better," said Eddie. "Win-win, right?"

Charlie chewed and nodded noncommittally. The trees *did* agree to giving up members of their community, after all. Maybe all his questions about the Greyfoxes were just making him overly suspicious of Eddie.

Eddie grinned. "That's more like it! I was thinkin' you could come out this weekend, see how it goes. Then if things work out you could come on part time, at least to start."

"Uh-huh." After all, he *had* just complained to his cousin about still working at the Cultural Center.

"We have to see how it goes," said Eddie. "We could train you in production too, depending on how fast extraction is goin'."

Charlie nodded and took another bite of his burger as the rich, fatty aroma of Eddie's grilled steak wafted into his nose.

"So, I'll pick you up at ten Sunday morning, okay? That's not too early, I hope. I hear you might be tied up in the evenings this weekend." Eddie winked at him and sliced off another forkful.

"Ten on Sunday," said Charlie, looking down quickly. That was one damn efficient gossip mill. He was probably the last person in town to find out he'd be seeing Liz this weekend.

Eddie seemed to know everything, didn't he? And he was doing all right for himself too. A nice house, nice family, juicy steak every now and then. Even said he was setting something aside for the kids' college, to help them go anywhere they wanted.

But did Eddie's job really pay enough to cover all that?

Charlie took another bite of his burger and tried to beat back his doubts, like he'd done a million times before. Maybe there was really nothing to know about Eddie and the Greyfoxes. That family wasn't exactly known for their honesty, were they? Here his cousin was trying to help him, and he returned the favor by imagining him taking kickbacks from a family of poachers. What kind of cousin was he?

"Shoot, Cuz, you eat too slow," said Eddie. "I'm ready for dessert!"

Eddie sure knew how to treat himself. And did that have to be a bad thing? He and his wife worked hard for their money. Maybe it was overly cynical to assume that the only route to a comfortable life was through corruption. Maybe he should trust his cousin more, and give himself a chance to find out what success actually felt like.

"Dessert, huh?" Charlie tilted his mouth into a sideways smile. "Pick one out for me too, would you? I feel like havin' a little something sweet."

CHAPTER 38

TAMIA SCANNED THE line of grim faces gathered around the conference table in the Executive Building that Friday afternoon. Men and women in suits and uniforms murmured to one another, poking at tablets and phones while waiting for the governor to arrive. A couple of them had printed copies of the report that had been e-mailed that morning. Tamia flicked on her phone and scrolled through her copy, recognizing some of the phrases she herself had written just a couple of months earlier.

She checked the time. Two o'clock on the dot. With every passing minute, she imagined a team of armed heavies bursting in and arresting her and Dr. Block in a display of shock and awe. The door opened and her body tensed, but instead of police, it was the chief of staff sharing a last few words with the governor at the threshold. Palmer switched his expression into "grim-but-friendly" mode and entered the room, shaking hands and patting shoulders as he worked his way to the empty chair at the head of the table. She'd heard this was his habit. Three minutes late, just enough time to make guests aware of the wait, but not long enough to be perceived as unprofessional.

Greg trailed the governor and chief of staff, carrying a large cardboard box with a notepad perched on top. He lowered the box to the floor and nodded discreetly at Tamia as he sat down in a row of chairs against the wall. She nodded back, strangely unable to relate to the Tamia of a few weeks ago who would have enjoyed seeing him relegated to the side taking notes.

The governor sat down and acknowledged the men and women around the table. "Thank you all for coming on such short notice. I know everyone's hands are full right now, so I appreciate your time. Is everyone here?"

"All but Dr. Nystrom," answered Greg, consulting a list. Tamia was, in fact, sitting in the seat that had been reserved for him. "He had a family emergency."

"I'm sorry to hear that," said Palmer. He looked around the table, his eyes only briefly alighting on hers. She wondered how much he really knew about what was going on. Was he the mastermind, or was Jones the real puppet master?

"Let's start with introductions," said the governor. Tamia listened to officials from the Forest Service, Department of Natural Resources, the State's Ecology Department, and the Bureau of Indian Affairs introduce themselves. One or two of the names sounded familiar; they might have been on that press list she used. The men in uniform were from the State Patrol and the National Guard, as she'd suspected, and the State FEMA rep sat to her right.

FEMA, thought Tamia. *Shit just got real.*

Introductions worked their way around the table to Dr. Block, who introduced herself and Tamia. Dr. Block hardly needed an introduction, however. A couple of people smiled at her, apparently eager to hear from one of the foremost experts on the issue that had brought them all together. Others responded with a flat stare, perhaps angry at having been proven wrong. The guy from the Guard looked at Dr. Block so intently, Tamia wondered if he actually blamed her for the whole thing.

Governor Palmer took the helm. "The report you have is the current stand as of this morning. Paul, could you give us an update?"

The Forest Service representative began his report. "State and local fire crews kept the blaze contained to a five-mile by one-mile swath, thankfully with low population density. Currently, five fatalities, ten critically injured. But those numbers will change as more residents are accounted for. The main blaze has been extinguished, but we're still dealing with flare-ups in a ten-mile radius, and growing. The trees are keeping the ground fires moving so we can't track them."

"Do you need more air support?" asked Palmer.

"That's not the core problem, Governor. Ground fires burn in *duff*, the layer of decomposed leaves and other organic debris *underneath* the surface of the soil, or inside decaying tree roots. These ground fires produce very little smoke, so air patrols can't always spot them. But if they come into contact with surface fuels, they can flare up at any moment."

"And you say the trees are moving these ground fires around?" asked the woman from FEMA.

"We can only assume it's the trees," replied the Forest Service rep. "Fires are, by nature, unpredictable, but this particular one is defying all previous patterns. We're seeing crown fires over terrain where we'd expect to see surface fires. And there was minimal wind last night, not anywhere near enough to push a fire in the direction it went. I can only explain it as targeted."

"Targeted?" asked the guardsman, transferring his glare from Block to the Forest Service spokesperson.

"Yes. Unless there's some kind of wind or crazy thermals going on, the fire should follow fuel sources, like dead trees and dry underbrush. But this thing leapt into the crowns and practically made a beeline for Tacoma. Ground crews can handle surface fires up to four feet high, but they can't get their arms around this. Digging a fire line won't help, in this case, and we're too close to watersheds and population centers to use aerial retardants. It's like the trees are choosing the most difficult type of fire to fight, in the most difficult terrain."

"Do we know how it started?" asked Palmer.

The Forest Service rep shook his head. "Still too hot to investigate. But to be safe, we've coordinated with Natural Resources to stop all scheduled burns until further notice."

"But what about private citizens?" asked the trooper. "Folks have to stop messing with the trees. That's what's escalating this."

"We're already working on a public service campaign," said the FEMA rep.

Governor Palmer tapped his pen on the table. "With all respect, Don, how many people really listen to those things? We have to get some private partners involved, get the media's ear."

Tamia was stunned. Just a few weeks ago, the chief of staff was trying to shut her down. Now the governor was calling for media partnerships?

"We need to figure out what triggers these trees," Palmer went on. "Why are they engaging in acts of destruction and what will make them stop?"

"Trees are not destructive by nature," said the BIA representative. "They are only reacting to hostility from us."

"That's right," said Dr. Block. "Wouldn't you defend yourself if someone were trying to cut you down? We're all panicking because now they actually can."

"But what's the alternative?" asked the woman from Natural Resources. "I mean, even if private citizens stop harassing trees, we still need lumber. What about our timber industry, our pulp mills? And what about prescribed burns? The longer we wait, the more dry fuel accumulates, and the worse future fires will be."

"The forest has managed itself far longer than we have," said the BIA rep. "Perhaps we should ask the trees what needs to be done."

"I agree," said Dr. Block. She set her jaw and looked around the room. "Richard Nystrom's son is one of those residents not 'accounted for.' Dr. Nystrom is out there right now, walking around a charred forest looking for him. Both of them would probably be home safe right now if we'd stopped to listen to what those trees want."

The officials in the room shifted and looked at one another.

"We'll find him, Ma'am," said the guardsman quietly.

The governor pointed at Dr. Block. "People, she's right. We can't just keep fighting the trees with brute force. We need to know what they want. Greg?" He looked over at his assistant. Greg opened the large cardboard box sitting on the floor and lifted out a smaller, metallic box about six inches in length.

"Pass them around, please," said the governor.

Greg handed out one rectangular metal box after another. The attendees murmured and passed them around the table until everyone had one.

Tamia turned the device over in her hands. Her eyes widened in recognition.

"These are translators," said Governor Palmer, "much like the ones our esteemed scientists have been using to monitor the trees thus far."

"Where did you get these?" asked Dr. Block, her face ashen.

"You must know, Dr. Block. These are from ArborTech."

Tamia looked at the faces around the room. She wasn't alone in her surprise.

"Excuse me, sir," said the Ecology rep. "But aren't they under federal investigation?"

Palmer nodded. "Yes. Keep in mind, however, we don't have all the details yet. ArborTech is still obliged to protect its clients." He looked directly at Dr. Block before going on. "In the meantime, they've been authorized to help us in this manner."

"Authorized by whom, exactly?" asked Dr. Block.

"Public safety is the main concern right now," answered the governor. "We have to do whatever we can to keep people safe."

"I agree," she pressed, "but is the State of Washington buying equipment from the same company that—"

"No, not buying. ArborTech is donating the translators to us. They are every bit as committed to saving lives as we are."

Tamia watched Dr. Block seethe quietly. It was just like she'd said. If ArborTech were able to come out of the investigation relatively unscathed, they'd have cornered the market on the only known solution to a—literally—growing international problem.

"Dr. Block," said Palmer, "I hope that you and Dr. Nystrom can put aside any differences you might have with ArborTech to help us with this new equipment. Surely whatever happened in the past is not as important right now as keeping more people from getting hurt."

"Certainly," said Dr. Block grudgingly. "But, Governor Palmer, based on our observations, it would be better to coordinate communication among ourselves before speaking with the trees. Each network of trees seems to have a group consciousness, and they may expect the same from us. It could be confusing and potentially dangerous to have multiple sets of negotiations going on, at least until we can map how far each network extends."

"So what are you suggesting?" asked Palmer.

"It would be best to have one point of contact for them."

"For the whole state?" interrupted the Forest Service rep.

"At least a unified strategy, one set of rules or guidelines," Dr. Block concluded.

"Hang on," said the trooper. "You're talking about these things like they're people."

"Well, they're raisin' Cain like people," muttered the guardsman.

"They're protecting themselves, as any living thing would," the Ecology rep argued.

Palmer raised his hand to quell discussion. "Dr. Block, can you and Dr. Nystrom come up with a set of guidelines for negotiating with these things?"

The trooper shook his head. "I'm sorry, sir, but we need more than just another report. People out there want answers, now. Every day that goes by without a solution, some yahoo out there is stuffing his family into a bunker, or organizing a militia, or worse yet, planning some kind of preemptive strike that winds up getting a whole neighborhood burned down."

Palmer tapped the table with his pen again. "Dr. Block, I'll need a set of recommendations on my desk first thing tomorrow morning. Meanwhile, folks, take these translators out there and establish contact with the trees in your jurisdictions. Tell them you mean no harm, try to get them talking. Coordinate between your agencies to get as much coverage as possible."

Dr. Block raised a hand in protest. "Governor Palmer, I really wouldn't—"

"We don't have time to dance around the issue, Dr. Block. The sooner you get those recommendations to me, the sooner we can review and distribute them." He addressed all the meeting participants. "We have more translators here, with instructions, so please see my assistant Greg and take as many as you can carry. We'll send more around to your branch offices as needed."

The scientist opened her mouth, but the chief of staff spoke first. "Dr. Block, I know we have more to discuss, so why don't we let all these people get back to work before we continue."

Dr. Block nodded, but her expression told Tamia she hadn't been expecting a second meeting.

Palmer stood and addressed the group. "Drs. Block and Nystrom will be available, as agreed, to answer any questions you may have about the translators. Their contact information will be included in the minutes of this meeting. We are very grateful for their assistance, and we will be praying for the safe return of Dr. Nystrom's son. Thank you all for coming, and let's keep each other informed."

A buzz of conversation rose as the meeting broke up. Greg continued to distribute translators while the governor circulated and shook hands with agency representatives. Tamia observed him working the room. His expression was grave, but he was likely congratulating himself inside. Whatever his reason, his goal must have been to get those things into as many hands as possible. Men and women filed out into the hallway, and Palmer nodded at his chief of staff just before he left the room.

Only she, Dr. Block and Derrick Jones remained. Greg hovered at the door with his tablet and an empty box.

"Thank you, Greg," said Jones. "Get those notes to me ASAP."

Greg nodded and smiled quickly at Tamia before closing the door behind him.

"Well," said the chief of staff expansively, "that was a productive meeting. I'm sorry Dr. Nystrom wasn't able to attend. I hope they find his son soon."

"We do too," said Dr. Block.

"Tamia, would you mind waiting outside?" asked Jones. "Dr. Block and I have some things to discuss."

"Tamia is working with me," Dr. Block countered. "I would like her to stay."

Jones observed the two women for a moment, his lips parted as if about to object. Then he sat down and gestured for both of them to join him. "This is, of course, off the record."

"Understood," said Dr. Block. She and Tamia lowered themselves into chairs across the table from him.

The chief of staff tipped his head and smiled at Dr. Block. His voice was warm and conciliatory. "Barbara—"

"Dr. Block," she insisted.

Jones' smile faded. "Dr. Block, our main concern is keeping people safe. That's what this is all about." He folded his hands on the table. "How you started communicating with these trees, using whose property, doesn't matter now. We just need you and Richard to concentrate on figuring out what they want. Leave the other questions be. We don't need the two of you in jail right now."

"Jail?" said Dr. Block, raising her eyebrows. "For disagreeing with ArborTech?"

And "right now"? thought Tamia. *Did that just mean they were saving prison for later?*

"The investigators haven't yet clarified who did what and when," said Jones coolly. "But you're not doing yourselves any favors by pushing on ArborTech the way you have been."

Tamia's stomach clenched.

"Let's be frank," said Jones. "It's pretty clear by now that ArborTech was involved in this, and perhaps Defense, and who knows who else. It's just a matter of time until they have to produce all of their records. The only question now is exactly what those records will reveal."

"What are you saying?" asked the scientist.

"This is a professional lab, Dr. Block. Don't you think they have contingency plans for this kind of thing? You have to know they're sitting down with their counsel right now, discussing a variety of options. One position they might take is that you and Dr. Nystrom were their eyes and ears the whole time, in accordance with responsible environmental monitoring. Then again, they might find grounds to accuse you of unauthorized possession and release of experimental biological material—something you might have wanted to track with the unreturned translators."

"You seem to know something about the science behind this phenomenon," said Block. Tamia wondered how she could keep her voice so steady.

"My staff keeps me up to date," replied Jones, smiling at Tamia. What kind of game was he trying to play here? She hadn't ever said anything to him about the science.

"I understand Dr. Nystrom was assigned to the project," he continued, "so he would be the first to come under scrutiny. But as a colleague, Dr. Block, you could also be implicated. Things could get very complicated for both of you."

Dr. Block's mouth tightened. "So what do you advise?"

"Well, I can't tell you what to do, but if it were me, I'd be a little less strident in my claims against ArborTech. And the DoD for that matter. I mean, you don't have any documentation about their involvement, do you?"

"It doesn't matter what I have or don't have," insisted the scientist. "Everything's got a paper trail. What do *you* think's going to come out in the investigation?"

"That's for other people to decide," he said calmly.

A chill ran down Tamia's spine. Could it really be that easy to rewrite the history of an outbreak?

The chief of staff looked intently at the older woman. "Dr. Block, we have to work as a team to make sure the people of Washington are safe. And we need you and Dr. Nystrom out in the field, not embroiled in some investigation. That wouldn't be good for anyone, would it?"

Dr. Block glared at Jones. "I'll discuss it with Dr. Nystrom," she said at last.

The corners of his lips curled into a smile. "Excellent." He rose and extended his hand to both women in turn. "You'll have to excuse me now. Please give my best to Dr. Nystrom. Let him know our thoughts are with him and his son." He escorted them out into the hallway. "We'll be looking for your recommendations tomorrow morning."

Tamia watched Dr. Block clench and unclench her fists, then followed her out toward the reception area.

"Looks like we've got to get moving," said the older woman. "I'll call Richard on my way home. Can you take him one of these new translators on your way back to Seattle?"

Tamia took a second machine from Dr. Block and trailed her down the stairs. She hated the way men like Palmer and Jones got everyone to jump whenever they wanted.

The two women stepped out onto the sidewalk. "I'm parked this way," said Dr. Block, pointing down the street. "I'll send you a first draft this afternoon, and then—" She stopped and studied Tamia's face. "I know, strange bedfellows. But we have to move quickly if we want to be part of the solution."

"The governor couldn't make a move without your recommendations," said Tamia. "*He* needs *you*, but they're still trying to make us look like criminals."

"Sometimes you have to play the game. You studied political science, you know that." She squeezed Tamia's arm before heading toward her truck. "I'll e-mail you this afternoon," she said over her shoulder.

Tamia walked to her car, so deep in thought she almost overlooked the little slip of paper fluttering on her windshield.

"Dammit!"

She ripped the ticket out from under her wiper blade. She should have put more money in the meter. No, Jones shouldn't have made her late. She could barely afford gas, much less a parking fine. Something had to change.

Tamia got into her car, threw her purse and the ticket onto the passenger seat and pulled away from the curb. Before she hit the highway, she reached back and grabbed a bottle of water from her back seat stash. She headed up the I-5 toward Seattle, brooding about still living with her parents, asking herself what those four years of college were supposed to have accomplished. As she reached for the radio, she glanced over at the ticket. Her heart sank at the thought of having to ask her mom for more money. She grabbed the slip of paper, crumpled it up and let it fall to the floor. Then she turned up the music and leaned on the gas all the way to Tacoma.

CHAPTER 39

WITH ONE HAND propping up his head, Ricky sat at the kitchen table and stared at his math homework. He stole a glance at Grampa Nystrom across the table, typing away at his laptop. Ricky swung his feet back and forth as he tried once more to focus on the numbers in front of him. But his thoughts kept floating back to his dad, lying helpless in a hospital bed all because of him.

Grampa reached over and placed his hand over Ricky's.

"Oh." He'd been tapping his pencil again.

Grampa smiled gently. "Need some help?"

"No thanks." Mom usually helped him with homework, but she was sitting with Dad at the hospital. And now Grampa had to babysit him. He'd messed things up for everyone.

"Okay, suit yourself," said Grampa Nystrom, turning his attention back to his screen.

Ricky sighed and tried to focus. He wrote down a couple of numbers under the easy questions. The question after that was almost as easy. Pretty soon he'd done the whole worksheet and had only thought about his dad a couple of times.

He looked up to see Grampa Nystrom smiling at him. "There, that wasn't so bad, was it?"

"I guess not," he said with a shrug.

Grampa Nystrom held out his hand and Ricky slipped the worksheet into it. After a minute he handed it back. "Very good! You have any more homework?"

"Reading."

"Well, Grampa has to do a little homework too," he said, checking his watch. "When I get back you can tell me what you read."

"Okay," said Ricky. He watched his grandfather rise from the table—he was going out to the woods again. Turns out he didn't need to go very far to do his work anymore, just to the edge of the yard. He said it was convenient for him, but Mom didn't like it at all. Ricky wasn't so sure what to think about it himself.

As he stared at his reading homework, he heard the front door open, followed by the clink of keys in the metal bowl by the door. His mother's familiar step sounded down the hall. She entered the kitchen, looking tired and worried, and put her grocery bags down on the counter. Setting her face into a smile, she came over to smooth his hair and give him a kiss.

"Grampa outside?"

"Yeah."

"Well, go let him know I'm back so he can go visit your dad."

"Can I go too?" he asked, already knowing the answer.

"I'm sorry, honey, he's still in intensive care. You're too young to go in there. And he's still not really awake yet."

Ricky slid off his chair and headed down the hallway to the rec room. Through the sliding glass door, he saw Grampa at the edge of the lawn, speaking with one of the maples. He didn't understand why all of their trees were still there, why they hadn't all burned up in the fire. Grampa said you can't always tell where a fire's going to go. His mom said they were lucky, but he didn't feel very lucky—not with his dad in the hospital.

Ricky opened the door a slice and slipped through. Grampa's back was still facing him as he tip-toed across the lawn to get close enough to hear.

"How long are you going to keep the fires burning?" asked his grandfather.

A calm female voice surprised Ricky. "As long as . . . needed."

"What does that mean?" asked Grampa Nystrom. "I hope you're not holding out for some kind of universal treaty. That doesn't seem to be in the cards."

"Better if all agree," said the flat, mechanical voice.

"Yes, yes, but agreeing isn't where we humans excel." Grampa laughed one of his short little laughs, when something wasn't actually supposed to be funny. "Creativity, tenacity, perhaps ingenuity, but not logic or efficiency."

Who's Grampa talking to? wondered Ricky. He took a step closer and leaned to the side to see around his grandfather. There was a new machine strapped to the trunk of the tree.

"How many people . . . must we speak?" The woman's voice came out of the machine.

Ricky's mouth popped open. *The trees can talk out loud!*

Grampa shook his head. "I don't know. But I want you to promise me something." His shoulders slumped. "Please don't hurt any more people," he said quietly.

"Your son . . . had saw."

"He was just afraid," answered Grampa.

"Humans must put down axes . . . put down saws . . . listen at trees."

"I can't promise that. I don't control everyone. Nobody does."

"How humans . . . keep order?" asked the tinny voice. "How humans decide about . . . resources? How you decide which humans survive?"

"Is that how you do it?" asked Grampa Nystrom. "You decide who gets to live and who doesn't?"

"When no human . . . interfere. Sick fall, dead rot. Their . . . nutrients feed community."

"Well, it's different for us," said Nystrom. "We like to think each person is important. It doesn't always happen this way, but ideally the strong help the weak to survive."

"Why sick tree not fall and . . . nourish others? That is natural way. Good is health of community, not . . . comfort . . . of one tree."

259

"Yes," sighed the older man. "Yes, perhaps we could use a little more community thinking. But that's not how our society works. And," he said, his voice cracking, "I could never just give up on my son." The old man took a deep, shaky breath. "Losing him wouldn't help at all."

Ricky's lips started to tremble and his eyes fogged with tears. Grandpa Nystrom turned around at the sound of Ricky's sniffling, and the older man's expression of surprise quickly melted into tears of his own. He knelt down and held his hands out.

"Oh, my sweet boy, come here."

Ricky rushed into his grandfather's arms and sobbed. "I'm sorry, Grampa. It's all my fault!"

"What?" Grampa Nystrom pulled him away to look at him. "No, no, come on now. What's your fault?"

"Dad!" bawled Ricky, barely able to breathe. His shoulders trembled in his grandfather's hands. "He was out looking for me."

Grampa Nystrom's rough thumbs rubbed Ricky's tears away. "That doesn't make it your fault, Ricky. You didn't set the fire, did you?"

Ricky shook his head, sniffling.

"Well, there you go, it's not your fault. Okay?"

Ricky nodded miserably.

Grampa Nystrom cupped the boy's cheek in his palm. "Ricky, your dad loves you very much, and he's glad you're safe. He's not looking for anyone to blame. All he's worried about is getting strong enough to come back home. The most important thing you can do for him is stay strong and help your mom, okay?"

"Okay," said Ricky, still shaking a little.

"Good," said the old man. "Now let's clean you up," he said, his hand hovering under his grandson's streaming nose. He raised Ricky's arm up to his nose and used the boy's sleeve to wipe it. "I'm sure this shirt was ready for the wash anyway," he said, smiling and patting Ricky on the shoulder. Ricky couldn't help but grin a bit too.

Grampa wiped a tear from his own eye. "There we are. Your dad will be fine. He'll be out of the hospital soon."

Ricky sniffed again. The word *hospital* reminded him of what he'd been sent out there to do. "Mom's home," he said. "She said it's your turn to go visit Dad."

Grampa Nystrom nodded and squeezed Ricky's shoulder once more before he stood up and collected his equipment. "We'll speak more tomorrow," he said into the woods. "Right now I need to take care of *my* community."

CHAPTER 40

TAMIA SAT AT the weathered desk in her old bedroom at her parent's house in Seattle. Her eyes flicked between Dr. Block's and Dr. Nystrom's faces on her laptop monitor. *It's Saturday,* she thought. She found it ironic that she'd never been important enough while drawing a paycheck to get called in to work on a Saturday. Now, suddenly, she was indispensable.

She circled her cursor around the first two items on the list of recommendations they'd drafted. "Palmer's not going to care about Points 1 and 2 yet. Those will take too long."

"But both are necessary," said Dr. Block.

"Genetic mapping isn't that time-consuming anymore," added Dr. Nystrom. "Not with the proper resources."

"I'm not saying we should take it out," said Tamia. "But let's not lead with it. Everyone will freak out if we start with 'microsatellites.' They won't know it's about genetic mapping. And we need more detail about harvesting agreements."

After all, she knew, harvesting was going to be the main issue when it came right down to it. Follow the money, as they say. Every day new groves of trees were *waking up* throughout Washington, Idaho, Oregon, and British Columbia and they didn't care one acorn about man-made boundaries. If people wanted to avoid more violence, they'd have to reach a compromise with each community of trees and the various human-defined regions through which it stretched. Tamia's head filled with the swarm of agreements that would have to be negotiated between overlapping state, federal, tribal, and international actors.

"The trees need more time," said Dr. Nystrom. "They don't know what they're in for. We have to get ahead of the process and teach them how to negotiate first."

Dr. Block looked impatient. "What makes us so sure they'll agree to anything? Why would they?"

"None of that matters, not for this document," said Tamia. "Palmer's looking for a list of short, medium and long term objectives from *our* side—I mean the human side. He didn't say that explicitly, but I know from experience that's what he wants. And all the agencies need metrics and action verbs so they can show their bosses and constituents what they're accomplishing."

"My dear," said Nystrom paternally, "we can't just assume a new species is going to squeeze its development sequence into our requirements. That's not how ecology works." He grunted a terse laugh. "Well, that's not how it's supposed to work."

"And we all know how much Palmer cares about ecology," grumbled Dr. Block.

"Well, he's going to have to start caring," argued Nystrom. "If he wants us to clean this mess up for them, he's damn well going to have to care."

Tamia glanced at the crumpled ball of pink paper on the corner of her desk, the parking ticket she'd been too chicken to throw away. It was hard to focus on the two scientists bickering about parameters for various experiments that would need to be done. In addition to the parking ticket, she had a student loan payment coming up, not to mention car insurance. And assuming ArborTech didn't go rogue and send hired thugs to dispatch all three them, at some point she'd have to think about restarting her career.

"What?" snapped Dr. Block.

Tamia refocused on the conversation.

"I'm sorry, Barbara," said Nystrom. "My lawyer's telling me to limit contact with other involved parties, so after we finish these recommendations I'll need to take a step back."

Tamia wondered if she should be talking to an attorney herself. Not that she had enough money for one.

"Are you serious?" Block complained. "What was all that talk about training the trees to negotiate?"

"Oh, it definitely needs to be done, but I can't be the one to do it. I need to think about my family," said Nystrom firmly. "And take care of my son."

Dr. Block's expression softened. "I am very sorry about Henry."

"But, Richard," said Tamia. She instantly realized that she'd used his first name, but didn't stop to correct herself. "The trees know you. They trust you. They trust *us*."

Nystrom smiled, Tamia felt, a bit indulgently. "Well, they seem to recognize people, but we have to be careful about assigning descriptors like 'trust' to them."

"But you said we shouldn't have just anyone talking to them," said Tamia. "And we've been speaking with them longest. We can help them."

"And I want to help them," said Nystrom. "But now is not the right time."

"Now is exactly the right time," Tamia protested. "Who do you think the trees are going to be dealing with, the botanists and ecologists who want what's best for them? No, they'll be up against the Palmers and the ArborTechs. And both sides trust us."

Dr. Block chimed in. "Richard, I know you have a lot to think about. Let's just finish this document first, then you and I can talk."

"When's our next meeting?" asked Tamia.

"We've got your input," replied Dr. Block. "Richard and I can take it from here. I'll copy you on what we submit."

An uneasy feeling settled over Tamia as she signed off the conference call. What were they going to talk about without her? She'd given up her job for this, but when it came right down to it, she was still just an assistant to Dr. Block. She wasn't a scientist. She'd barely understood half of what Block and Nystrom had been talking about. And if Nystrom could just bow out like this, maybe she should start thinking about moving on with her own life as well.

Except what exactly was she qualified to do? And who would even hire her now?

Tamia closed the laptop and drummed her fingertips on the desk. She grabbed the translator she'd gotten at the governor's meeting and went outside. Good thing DeShaun was still at football practice. His college-graduate big sister, fired from her job, spending her days skulking around the forest—great role model.

She wanted to know more about the Tacoma fire. With all the talk about it, the local trees would have learned of it from humans by now. But is that the only way they would have heard? How long did it take for messages to travel between tree communities? Was it possible that all the trees planned the Tacoma fire together, or did the Tacoma trees act first and spread word to other communities later?

Her step slowed as she approached a stout maple in her parents' back yard. The neighbors had just mowed their lawn, and Tamia remembered what she'd read about that fresh-cut smell being the chemical scream of the butchered grass. Would the trees hear it and blame her?

Relax, they won't hurt you, she told herself. *At least, they haven't yet.*

Tamia put her palm against the maple's trunk, her fingers tracing up and down the furrows in its bark. She held the translator up to the tree and said hello. The new display was small and dark. That was going to be a pain in the ass to read.

"Hello, Tamia," said the maple.

Tamia gasped at the synthesized female voice coming from the machine. ArborTech must not have buried this project very deep. They couldn't have just whipped this up in a week.

"Wow, um, hello," Tamia replied. "You're speaking now."

"Yes. Translators updated."

"Hang on," said Tamia, fastening the strap around the trunk. "Look, a lot of people are freaking out about everything that's been going on. People are getting hurt, and that fire down in Tacoma did a lot of damage."

"Is not good," said the neutral voice. "But Tacoma tree community not start fire. Tacoma trees only . . . move fire so people can see. Humans need very big . . . signals for get . . . attention."

Tamia marveled at the tree's vocabulary and ability to form sentences. This was much more than an updated translator would explain. "You sound different. How did you learn to speak so well, so quickly?"

"Trees remember. Before speak, before move, trees hear. But we not . . . understand then. Now we wake. Now we speak, move, hear, remember . . . think."

Tamia felt a tingle of alarm. If they were just waking now, how much more could the trees be capable of in the future? In fact, maybe they would do more than simply react. What if they were already on the offensive?

"Do you know how the fire started?" she asked warily.

"A human was afraid."

"Of course," Tamia sighed, feeling sheepish for even thinking the trees could have ignited it. But who knows, they must have seen boy scouts do that trick with two sticks. "No one is supposed to be setting fires, but people aren't always good about following rules."

"Yes, we know. How can human community work if people do not . . . agree about rules?"

"Well, in general, people do agree. Like you, we want to live in *peace*," she said, emphasizing the last word for the tree's benefit. If trees could think now, she had to focus on all the things they had in common with humans. "We want our family and friends to be safe. Love is important to us, and *community*, which is important to you too. And everyone wants to improve their lives a little bit, you know, feel like they've accomplished something." She was babbling by now, and pretty much mangling Maslow's hierarchy of needs. It was a little odd explaining human wants and needs to a tree, after all, and the machine's toneless voice made her feel like she was debating a GPS unit.

"If you all agree, why people not share . . . resources?"

"But we do share."

"But human share is with . . . disagree," intoned the tree. "Give-take-argue . . . negotiate. Sometimes share, sometimes no share. We cannot understand human rules."

"Yeah," she admitted, "our rules are confusing, even for us." Negotiation would be a challenge. Firs and birches, for example, were used to swapping nutrients in summer and winter, simply according to which had more to spare. Neither one had to worry about the other one stockpiling or holding out for a greater price, and there was no such thing as Senator Tree withholding a packet of sugars until some other tree gave it a bagful of money. "People want to satisfy their own needs, but we also have to work together in larger communities. And sometimes individual needs conflict with group needs."

"This is problem. One person can hurt all. When trees use energy to . . . defend and repair, no more energy for . . . wood and food for people."

Tamia was heartened. At least trees still wanted to give things to humans. "I guess our weakness is that we don't notice problems until they get extreme. Like almost setting Tacoma on fire. That certainly got our attention— not that you should do that again," she hastened to add. "I'm just saying that people seem to need a crisis before they pay attention. But I think now they're listening."

"Maybe humans listen," said the tree. "But how much understand? Humans want to make rules for trees . . . where to grow, which to cut. Not always right decisions."

"But that's changing," argued Tamia. "There are more regulations and protected areas now. We're getting better."

"Better for trees or for humans? For humans, how to . . . control fire means how to protect humans, houses, cities. Before, you stop all fire, every time. Now, you burn some trees sometimes. But you choose trees for burn."

"You're talking about controlled burns, right? It's not just about us, though. We do that because it's also better for the health of the forest."

"Yes, your forest people set us on fire, clear out our dead. They say this protects us. Recycle nutrients. No more . . . overcrowding. Kill eating insects and . . . plant invaders."

"You mean harmful insects and invasive plant species?" Tamia asked. "Yes, controlled burning does all those things."

"So how trees survive . . . before humans?"

Touché. "Fires have always happened. No one's saying they haven't. But people get killed when they get out of control."

"Trees get killed too. But both . . . species survive. Better . . . conditions after fire."

She hesitated. "So, what are you saying, we should just let everything burn?"

"If need to," said the tree.

Tamia's breath caught. She'd heard about a recent study estimating that there were over *three trillion* trees on the planet. Now, North American trees were gaining speech, movement, memory, and logic. Could those abilities spread to every tree in the world? Would they eventually reach all plants as well? If so, would they need, or even tolerate, people on earth at all?

"What do you want?" she said, almost in a whisper.

"We want peace," said the tree. "No fighting. No more humans decide for trees. *Trees* decide for trees. You must organize people, follow new rules. We give you what we can . . . food and wood . . . with no harm to community. But we decide which trees. We teach you how to know which to take. For trade we want . . . care and protection."

Tamia furrowed her brow. "But I thought you didn't need us."

"Trees survive always. But humans sometimes . . . beneficial. Help fight harmful insects, disease, invasive plants. Better for trees, better for humans."

It seemed Dr. Nystrom's concern about the trees not being prepared to negotiate was unfounded. In fact, Tamia didn't see much room for humans to counteroffer. But she knew others would be more difficult to convince. People were used to managing resources, not taking orders from them.

"I don't know if everyone will see it your way," she sighed.

"Then more fighting. More trees and people hurt."

The maple was right. Considering the havoc they could wreak, they were being incredibly generous, and she had to make the most of it. Tamia crossed her arms and paced, head down in thought. "We need to come up with a non-threatening way to convince folks that they have more to gain from working with you than trying to fight you. But how?" And what made her think she would be more successful than the generations of environmentalists before her?

Tamia stopped pacing and pulled her phone out of her pocket. Her finger hovered over the speed-dial for Dr. Block.

No. No more running to Block at every juncture. She had to learn to take initiative, come up with a plan: something that would make an impression.

The phone rang in her palm, and she was surprised to see Greg's extension pop up on the screen.

"Greg?" she answered.

"Hey, Tamia. This is some crazy shit, huh?"

"Yeah." She let an awkward pause hang in the air.

"So, I know it's the weekend and all, but Jones wanted to make sure you guys are on track with those recommendations."

Her temper flared. "You know we just got the assignment yesterday."

"Hey, you know what he's like."

She remembered all too well. "So, what time does he want it?"

270

"Any time before, like, seven tomorrow morning is fine. He wants to read through it before the apple thing."

"Apple thing?"

"Yeah, he's going out to Pilalla County to talk to apple farmers about the whole tree crisis. It's our top crop, you know, so he's got to put them at ease."

Pilalla County! "Out where, exactly?" she asked innocently. She liked the idea of Palmer surrounded by an orchard of trees. The press would be there too.

"Some orchard, Happy something or other. I had no idea what a big deal the Washington Apple Commission was. I hope he's tapping them for campaign funds."

"Always thinkin', aren't you?" said Tamia. This was her chance. She would come up with a plan to show people that the trees were to be negotiated with, not messed with. And while she was out that way, who could blame her for taking a small side trip to the Palalla Nation to finally track down Charlie Meninick? "So Greg, Dr. Block lives kind of out that way." Not really, but how was he to know? "What's Palmer's schedule? I mean, in case he wants to meet with her about the recommendations?"

He hesitated.

She knew Palmer's schedule wasn't supposed to leave the office. "I just thought he'd want to have someone on call," she said, ignoring the twinge of guilt in her chest. "You know how he is about face-to-face."

"Yeah," said Greg, stretching the word out as he came around. "Good point, we should have someone ready to jump. I'll send you his schedule."

"Cool. Listen, don't mention this to anyone yet, okay? I still need to check with Block. Don't want you to promise something you can't deliver, you know?"

"Totally," he said. "Hey, uh, I'm glad you landed on your feet."

"Thanks, Greg."

"I thought you were fucking crazy at the time, but looks like you were right. And this new guy they hired in your place? Pshhh."

"Oh, now . . ." He was being so nice, she felt even sorrier about pumping him for intel.

"Seriously, man," he said. "This is your break. You're going to be Washington State Tree Czar. Or, Czarina, I guess. And then, who knows?"

"Well, I don't know about that." It was always about power with him. That's not why she was doing any of this. But then again, having a little more influence wouldn't be terrible.

Minutes after they hung up, her phone pinged again. *That was quick.* She opened up the governor's schedule and copied the orchard's address into a map. It'd take her a little over two hours to get there, so she'd have to set out early to arrive before Palmer and his people. And between now and then she had to finish hatching this idea. The plan coalescing in her mind wasn't really her style. She was used to helping big people think up their big ideas. Was she really ready to act like one of those big people herself?

She put her hand against the craggy bark of the maple and asked, "You know any apple trees in Pilalla County?"

CHAPTER 41

CHARLIE TURNED HIS mug between his palms as he waited for Liz. He looked out the window at the dimly lit park across the street. Dad's Diner wasn't exactly a hotbed of excitement, but there weren't a lot of options within walking distance, and asking to borrow the car that evening would have generated too many winks and nudges from Eddie. A waitress floated by with a fresh pot of coffee, but Charlie put a hand over his cup.

He checked his watch. He'd gotten there early. He hadn't been able to sit and wait in his new apartment any longer. The place was clean, but small, and the odds and ends his landlord had left him were cheap and scratched. The threadbare couch, the wobbly table, and sad little twin bed hardly felt like progress. He and Jenna hadn't been high-rollers, but she could always find the good deals. She would have found this place depressing, not that *that* was supposed to matter anymore. More to the point, it wouldn't impress Liz at all. But then, he was getting ahead of himself.

"Hey, Charlie." He looked up as she waved from the doorway.

"Hey." He was careful not to smile too eagerly as she approached his table. He rose into an awkward crouch as she sat down, unsure of dating etiquette here, and with her. "Welcome to the fast lane," he quipped.

She smiled and sat down, looking at the menu for a moment before tossing it back onto the table. "I'll just get a coffee. Mom's been stuffing me with frybread ever since I got home."

Charlie flagged the waitress and placed the order.

"So," asked Liz, "have you heard the news about the Nystrom family?"

"No."

"Ricky's dad was injured in the fire. He's in the hospital, pretty badly burned. He inhaled a lot of smoke, too, but he's alive."

"Oh my god. He's gonna be okay, though, isn't he?" He couldn't even imagine the alternative. Ricky was too young to face something like that.

"We all hope so," said Liz, nodding thanks as the waitress arrived with her coffee. "As far as I know, he's still in intensive care, but he's stable."

Charlie shook his head. What happened to the benevolent trees that had saved him when he crashed his truck; the ones that kept Ricky safe when he climbed, and bowed down to Minnie Littledeer? How had everything gotten so messed up?

"We're all still in shock," Liz said, staring into the steaming mug in front of her. "I'm sure poor Ricky's a mess. He hasn't been back to school yet. I hope they're getting him some counseling."

"Jeez," said Charlie. "I'm sorry." They were both silent.

Movement outside caught Charlie's attention. He looked over just in time to see Louis Greyfox passing by the window with two other boys, shoulders hunched against the cold. One of them stuck a cigarette in his lips and pulled out a lighter. They all stopped in the light of the window while the kid cupped his hand around the flame.

Charlie could see in the reflection that Liz was watching the boys as well. The smoker puffed on his cigarette as a girl walked by. Charlie heard a muffled comment through the glass followed by a hyena-like laugh. While the two other boys turned to watch the girl, Louis stopped and leaned toward the window. He squinted his eyes and looked right at Charlie. To his surprise, the kid seemed to recognize Liz as well. Charlie glanced over and saw her looking back at Louis with an expression of concern.

"You know him?" he asked.

"Yes," she said, her eyes troubled.

"How?" He looked back out the window and the boy's face creased into contempt. Louis led the pack of boys away from the diner window.

"I knew his family," said Liz.

They watched the boys cross the street and settle under the light of a streetlamp on the opposite side. Two of the boys leaned against a wall. Louis pulled out a cigarette and glanced over again before turning his back.

"Excuse me," said Liz, her eyes still on the boys. "I'll be right back."

Charlie grabbed her hand as she stood up.

"I'll be fine," she said, gently pulling away.

Charlie watched her cross the street. The young men shifted as she approached, easing their backs up off the wall to stand straight. Louis glared at Liz, while the other two shoved their hands in their pockets and looked down. Charlie tried to put his mind at ease, reminding himself they were basically harmless. One of them would be talking about how far some girl let him go last night. All of them would be complaining about how lame Nakalish was, how everything was better in Seattle—the nightlife, the women—and fantasizing about what they'd do once they got there. All nothing but talk. But still, Charlie stayed alert, ready to spring if necessary.

Liz kept talking, but Louis was still as stone, arms crossed over his chest. She finally came back in to the diner, looking defeated.

"What's goin' on?" he asked as she sat back down. "How do you know him?"

She sighed and folded her hands around her mug. "There's nothing I can do. He's too determined to hate." She took a sip of coffee and spoke in a low voice. "I used to date his older brother, Ray."

They exchanged a glance. Charlie knew the name from the reports that came out after the accident. As cruel as it seemed, he hadn't devoted much time to mourning the poachers. But there's no way he would ever forget Ray Greyfox's boot under the fallen red cedar.

"We dated a long time ago," Liz said. "But then I went away for school and started teaching, and I never came back. Ray wanted to move to Tacoma, but I . . . I didn't see a future with us, you know? I wouldn't have felt right having him come out to be with me when I didn't feel that way." She sighed and stared into her cup. "Then his family started talking about how I did him wrong, how I was ashamed of where I came from, and looked down on my people."

"That's a load of crap. You're here all the time."

"Now, yes. But not back then."

They both glanced over at the boys across the street. Louis had his back to them again. One of the others put a flask to his mouth and tipped his head back.

"There was probably a little truth to it then," she said. "I did want to get out and have a better life. And I was young. I guess I kind of felt like Ray would hold me back. He wasn't ambitious enough. He didn't seem to know what he wanted out of life."

Charlie grunted. "I can relate."

"That was just me being young and proud," she admitted. "Then life went on, I became a teacher, and shoot, those kids really give you a reality check." She flashed a crooked grin at Charlie. "I started coming back to Nakalish, and Ray thought that maybe we could try again. But I just didn't feel that way about him anymore. I'd moved on, but I guess he hadn't. So in his family's eyes I hurt him all over again."

"Yeah, but you couldn't just—I mean, you know what he was in to, right?" Charlie felt like an asshole as soon as he asked the question, like he was kicking the dead man's body.

"Yeah," she said. "I do now. It was just rumor for a long time, but when they found him—when *you* found him—everything came out in the open." She cocked her head. "I guess that's why his brother's mad at you too."

"Seems to be," said Charlie. He wanted to ask her more questions. There were more ways his family was involved with the Greyfoxes, but he wasn't getting any info out of Eddie. She probably knew something, but he wasn't sure he could stand to hear any of his family's secrets coming from her lips.

"So," he asked, shifting in his chair, "is your whole family still in Nakalish?"

Her expression brightened with the change of subject. "My parents are here, but I have a brother in Seattle, an electrician, and a sister in Olympia. She works for the State. And then there's me in Tacoma. So all of us kids left."

"Yeah, well, it's kinda hard to stay."

"Hard to stay away, too," she added. "How about your family?"

"Well, my folks split up and my dad went to Seattle. I went up there to live with him when I was about fourteen." He took a sip while he considered how much to tell. But then, she'd probably already heard everything through the grapevine anyway. "I had a younger sister, but she died when I was six. She was five. Car accident."

"I'm sorry," she said.

"Thanks." He never knew what else to say when he told people about his sister, which was why he never did. He looked at Liz. He wasn't sure why he felt compelled to go on. Maybe because she'd already shared so much from her past.

"My mom took it really hard," he said, looking down into his cup, as if it would tell him what words to use. "Things got pretty rough between her and Dad. She started drinking, I mean, they always did a little, but she got serious about it after Lilly died. After a while, they split up. And then once I left, she just kinda gave up. No more kids to take care of, you know, and she didn't feel like takin' care of herself at all. She was in really rough shape."

"I'm sorry," said Liz. She sounded so sincere. Charlie doubted she could fake that level of concern if she'd already heard the story. He kept going.

"Dad tried to come down and help a couple of times. He didn't really talk about it that much, though. Nothing seemed to help."

"Did you visit her?"

"Nope. Dad didn't want me seein' her like that. And, at that age, I thought everything was better in Seattle anyway. By the time I grew up and got my head out of— on straight, she was gone."

Liz put a hand to her mouth. "I'm sorry, Charlie."

"No, not 'dead' gone, just not here. She kinda comes and goes without tellin' anyone where she's heading. She'll call from time to time, say she's getting better, say she's comin' back. But it's been a while. I'm not sure where she is now."

He narrowed his eyes. "Come on, you didn't know about any of this already? Your mom or Auntie didn't say anything?"

She shrugged her shoulders. "I try not to listen to too much gossip. There's a difference between staying connected and getting into the mud. But Charlie," she said, putting her hand on his, "I really appreciate your sharing that with me. I can only imagine how hard—"

A loud bang at the window made them both jump. Louis Greyfox's angry face was just outside, sneering in at them. He beat on the window with both fists again before his friends pulled him back.

Liz gasped, her hands fluttering to her chest.

"He's drunk," growled Charlie.

Louis shouted something from the sidewalk, looking right at Charlie through the window. All they could hear through the glass was, "Your mother . . ."

Charlie's blood boiled. *Fuckin' punk.* Fists on the table, he rose from his seat.

Liz pulled thin sheets out of a clanking napkin holder to mop up her spilled coffee. "Charlie, please."

"I'll be right back." He stepped away from the table, seething. *Poacher's kid has the nerve—*

"Let it go."

The Greyfox kid was yelling even louder now. As soon as Charlie opened the door, he heard the whole thing. "Charlie Meninick, your mother's a dirty, fuckin' whore!"

Charlie bolted out of the coffee shop, breathing hard. In a second he was out on the street, steaming up to the kid, right fist cocked and ready. Louis' friends stepped back, but the boy kept on yelling.

"She's a two-bit hooker down south! Charlie Meninick, your mother's a dirty—"

Charlie's fist landed on Louis' cheek and sent him flying out onto the street. The impact jolted Charlie out of his rage. He stood over Louis and uncurled his hands. Liz called out, running toward them.

Louis moaned and rolled up to a sitting position, a hand on his cheek. Liz knelt down beside him. A wave of shame rose up inside Charlie. Louis was just a kid saying stupid shit. He massaged his hand and stuck it out toward the boy. "Dammit. You okay?"

Louis' gaze settled on Charlie's hand, then traveled up to his eyes. "I ain't hurt," he snarled. "And your mother's still a whore."

"Stop it!" yelled Liz.

"Just ask Eddie," spat Louis. "He knows."

"That's enough!" Liz grabbed Louis' arm and pulled him to his feet. "Go on, get home." She shoved him away from them. "Go on now."

Charlie watched Louis stumble off down the street. Just one punch and the skinny little kid could barely walk right. The tight, hot anger in his chest loosened and regret burned down through his stomach like molten lead.

The boy turned back around with a sneer. "Ask Eddie!" he shouted. "He'll have to tell you everything now!" He turned away again, and his friends slunk back to his side.

"Come on," said Liz, putting a hand on Charlie's arm. "Let's go back inside." He stared at the boy's back and tried to calm his breathing. Liz tugged gently on his arm until he let her guide him back into the café. But the rest of their date was an awkward, stilted wreck.

Charlie realized on the walk home that his shame wasn't really about hitting Louis. No, he'd punch the little bastard again if he had to. Shame was burning him up because, for a moment, he had let himself wonder if the kid was right.

CHAPTER 42

"GRAMPA?"

Ricky sidled into the kitchen clutching the translator behind his back, half hoping his grandfather wouldn't be there. He knew he should tell Grampa Nystrom what the trees had said just now, but he also knew he'd be in trouble for using the translator without permission.

Grampa sat at the kitchen table with a sandwich and a glass of water. He broke into a smile as soon as he looked up at Ricky. "I've got some good news." Grampa turned his chair to face him. "I just got back from visiting your father, and they say they're going to move him out of intensive care tomorrow. That means he's getting better."

Ricky's heart leapt at the news, but the edge of the translator dug into his back. He had to tell Grampa.

Grampa Nystrom's smile dimmed. The older man looked closely at him. "I know this has been hard on you, not being able to see your dad. But when they move him, you'll be able to visit. We'll go tomorrow afternoon, how about that?"

Ricky nodded. He was excited to see his dad, even though he was a little nervous to see how badly he was hurt. And his arms, twisted awkwardly behind him, felt tight.

Grampa Nystrom reached out to him. "What's the matter? Come here."

Ricky looked down and slowly produced the translator from behind his back. He peeked up at his grandfather, and his stomach tied itself into a knot at the stern expression on the older man's face.

"What are you doing with that?" he demanded. "What did I tell you about taking other people's things?"

"I . . ."

Even louder: "Did I give you permission to use that?"

Ricky shook his head.

"No," barked Grampa. "So then, why did you?"

Ricky buried his chin in his chest.

His grandfather sighed. "I'm sorry, I didn't mean to yell. But this is valuable equipment. You should know better." He held out his hand for the translator, and Ricky shuffled over to give it to him.

"I'm sorry, Grampa," mumbled Ricky. "I was wrong."

Grampa set the translator on the kitchen table and patted Ricky's shoulder.

"But Grampa, I think the trees are in trouble. I think you should hear."

The older man frowned. "So you still want to help the trees? Despite what happened to—despite everything?"

Ricky nodded. He wouldn't forget sitting up in the treetop on the edge of town, watching waves of branches pass the fire along from tree to tree. But those were just some bad trees, he'd decided, just like there were bad people. Not all of them were like that. He hoped.

"Come on, then, let's go," said Grampa Nystrom.

Ricky ran out of the kitchen to the back room, throwing the sliding door open and bolting into the back yard.

"Hold on, Ricky, slow down," said Grampa Nystrom, following with the translator. "They're not going anywhere. At least, not yet."

Ricky picked out a knotted old oak, one of his favorites to climb because of its broad, sloping trunk and low branches. "Hey, Gina!" he said, patting the scaly bark at its base.

"Its name is Gina?" asked the old man.

"Well, that's the name I gave her. If they can talk, it seems like they should have names." He was too embarrassed to tell his other reason—that maybe if you named them and were nice to them, they wouldn't go bad.

The old man nodded thoughtfully as he looped the translator around the trunk. Ricky pressed a couple of buttons and brought the translator to life.

"Richard Nystrom, you must talk to human leaders," said the tree. "Now."

"What is it?" asked Grampa Nystrom with alarm. "What's going on now?"

"Humans will do much harm. We hear them say much . . . mo-di-fied fire retardant to hurt trees. Now bring modified fire retardant more and more from other places. We also feel ground move, many big cars. They say tanks."

"Well," said Grampa Nystrom, "you can't really blame them—us—for being worried. The last fire still isn't completely out."

"Is something bad going to happen?" whispered Ricky, looking from the tree to his grandfather and back.

"We want Ricky Nystrom safe," said the oak. "Ricky Nystrom will help us. But now he must go be safe."

Ricky's heart beat faster. "Why?"

"Your leaders plan dangerous thing," said the tree.

"They're just fighting the fires," said Ricky.

"They fighting us."

"They wouldn't have to fight you," interjected Grampa Nystrom, "if you would let the fire go out."

"Fire defend us," replied the oak.

Ricky's heart sank. Was Gina turning bad too? "But you're hurting people," he said. "You hurt my dad. You have to stop!"

"No other way, Ricky," said the toneless female voice.

"The boy's right," Nystrom argued. "If you let the fire go out, they'll stop coming after you."

"Too far now, Richard Nystrom."

"Too far?"

"Your leaders fight too far. Ricky Nystrom must be safe. Away from here."

"What? No!" shouted Ricky. "I have to stay and see Dad!"

The tree remained silent.

"Why do I have to go?" demanded Ricky. "You're going to start another fire, aren't you?"

"You must talk to your leaders."

"You're just like the rest of them!" yelled Ricky. "Just like the ones who hurt my dad. You're all bad!" He picked up a rock and threw it at the tree. He picked up an even bigger rock. "I'm not going anywhere, stupid tree! I'm staying here. I'm going to see my dad!" He threw the second rock, feeling satisfied at the *thunk* it made against the old oak's trunk.

"Ricky!" yelled his grandfather.

A cacophony of pops and cracks drowned Grampa Nystrom out. The old oak lowered its branches and wrapped them around Ricky. He struggled against the grasping tree limbs, scraping his hands as he tried to pry himself loose. He gasped, his feet now pedaling air.

As he soared upward in the branches' grasp, he looked down and saw his grandfather reaching up to him. Writhing twigs descended from the top of the tree, wrapped themselves around his waist, and took him even higher.

"Let me go!"

Wood popped and branches clicked against one another as they carried him higher. He felt woozy, like everything was leaning to one side. He put his hands over his eyes as he tipped farther and farther over. Suddenly he smelled pine, like his face was being pushed into an air freshener. He peeked through his fingers. As the oak let him go, the pine lifted him straight up in the air before arcing over to tip him into a waiting maple.

"Grampa!" he yelled. He heard his grandfather's cries, far away through the groaning trees. The branches supported him, scooping him out of one tree and handing him off to the next, knitting themselves into each other and pulling themselves out again. Ricky jostled from oak to fir to maple and beyond, covering his head as needles and pinecones scraped by. It was like a rollercoaster, going up and down and forward and backward. He held his breath and tried to roll himself into a ball as the branches slid around his body, weaving in and out underneath him, rocking him from tree to tree on an undulating carpet of wood.

The stiller he stayed, the smoother the ride got. As the rocking calmed, he cracked his eyes open and braved a look down. Patches of ground flew by through layers of bare branches. Ricky had no idea where he was, but he was up high—too high to do anything but hold still and see where the trees would take him.

CHAPTER 43

CHARLIE TURNED OVER in bed, struggling against the first strains of Sunday morning light. He hadn't slept much, and not because he'd stayed out late.

The evening with Liz was pretty much over as soon as he'd punched the Greyfox kid. Eddie hadn't answered the phone and it had been too late to bother his family by going over in person. After walking the streets for hours, he'd tossed and turned and watched the clock until dawn. The only thing on his mind all night had been getting the truth from Eddie.

Why was he letting that goddamn Greyfox kid get to him? It was just a stupid school ground taunt meant to get a rise out of him. But then . . .

He'll have to tell you everything now, the kid had said. What was there to ask Eddie about? Could he really be running some game with the Greyfoxes, cheating the Nation with that band of poachers? And if so, what the hell could his mother have to do with it?

He opened a gummy eye and looked at the clock. It was still hours until Eddie would be over to pick him up for their Eco-Wood experiment. No use pretending to sleep, though. Charlie got out of bed and pulled on some clothes. His apartment felt too small again.

A couple of early birds were heading to church as Charlie stepped outside. The fresh air and clear light were bracing. Not a trace of fire over their way. He should probably just concentrate on that, focus on keeping the peace with the trees. Why should he be so quick to believe what some punk kid said? The Greyfoxes clearly had a grudge against his family, and Liz's too. He'd been a fool to let it escalate. He'd talk to Eddie, and Eddie would just *haw, haw, haw* in his face and tell him he'd fallen for a crock of shit.

Charlie's mind churned while his feet took him on autopilot to Eddie's. He stared at the door, wondering if he should knock. He scanned the porch. Sunday paper was already taken in. Or someone had stolen it. He rapped quietly at the door.

The door opened, and to Charlie's relief it was Eddie standing in the doorway in his robe and slippers. "Hey, I thought I was pickin' you up at ten."

"Yeah, but I got something I want to talk to you about."

Eddie sized him up. "Step inside while I get some clothes on."

It was cold, but Charlie shook his head. He didn't want to face a lot of inquisitive eyes at this time of morning.

Eddie furrowed his brow. "Okay, Cuz. Hang on." He closed the door but was quick to return, dressed and carrying a thermos of coffee and a couple of doughnuts in a paper bag. "Breakfast of champions," he quipped. Charlie felt a little low for making him miss breakfast with his family.

"May's well get on the road," said Eddie, heading toward his truck. "It's not far."

"I guess," said Charlie. He didn't feel up to "conjuring" lumber today, but he'd already dragged his cousin out of the house.

They climbed into the truck and Eddie handed him the doughnuts. "Don't eat 'em all."

They backed out of the driveway as the cheerful patter of an early morning radio host filled the cab. Eddie didn't push. Once they were on the highway out of town, Charlie turned down the volume.

"Eddie, I have to ask you something, and tell me the truth. Last night, I heard something." He took a deep breath. Once he started this, there was no going back. "About my mother."

Eddie's face folded into a frown. "What about her?"

"You tell me," said Charlie. "I was told you would know."

"What're you talkin' about?"

"You know anything about my mother bein' somewhere down south? About her bein' a . . ." Charlie turned the radio off completely. "You know what they're sayin' about my mom?"

"What who's sayin'?" snapped Eddie, his eyes darting between the road and Charlie's face.

"Well, Louis Greyfox for one."

Eddie scoffed. "That kid? Come on, Charlie," he said, gripping the wheel.

Charlie studied his cousin's profile. "He said you'd know something, about it. About her."

"Why do you care what some snot-nosed punk's sayin' about your mother?"

"Because it seems like there's something to know about her. And the Greyfoxes. And you."

Eddie shook his head in disbelief.

"Come on, Eddie. I feel like you been keepin' secrets, sayin' mind my own business about this and that. And I have been, but now *this* is my business. Whatever dealings you may have with the Greyfoxes—"

"Me and the Greyfoxes? Where'd you get that?"

"Is it true?"

Eddie stared straight ahead as the truck rolled down the road, tires humming on asphalt.

"Eddie. Come on." Charlie gritted his teeth and looked out the window. "Shit, I don't even know if I can trust you anymore."

Eddie kneaded the wheel in his hands. "Okay, Charlie." He pulled over and cut off the engine, then twisted in his seat to face him. "So, you know your mom used to live in Tucson, way back."

"Yeah." Charlie swallowed, hard. Until that moment, there had still been a chance that there was really no secret to tell.

"Well, a little while before the last time she left, a guy name of George Greyfox came to town. He's Louis Greyfox's uncle, and he came up here from Tucson, too.

Pretty soon people thought maybe something was goin' on between him and your mom, the way they looked at each other, but no one knew what."

Charlie clenched his fists in his lap, waiting.

"Well, turns out they knew each other from past days. He used to be her—" Eddie looked down.

"Spit it out," Charlie snapped.

"He used to be her pimp. She used to be a prostitute, Charlie."

Charlie couldn't breathe. He didn't think Eddie would lie to him, not about family.

"It was a long time ago," said Eddie. "She got out of all that, though. Married your dad, had you kids, put that life behind her—at least, until George Greyfox came to town. That fucker'd played his shit out down south and crawled up here. Minute he saw her, he must've started calculating to see what he could get out of her."

"And she told you this?"

"No, he did," said Eddie. "Soon as he figured out who her people were, he came and threw it in our face. His people had been fined for poachin' timber before, and now he thought he had something on us. Between me at Land Enterprise and our uncle on the Council, he thought we'd be able to overlook a few things to keep your mom's past a secret."

"Well, you guys got duped," said Charlie, nostrils flaring. "He cheated you over nothing."

Eddie looked at Charlie solemnly.

"He's lying!" Charlie yelled.

Eddie shook his head. "He's got proof."

Charlie searched his cousin's eyes for a scrap of doubt, but what he found was certainty. And pity. He threw open the door and jumped out of the truck. He felt sick. He didn't want to think about what kind of proof that bastard was holding on to—and how many people had seen it. He leaned over, hands on his knees.

Eddie's door creaked open and slammed shut. The engine ticked in the crisp autumn air. Charlie stared into the brown grass lining the highway. Eddie's boots clomped on pavement, then crunched in the broken asphalt on the side of the road.

"I'm sorry you have to hear about all this, Charlie." Eddie leaned against the side of the truck. "If only he'd of kept it small. But he got greedy, got more people involved, started taking more trees. I thought havin' you out there would send him a message. Never thought he'd actually send poachers your way."

"When did all this happen? How long has that Greyfox bastard been here?"

"Two, three years. She left town again a few months after he got here. Guess she could only take it for so long."

"Why didn't you tell me?" asked Charlie, simmering.

"Jesus, Charlie, the whole point was keepin' it secret."

"But I could've looked for her, helped her."

"What was stopping you before?"

Charlie's eyes bored into the dried grass, hot enough to start a blaze.

"Dammit," cursed Eddie. "You weren't much good at finding your way out of a bottle, much less helpin' us find your mother. Till recently you weren't much use to anybody. But this was about family, so we kept it quiet for as long as we could."

Charlie stood up to face Eddie, and his head whirled with the sudden motion. "And you think that was your decision to make, huh? You didn't think I would've—that's my mom, Eddie."

"Sit down, Cuz. Come on." Eddie stood by the passenger door and held an arm out to him. Another truck clattered down the road past them. Charlie didn't move. Eddie left the door open and leaned against the side of his truck.

"Look," Eddie said after a while, "it wasn't my decision to make. I was just caught in the middle. But I agree with what they decided—including not telling you."

"It wasn't right, Eddie," fumed Charlie, stepping closer to his cousin.

Eddie's eyes flashed with anger. "Oh yeah? You think so? You're mad at everybody, huh? Mad at her for leaving, mad at us for not getting her back or tellin' you anything. Well lemme ask you this, you ever stop and think maybe she kept runnin' for your sake? If you was her, would you want your son to know?"

"Yeah, well how's runnin' away supposed to help?" he yelled. It took a minute, looking at Eddie's incredulous expression, to realize his own hypocrisy. After a lifetime of running, who was he to accuse her of anything?

Eddie collected himself and continued calmly. "Charlie, I been thinkin' about this for years. I don't think you realize how much your mother loved you. You're all she talked about. Only reason she ever would have left was to try to protect you."

"But . . ." Charlie's voice faltered. If that was true, if there was any chance he was the reason she stayed away . . . "Where is she now?"

Eddie shook his head. "No sign of her since. She's a smart woman. She knew someone would try to bring her home. Guess that wasn't in her plans."

Charlie's gaze slid away from Eddie's face to another car traveling the highway. For the first time, he noticed the chill wind stinging his ears and nose.

"Cuz," said Eddie. "We did what we thought was best for you, your mom, and the whole family. And I think, in her mind, that's what she did too when she ran off again. Whatever she did was for family—for you."

Charlie stared down the highway at nothing. His limbs felt heavy, his feet glued to the ground.

"Hey, look at me," said Eddie firmly. He waited until Charlie looked him full in the face. "This isn't just about you, you know. There's other people at stake too."

He was right. Land Enterprise and Council covering for poachers was no small thing. While he was fucking around up in Seattle, his cousin and uncle had risked their careers to keep this secret for the whole family.

"I know," he murmured. He pulled himself together and headed for the open passenger door.

Eddie nodded. He walked around the back of the truck toward the driver's side, digging his keys out of his pocket. Both men climbed in and shut their doors.

Eddie turned in his seat to face Charlie. "Hey, like I said, I'm sorry you had to hear this. But I have to admit, I'm glad we don't have any more secrets between us. And if I'm selfish for a minute, I'm also glad to be out from under the Greyfoxes' thumb."

"But are you really out from under it?" asked Charlie.

"Well, poachin' won't work anymore, will it? Not now that the trees can fight back."

"So you think it's over?" asked Charlie. "I mean, won't they try to find something else to get out of you?"

"Oh, I suppose they could," mused Eddie. "But sounds like their boy is out there throwin' away all their bargaining chips." Eddie started the engine and pulled back onto the road.

Charlie watched the yellow and white lines slide past the truck as Eddie picked up speed. "But, Eddie," he asked, "what if they tell everyone what you did, how you covered up for 'em?"

"Don't know. Guess we'll have to figure that one out." He smiled ruefully. "Anyhow, I'll be in a better bargaining position if you can sweet talk those trees for me."

Charlie shook his head. "You always got a plan, don't you, Cuz? I'll do my best."

"Look," said Eddie, turning serious again. "Whatever happens, it's probably gonna get rough. There's gonna be a lot of shit talk about our people—not from everyone, but enough—and folks makin' stuff up on the side. But don't you ever forget, your mom always loved you, no matter what. I was here the whole time and I saw it." Eddie cleared his throat and kept his eyes on the road. "She always loved you, and wherever she is, she still does. And I do too. We're family, and that's what matters. That's the only thing that matters."

CHAPTER 44

TAMIA GRITTED HER teeth and pulled into the gravel parking area of the Happy Acres Apple Farm. That stupid accident in the pass had snarled up traffic, adding almost an hour to her trip from Seattle. She wheeled abruptly up to a line of cypress trees, parking her Toyota at the edge of the lot.

Tamia stepped out of the car and was instantly dazzled by sunlight. A cool, sweet-smelling breeze ruffled her hair as she looped her purse over her head and across her chest. She'd been so focused on traffic, she'd barely noticed the change from gloomy, cloudy Seattle to the sunny plains east of the Cascades. But there was no time for reveling in sunshine. She had less than half an hour before the governor was supposed to arrive. If she could get the apple trees to agree with her plan, they might be able to show the governor and everyone how much easier it would be to negotiate with trees than fight them.

She spotted signs for U-Pick and hurried toward them, annoyed to see a couple with two small children ahead of her. Tamia scanned the signs and fished out the right amount of cash, grumbling inwardly at the family for not just getting their apples at the store like normal people.

As soon as the parents and children toddled off with their baskets, Tamia stepped up to the window and thrust her money toward the middle-aged woman behind the counter. "One, please."

The woman pushed up her glasses and smiled warmly. "Mornin'. All by yourself today? It's a beautiful day, whyn't you bring your friends?"

"They didn't feel like it. One, please." Tamia reminded herself not to look too impatient, since that seemed to make people move even slower.

"I understand," said the woman, calmly taking the cash from Tamia. "Folks are a little skittish about trees nowadays. We haven't had a bit of trouble with ours, though." She stood a little taller. "I believe that's why they picked Happy Acres for the governor's visit. No one said as much, but I like to think so."

Tamia raised her eyebrows. "No one here's had any tree problems?"

The woman discreetly splayed the bills out in her palm to count them, then tucked them into the pocket of her Happy Acres apron. "No, not that I've heard of. But then, we all hand-pick out in these parts. Machines are efficient and all, but they're always going to be rougher on a tree than a person. I kinda feel like if we're gentle with 'em, we can still get along with 'em, even if they have—changed."

Tamia hadn't thought of that possibility. What if these trees hadn't been affected yet? What if they couldn't move or talk or understand what she was saying? So much for her grand plan. "So, *are* they changed?" she asked. "Have the owners gotten them tested?"

"Well, speaking as one of the owners," said the woman, "no. We don't need to know, really. Just keep doin' right by 'em, and they'll do right by us, is our philosophy." She handed Tamia a basket and a map. "I tell people if you're gentle with the trees, you'll be fine. But here," she said, giving Tamia a whistle on a lanyard. "We got these special in case anyone has any concerns. Just give it a blow if you run into any problems—not that we expect you to," she said with a smile. "Red Delicious are at their peak now, you might want to start with them."

"Thanks," said Tamia, hoping her blush wasn't too apparent. She'd pegged the owner as a rank and file employee, and had come across as a paranoid city-dweller who needed a panic whistle. Great. She gave the woman a quick smile and headed out to the fields. After briefly consulting her map, she shoved the whistle into her bag and made her way toward the furthest grove from the counter.

Tamia strode quickly down the wide, rutted trails between plots. A fragrant gust of wind tossed the leaves, and the sun coaxed its rays into her, starting to undo the knots of anxiety in her chest. She didn't have much time to establish contact and get the trees to buy into her plan, but maybe she should follow the lead of the unhurried woman at the counter. If the trees picked up on her anxiety, they might be on guard.

She worked her way to the far side of the orchard, amazed at the contrast between sagebrush and scrub growing alongside all these lush, green crops and orchards. And so sunny! It was beautiful, the perfect place to turn this conflict around—as long as she could get the trees to cooperate.

Tamia consulted her map again. This was the last plot. Red Delicious. She turned around to make sure she had some privacy, then threaded her way several rows into the field and took her translator out of her bag. These trees were tiny compared to the ones she'd been dealing with, and she had to cinch the belt in quite a bit for the machine to stay on the trunk.

"Hello?" she said quietly, making sure the volume was down.

"Mornin'."

Tamia cocked her head. She was used to the trees greeting her by name. "Do you know who I am?"

"No. You from these parts?"

Her mouth hung open for a second. "Have you heard of Tamia Bennett? Or Barbara Block, or Richard Nystrom?"

"Block maybe. But politics not for us."

Tamia pursed her lips. "Well, there's a lot going on right now, so you might want to start paying attention."

"Everything fine here."

"Maybe it has been, but things are changing. Haven't you heard about all the fighting? The fires?"

"Nothing change here. Farmers do right us, we do right them."

Tamia shook her head. These trees sounded just like the woman who had raised them. Tamia thought back to the arguments the forest trees had made. "But don't you want to be in charge of your own existence? As it is now, someone else decides where you'll grow, how many of you there will be, and how big you'll get. Then your fruit is taken away and you have no idea what happens to it. You never feel like you're being taken advantage of here?"

"Give and take. Farmers care, protect us. Good for us."

Tamia racked her brain. "But don't you want to decide what's best for your community?"

"This way best for community."

This wasn't at all what she had expected. These apple trees had no appetite for unrest. "You may feel this way," she said, "but you have to know other trees feel differently. Do you really think you'll be able to stay out of the conflict?"

"Community . . . content. No conflict here. Why change?"

"Maybe the choice won't be yours to make," said Tamia. "At some point the orchard ends. What are you going to do when trouble crosses your borders?"

"Safe here. Not want . . . get involved."

"But—"

"Stop talk. You want apples, pick. But go to other trees. Bad talk make for bitter apples."

"I'm sorry," said Tamia.

The tree didn't respond.

"I'll leave you in peace," said Tamia, unlatching the machine.

She walked out of the orchard feeling disappointed, and petty in her disappointment. She should be happy to see a sign of hope, an example of coexistence between man and tree. Instead, she was angry at the orchard for being so insular, condemning them for turning their backs on the rest of their kind—not that they had backs to turn. She had to stop thinking about them like people.

For them, this wasn't betrayal. It was survival. It was the natural way of things, give and take. These apple trees weren't the ones who had disturbed the natural balance by trying to take too much.

By the time Tamia got back to the parking area, it had filled in with cars and trucks. Apple farmers from around the county were stepping out of their vehicles and heading up a grassy slope at the end of the lot. Reporters followed them, chatting them up and scribbling down notes as they climbed toward the tent set up for the press conference.

Tamia ducked her head and walked away from the commotion toward her car by the cypresses. She should have prepared an excuse in case Palmer saw her. The last thing she needed was for him to think she was tailing him instead of working on his recommendations—which is exactly what she was doing.

Dread yanked at her gut as she approached her car. So many vehicles had pulled into the lot while she'd been talking to the apple trees, there was barely enough room to open her door, much less wiggle her car out. Tamia looked dumbly at the tiny space. Another car door closed nearby, and she heard a voice say, "This way, Governor."

Shit!

Tamia ducked down, crouch-walking across the gravel to the small gap between the front of her car and the row of cypresses. Footsteps crunched away from where she was hiding, and a few minutes later she heard a polite round of applause. By the time she heard opening remarks drift out of distant speakers, her legs had started to cramp up. She stood and peeked over her car. The parking lot was clear. After another round of applause, snippets of Palmer's speech floated across the lot. She couldn't hear every word, but she caught enough to recognize the typical phrases of concern and pledges to perform. At any rate, she was safe while he was on stage.

She sat down on the hood of her car and stared at the row of cypresses flanking the lot. Nothing to do now but sit and watch them wave in the breeze while she waited for the lot to clear.

What the—?

One of the cypresses stuck out a limb, beckoning to her like something out of Looney Tunes. She slid off the hood of her car and burrowed through dense, bushy fronds to attach the translator to the trunk.

"Hello, Tamia Bennett," said the cypress.

"You know who I am?" she asked.

"Yes, most trees know."

"The apple trees didn't."

"Apple trees . . . pretend much not know," replied the cypress. "Want no . . . conflict."

Tamia frowned. "I always thought you agreed on everything."

"Most things. But human-make, human-care trees . . ." The cypress paused to sound out the next word: "do-mes-tica-ted trees have different ideas about community."

"So you agree with the forest trees?" she asked. "You would help them?"

"Trees help trees," said the cypress.

"I wish the apple trees felt that way. I wanted them to help me make a point to the governor—to everyone really. I thought they could provide a reminder of how much we need trees, and how we really need to work together with them."

"What you ask?"

Tamia scoffed. "I didn't even get that far. They basically told me I was in the tree equivalent of Switzerland and said I could take a hike with my plans."

"What you want ask?"

"Well, at some point this morning, Palmer's going to go out and tour around the grounds, look at the picking operation and the cranes and so on. Then he'll pick an apple himself—photo op—and that's when I'd have all the apple trees raise their branches out of reach, not allow any picking."

"No more apple pick?" asked the tree.

302

"Not forever, just until people saw what it would be like if they didn't try to make peace with the trees. Then, once that started to sink in, I would have the trees bend down and offer their fruit to everyone."

"Tamia Bennett is now tree master?"

"No!" Tamia protested. "I'm not trying to be anyone's master. I just want to help you negotiate. But it would only work if people saw that you recognized me."

"We . . . recognize you, Tamia Bennet," said the cypress. "You are important for us. Trusted one."

A pleasant warmth spread through her chest. "You trust me?"

"Yes. We read your . . . signals."

"My signals? You mean my volatiles?"

"Yes . . . vo-la-tiles. Every tree, human has chemicals. Yours say you are friend. Ally."

Her heart swelled. "So, how can I help?"

"Speak for us," answered the tree. "But not only you. Stronger with more. You work with other trusted one, Charlie Meninick."

Tamia's eyes brightened. "I've been looking for him! Where is he now?"

Applause erupted from the tented area in the distance, signaling the end of Governor Palmer's remarks. Tamia listened closely to determine what was going on next. Sounded like Q & A.

"Palalla Cultural Center," said the cypress. "Find him. Whole forest stronger than one tree."

A buzz of voices rose from across the lot. Tamia looked up to see a trickle of people from the presentation hustling toward the parking area. *Why is it ending so soon?* She squinted at the growing crowd—was that Governor Palmer at the head? With a start, she dove back into the tangle of cypress branches. Panic made her fingers clumsy, and it took forever to unlatch the translator and slip it into her purse. She barely had enough time to crack open her door and squeeze into her car before the crowd hit the parking lot.

She faced straight ahead, away from the approaching throng of people, and waited. The stale smell of her old,

303

dined-in, always-parked-out-in-the-rain car was more noticeable now, compared to the fresh, sweet air of the orchard. She stared at the wall of green in front of her, willing no one to see her.

The crunch of gravel under feet intensified as a garbled murmur of voices grew louder. Car doors opened and shut, engines started. Tamia twisted around in her seat to watch grim-faced people making an orderly, yet hurried exit. She rolled down her window as a couple approached the dusty blue Subaru next to her.

"What's going on?" she asked.

"Flareups around Mt. Rainier," said the young woman, opening up the Subaru's passenger door.

"Flareups? You mean fire?"

"Yep." The woman slid sideways into the car and shut the door.

Tamia's stomach tightened. Mt. Rainier was about seventy miles to the west, back toward Seattle.

Someone tapped at her rear window. She craned her neck and looked back. It was Jackie, from Palmer's Public Affairs office.

Busted! Tamia slipped out of her car. "What's going on here?" she asked, hoping to preempt any questions Jackie might pose.

"We got a report the hotspots west of here are getting hotter. From Rainier north, all around the SeaTac area."

Tamia put a hand over her mouth. Did her parents know? Where was her brother?

"Hey, don't panic," said Jackie. "We've got crews on call, and we're getting the word out in the affected areas." Her eyes flicked around to the trees bordering the parking lot. "Tamia, if there's anything you recommend . . ."

Tamia shook her head, feeling useless.

"Well, come with us then," said Jackie. "We've got a helicopter on the way for Palmer."

Tamia was torn. If she took the helicopter, she'd be back home, but without a car—and without any further plans. But if she could find Charlie Meninick, she might have another chance to stop whatever action the trees were taking.

Tamia heard Governor Palmer's voice and spotted him approaching. "Tamia, I didn't expect to see you here."

She nodded and braced herself for questions.

"You've heard what's going on?" he asked. "Come back in the chopper with us. Jackie, let them know we'll have another passenger."

"Already on it," she said, radio to her lips.

"I appreciate it, Governor," said Tamia, "but I don't think—"

"Don't be ridiculous, you can't drive back to Olympia in these conditions."

"Well, I'm actually up in Seattle now, since . . ." She looked down and cleared her throat. "Anyway, I still have some business down here at the moment. And my car."

"Don't worry, we'll get your vehicle back to you later." Palmer put a hand on her shoulder, lightly guiding her away from her Toyota. "Jackie, where's the chopper picking us up?"

Jackie pointed. "In the northeast field, sir, five minutes' walk."

"That's fine," said Palmer, pressing Tamia's shoulder more firmly.

Tamia planted her feet. "Sir, please, I have some things to take care of here."

"I'm sure it can wait. Safety first, Tamia. By the way, what about those recommendations from Drs. Block and Nystrom?"

"I don't know, sir, I'll have to check." A faint cracking sound reached Tamia's ears.

"Helicopter's on its way, Governor," said Jackie. "We should head to the pick-up site."

"You heard her," said Palmer, clenching Tamia's shoulder. "Time to go."

Tamia winced. "Governor, please."

The popping and rustling grew louder. Tamia wheeled around to face a phalanx of cypresses toppling toward the governor and his public affairs official. Palmer froze in a crouch while Jackie screamed and pulled on his arm. Tamia gulped in a deep breath, held her hands up to the trees and yelled, "Stop!"

And, with a long, loud creak, they did.

Palmer and Jackie stood slowly upright and stared at Tamia, still holding her hands up to the giants she'd stopped in mid-air. A trickle of green fronds fluttered to the ground as she lowered her arms.

"Thank you, Governor," said Tamia, heading toward her car. "But I think I can help you more out here." She climbed in, feeling like Wonder Woman, and started the engine.

The heroic soundtrack in her head stopped briefly while she pulled up the route to the Palalla Cultural Center, then started again with a flourish when she backed up and pulled out of the parking lot, spraying gravel to boot.

It was time to find Charlie Meninick.

CHAPTER 45

RICKY HAD NO idea how long he'd been traveling, or how far. The ride was smoother now, because they were in thicker woods where the trees didn't have to lean over so far to pass him off. He'd stopped yelling for help, focusing instead on shifting with the movement of trees and looking around for clues as to where he was.

Needles rustled, branches clacked and birds squawked as they were rousted from their nests. The rocking motion slowed at last, and Ricky heard something new. An engine, far off. It sounded like an airplane. The trees stopped moving, and he took the opportunity to stand up and look around.

Off in the distance—to the south? west? he had no idea—he saw a big, white airplane flying low, just above the tree line. There was a second one behind it, and a third one on its left. They were flying in formation.

Ricky yelled and waved his arms at the planes until the platform of branches supporting him began to sway. He gasped and ducked into a crouch, panting. When the rocking subsided he stood up again and slowly circled his arms to catch the pilots' attention.

Suddenly a big blue cloud spilled out of the bottom of the first plane. He knew right away what it was, even though the color was different than in all the videos he'd watched. The fire retardant was light and heavy at the same time, floating in a big foggy trail behind the plane, then drifting slowly down into the forest. The second and third planes released their plumes of retardant before all three curved away from Ricky and flew off into the distance.

But where was the smoke? Where was the fire all these planes were supposed to be putting out? He turned around, confused. All the videos he'd watched had smoke, but he didn't see any here. So why were those planes dumping retardant?

The forest grew quiet as the planes disappeared. Really quiet. Ricky realized the tree still wasn't moving, and he was wasting his chance to get away. He clambered down the tree, hoping it wouldn't change its mind with him halfway down. To his surprise, a branch lowered itself to help him to the ground. He landed with a crackle of dead leaves, his head still spinning from his trip through the treetops.

There was a road nearby. He crunched toward it through twigs and debris, lurching like he'd just gotten off a carnival ride. As he got closer, he saw a maroon SUV parked on the shoulder.

"Grampa?"

"Ricky? Ricky!"

Ricky stepped out to the roadside and his grandfather jogged toward him. "My god, Ricky!" The older man knelt down and squeezed him.

"I'm dizzy, Grampa."

"I'll bet you are. But you're okay? You're not hurt?"

Ricky slumped against his grandfather. "Yeah, I'm okay. Where are we?"

"Near Issaquah. Do you know how far that is?" said the older man, leading him to the car. "It's pretty far. It took me over an hour to get here."

Ricky was glad to sit down in Grampa's SUV. It made him less dizzy.

"The trees told me where you would be," Grampa told him. "They didn't want to hurt you. They thought they were doing a good thing by getting you out of harm's way."

"Why, what's going on?"

The older man hesitated. "Everything will be fine. They're just being very careful. It's what you call an abundance of caution. Here, seatbelt."

"Grampa," he asked, buckling himself in, "is there a fire around here?"

"No, not yet."

"Well, then why are they spraying here?"

His grandfather stopped, his key hovering by the ignition. "Spraying?"

"Yeah, didn't you see the planes? There were three, and they were flying really low. They sprayed this bright blue fire retardant all over the trees."

"Blue? Are you sure?"

"Yeah. What's wrong?"

"They were right," he said quietly. He started the car and pulled onto the road.

"Who were right?"

Ricky watched his grandfather consider what to say, the way grownups do when they think they can't just go ahead and tell you what's going on. "The trees told me they were being poisoned with—God knows what. It's retardant, but it's been altered to kill the trees."

Ricky didn't know what to think. He knew he should be angry with the trees for spreading fire and burning his dad, but he didn't think they should be killed either.

"The way the trees describe it," his grandfather went on, "it's like they're overheating. Like their metabolism is being sped up and burned out. Maybe nitrogen. I don't know." He jerked the steering wheel angrily to take a curve. "It seems our firefighters are trying to create a dead, fire-resistant perimeter around the cities. Pretty ingenious, actually, unless you have any qualms about killing off the whole goddamn forest." He glanced at Ricky. "Sorry."

"They can't do that," said Ricky. "They can't kill all of them. Why don't they just put out the fire?"

"The trees are spreading it too fast. The firefighters can't keep up with the trees so now they're killing them, and whoever else happens to live around here." He glanced at Ricky again. "Never mind, I'm sure whatever they're spraying is safe. I'm sure they've tested it."

The older man's phone rang. He fished it out and answered. "Marla, I just found him, he's safe. He's not hurt." *It's your mom,* he mouthed to Ricky. "Yes, he's perfectly fine. We're heading east." He listened. "No, I haven't said anything yet." He listened again. "Yes, I will. Marla, we're all going to make it. Yes, here he is."

Ricky's grandfather handed him the phone.

"Ricky, baby, thank god! You okay, sweetie?"

"Yeah, I'm okay."

"They didn't hurt you? You're all right?"

"Yeah, Mom, I'm good."

"Okay, Ricky. You be a good boy, now." Her voice sounded funny. Sad. "Daddy and I love you. Remember that, all right?"

"Yeah, Mom." Her voice made him nervous, like something bad was about to happen. "You okay, Mom?"

"Yes, honey, I'm fine." She sniffed, like she was about to cry. "Listen to your Grampa, okay? He's going to take you on a little trip. Call us later, all right? Mommy loves you, honey. I love you so much."

"Mom?" Why was she so upset? He looked up at his grampa. "We're going on a trip?"

Grampa Nystrom held his hand out for the phone. Ricky gave it to him, confused.

"Listen, Marla, I'll explain it to him," he said. "But he's still a little stunned from the trees, I think, probably dehydrated. I'll get him something to eat first. Yes, we'll be careful. I'll call you later." He hung up and stuffed the phone back in his pocket.

"Is Mom okay?"

"Yes, she's fine. She's with your father and he's doing well."

Ricky waited for more, but his grandfather just kept brooding and driving. "Where're we going, Grampa?"

"I thought we'd head into Nakalish."

"Really? Can we go see Charlie? I bet he can help us!"

"That's exactly what I'm thinking," said Grampa. "It's almost like they're pushing us together."

Ricky could tell he was talking about the trees. "Is that what they said?"

"No, they didn't talk about Charlie. They just wanted to get you away from Tacoma. They said—"

Ricky didn't like the way his grandfather's expression changed. "What?"

"They seemed to think you would be better off out here, for the time being."

"But why?"

"I don't know, Ricky. Let's see if we can talk to Charlie about it." He smiled over at Ricky. "So, what do you feel like eating?"

Ricky shrugged and looked down at his lap. Grownups always changed the subject when there was something they didn't want you to know. He'd just have to wait till Grampa forgot he was keeping it secret. He sighed and twisted back around to where he'd seen the planes, wondering if there would be more. His eyes grew wide.

"Grampa?"

"What?" Ricky pointed behind them, and his grandfather looked into his rear view mirror. His face froze.

A tendril of smoke twisted up from the treeline behind them.

Ricky lurched in his seat as Grampa Nystrom stepped on the gas. His eyes flicked to Ricky, then back to the road. "We're okay. We're fine." His words were meant to be reassuring, but his tone was sharp. "We just have to keep going east."

"But what about west? What about Tacoma?"

Grampa didn't respond.

"What if the fire comes back?" Ricky leaned forward in his seat, trying to catch his grandfather's eye. "What about Mom and Dad?"

His grandfather kneaded the wheel and kept driving. "Ricky, your mom's going to stay in Tacoma for now, just in case your dad needs her."

"But why can't they come with us?"

"Ricky, honey, your dad's not quite ready to leave the hospital yet."

And it's all my fault! "But what if the fire comes back?"

"They'll evacuate the city if they have to. Everyone will get out, and your mom will help your dad."

Ricky tried to swallow the lump forming in his throat. "But what if—"

"I don't know!" his grandfather snapped.

Ricky sniffed, tears brimming his eyes.

Grampa Nystrom took a deep breath in and out. "I'm sorry, Ricky." He reached over and ran a hand over Ricky's hair. "I don't mean to scare you, but it sounds like the trees have some dangerous plans."

"What did they say?"

"They didn't say much, just where to stay away from in order to keep you safe." He gripped the wheel and stared out the windshield. "You don't give your enemy details when you're about to start a war."

CHAPTER 46

CHARLIE GRUMBLED TO himself as he clicked and nudged powwow events around on the screen. Damn his soft heart once again. He shouldn't even be at the Cultural Center anymore. The trees had understood him and Eddie, and they'd given them a sign. Three more trees went down, so as far as they could tell, Eco-Wood was a go.

But his boss had looked like she was about to have a heart attack when he'd told her he was leaving, so here he still was. Well, at least it was just one more week till the powwow, then he was out of here. And then he and Eddie and that forest were in business. No fires, no panic, no mayhem like everywhere else.

He'd been keeping tabs on the fire situation, what with Liz driving back and forth to Tacoma, and things were looking dicey. Little brush fires kept springing up in a line west of the Cascades, north to south, a 200-mile hot zone from Bellingham down to Centralia. Firefighters going crazy, reinforcements from Oregon, Montana and Idaho. Guard standing ready to deploy, talk about recruiting private citizens as emergency firefighters.

If he and Eddie could keep the peace with their trees, the Palalla would be safe. Maybe even rich in the process if Eco-Wood took off. And then perhaps, if he could find his mother again, he'd finally be able to take care of her like she deserved.

He looked up as the front door opened. A young woman with light brown skin walked in, smoothing a hand over her thick, dark hair. She approached the desk with a serious expression on her face.

"Excuse me," she said. "I'm looking for Charlie Meninick."

He kept his face blank. "Who are you?"

"I'm Tamia Bennett," she said, extending her hand.

Charlie looked at her hand for a moment before shaking it. "And what brings you here, Ms. Bennett?"

"Tamia," she insisted. "Are you Mr. Meninick?"

He wasn't a great liar, especially while shaking someone's hand. "Yeah. Call me Charlie."

"Finally!" She squeezed his hand even tighter. "I've been trying to reach you for weeks! I'm here because of—" She let go of his hand to pull a chair up to the desk. "May I?"

She sat down, and Charlie settled his expression between welcoming and wary.

"I was referred to you," she said, "by the trees."

"The trees?" Something in his brain clicked. "Tamia Bennett. Aren't you that girl that got canned from the governor's office for the video?"

She flashed a tight, embarrassed smile. "Yes, I used to work for Governor Palmer, and now I work with Dr. Block."

"So, the trees told you to find me?" he asked. "They say why?"

She leaned forward. "They want us to work together."

"Work together? On what exactly?"

"Charlie, things are getting bad out there. Between the attacks and the fires, people are getting hurt, even killed." She kept her voice low, earnest but discreet. "Did you hear about Covington?"

He nodded. He'd seen the footage while flipping back and forth between the powwow schedule and the news. The small community halfway between Tacoma and Seattle was being evacuated because a small brushfire in its outskirts had erupted into a major blaze.

"They can't put it out," she said. "Every time they try it moves. *The trees* move it."

Charlie looked down at the desk. Eddie had told him not to say too much about tree activity before he got the Eco-Wood patent. But the young woman was right.

Those trees were making some kind of maneuvers. Planning.

"Charlie."

He looked up.

Her expression was stern. "I talked to Dr. Block on the way here. She and Dr. Nystrom—yes, the same one who visited you before," she clarified when he raised his eyebrows. "They have an idea of what the trees might be up to." She swallowed. "It's terrible. I hope it's not true. But we need to do something to make sure it doesn't happen."

"I . . ." He trailed off, shaking his head. This young woman looked seriously afraid. But could he afford to get involved?

"Can I show you something?" She dug her phone out of her purse and tapped it a few times, then turned it his way. She'd called up a Washington fire event map showing a line of flame icons running up and down the state. "Dr. Block and Dr. Nystrom think that Tacoma and Covington were just test runs. They think the trees are lining up a perimeter, and that soon they're all going to go on the offensive." Her hand was shaking, so she laid the phone on the desk, facing him. "They think at some point the trees are going to flare up, perhaps all at once, and burn everything from the mountains right through to the coast."

"That's crazy!" Charlie sputtered. "Why would they do that? They'd be killing everything off, including themselves."

"I know, but the trees warned both Dr. Block and Dr. Nystrom to get east. They were the ones who told me to come here—I think they just wanted to keep me from going back to Seattle. I think they're planning something huge."

Charlie pushed back from his desk and shook his head. This was impossible. Crazy. And if by some wild chance it was true, could he risk having the Palalla trees think he was siding with the humans? Wouldn't that just put the Nation on the trees' list of places to burn?

"Miss," he said. "I can't believe they would do that. We have an agreement with our trees. A peace agreement. So I can't believe they would do something like that."

The young woman stared at him, lips tightly pressed. "Why don't we ask them?" She pulled a small metal box out of her purse.

"Wait, is that one of those translators?"

She nodded.

Eddie had told him about them. BIA supposedly had some, but nothing had made its way around to them yet.

"Hang on," he said, picking up the phone. He called Eddie's office but he was at lunch. He didn't pick up his cell either. Charlie didn't feel right about making decisions about the trees without Eddie—especially not one that could put the Nation on their bad side.

"Sorry, Miss," he said, putting down the phone. "We're gonna have to wait."

"How long?"

"I don't know."

"That's not good enough!" she insisted, her voice rising. "Didn't you hear me? There could be a forest fire out there right now, heading straight for Seattle!"

"I'm sorry, but—"

"My family lives in Seattle. My mom and dad, my little brother—" Her voice caught. She blinked rapidly, but not quickly enough to hide the tears starting to well up.

Charlie felt his resolve weakening.

Tamia straightened her back and set her shoulders. "Here," she said, holding the translator out to him. "If you help me stop these fires, I'll give it to you. I'll show you how to work it, and it's yours when we're done. Please."

He stared at the translator. Eddie couldn't fault him for getting his hands on one of those, could he? And neither could the trees—it was just a way to understand them better. He dialed his boss' extension. "Ruth, I'm headin' out for lunch. I'll be out a little longer today."

Charlie felt a little buzz of excitement as he swept up his wallet and phone and stuffed them into his pockets. Eco-Wood could get off the ground even faster if they could talk directly to their trees. He didn't believe they would really burn up the whole western half of the state. They only acted in defense, and anyway, they'd have to burn too many of themselves to go through with it. There had to be some other explanation for all this. He motioned for Tamia to follow.

As soon as they hit pavement, Charlie hurried her down the street.

"Wait, where are we going?" she asked.

"To the river. Follow me."

"Shouldn't we drive?"

Charlie stopped dead in his tracks. He'd gotten too used to life without a vehicle.

As they drove to the river, Tamia briefed him on her latest conversations with the changed trees, telling him about their rapidly increasing language skills, their spread into Canada and down into Oregon, their increasing consciousness and understanding of the world around them.

The closer they got to the river, the tenser he felt. Was there any way to guarantee his people would stay on the trees' good side?

They parked on the opposite bank from where the three fallen alders still lay. Charlie held Tamia's arm as they passed over the wooden planks to the other side. In all this time, no one had moved the downed trees. While there were fewer visitors, the candles, dried flowers and other mementoes remained.

"Is this a sacred place?" Tamia asked quietly.

"For some. This is where we first learned how to live in peace with the trees."

"How did you do it?"

He hesitated. "I can't tell you," he said. "I mean, I can't tell you what they want from your people. They'll have to tell you themselves." He gestured to the translator in her bag.

She pulled out the machine and approached the forest, carefully avoiding the fallen trees and the offerings. Charlie watched her loop a strap around the platy, grey bark of a pine and cinch it into place.

"Hello, Tamia Bennett," said the tree.

Charlie's mouth opened. He didn't know how he'd imagined trees sounding, but it sure wasn't like Siri on his iPhone. The young woman waved him closer, and the pine greeted him by name.

"Hello," he said, feeling a little foolish. He watched the girl make some adjustments to the unit.

"Okay," Tamia said, "I found him like you told me. Now what can we do to settle this conflict?"

"Too late," said the tree.

A wave of panic washed over her face. "Too late?" she asked. "What does that mean?"

"Your people start . . . war. We cannot stop them."

"Whoa, whoa, whoa, what war?" asked Charlie, raising his hands toward the tree. "Nobody's askin' for war."

"Cities Seattle, Tacoma, Olympia. Kill before talking peace."

"We don't want any part of it, whatever it is." No way he was going to drag the Palalla into a war.

The female voice was flat and matter-of-fact. "No choice. Humans use poisons, new fire retardants that kill us."

"New kind of pox blankets," said Charlie bitterly.

Tamia frowned, then addressed the tree. "What did you expect them to do, just sit there and wait for the city to burn?"

"You not understand," said the pine. "No fire until human poison come."

"That's not true!" argued Tamia. "You were the ones who kept the fires going."

"We must keep fire. Our only defense. Now . . . fire retardant take away our defense."

"You used it as offense in Tacoma," she said hotly.

"Tacoma warning."

"Or a test?" she prodded.

The tree ignored her. "Humans still cut us, poison us, burn us. Warning is no good for people. No respond. Now we must have new start."

"New start," Charlie repeated. "You're talkin' about fresh negotiations, right?"

"No. Too late. We need new start. Shape land for right humans."

"Enough riddles," he said, frustrated. "Just say it straight. What do you want?"

"No riddle," said the tree. "Humans use fire to clear land, get rid of bad insects and plants . . . invasive species. Now we do same."

Charlie looked at Tamia, stunned.

The tree continued: "We must clear . . . infestation of harmful humans, create room for beneficial humans. Need . . . fertile conditions for new growth."

"That's crazy," he countered. "You'd be destroying yourselves too. That's not self-preservation."

"Good is health of our kind, not . . . comfort of single tree. After fire, we sprout, we live again. So will you."

Charlie's head felt light. He couldn't be hearing them right. Were they really talking about destroying everything west of the Cascades?

"Please, wait!" Tamia urged. "Can't you wait? Can't we talk about a solution?"

"Your leaders poison us," said the pine. "We must fight now. Soon too late."

"But I have another idea," she said. "Why can't you use your root systems to disable ours? Get city trees to dig up power lines and sewer lines, disrupt water. That'll get the cities' attention, show them who really has power."

"Roots only for communicate."

"But you've used them before," she argued. She passed a hand over her mouth in thought. "They must have changed tactics," she told Charlie. "Dislodging their roots disrupts their communication system, so they must have learned to use them only when there was no other option."

"Roots grow back! They'd rather burn up a whole state than have a little spotty reception? That doesn't make sense!"

Tamia shrugged helplessly. "It must to them." She crossed her arms and looked down. "Maybe they think *we* need *our* 'roots' to survive, and they're helping us by keeping them intact. Or maybe—"

"We have to stop them!" Charlie blurted.

"That's what I'm trying to do. We have to figure out how to reason with them."

"Trees think and think," the pine said. "Fire only way. Your population is . . . overgrown with . . . invasive humans. We make room for new stock, best conditions for future peace."

"So everyone has to die because some are bad?" Tamia asked angrily.

"Enough will survive. We move some. We bring you here, Tamia. Keep you safe."

"What about my family? You think they deserve to die?"

"We move most . . . promising specimens."

"What about my family?" she asked again.

Charlie waited for an answer. What about his own family? His dad was still in Seattle, and his mother could be anywhere out there.

The tree remained silent.

So the trees had decided, Charlie thought with a chill. There was no talking them out of it. So how would he get Liz out of Tacoma? What about Jenna, vulnerable and alone up in Seattle?

And what would keep them from turning on the Palalla someday?

Tamia pivoted and stalked toward the riverbank, digging around in her purse. Charlie watched her take out her phone and make a call, cupping a hand over her mouth. The tree still hadn't responded. Charlie reached for his own phone and dialed Liz, waiting through the rings before it went to voicemail.

Dammit, she's in class! "Liz, call me as soon as you get this. It's important."

Charlie looked over at Tamia, pacing around with the phone to her ear. He still had another call to make himself. He felt worn out just at the prospect of hearing that voice, but he had to call. He took a deep breath and dialed the number he thought he'd never have to dial again. The rings bleeped in his ear, and he prayed for the click of voicemail.

"Hello," said Jenna.

Shit.

"Hello?" she repeated. "Who'ssis?"

The slip of the "s," that little blur between words—she was drunk. He pulled the phone away from his ear to check the time. Not too long ago, he'd have been in the same condition right about now. Not too long ago at all.

He heard a deeper voice in the background, and then hers, muffled, as though she were holding her hand over the phone. He knew she'd find someone else sooner or later, but that didn't make the punch in the gut feel any better.

"Okay, who iss'is?" she said into the phone. "I'm gonna hang up—"

"Wait!"

"Who..." Her voice became a little more lucid. "That you, Charlie?"

He swallowed. "Yeah, it's me."

"Huh. Go figure," she said. Then, fainter, away from the receiver: "It's nobody."

Charlie's throat tightened.

"What d'you want?" she asked gruffly.

"Jenna, you got to get out of Seattle. It's too dangerous there."

"Ha, you don't have to tell me that."

"No," he said, "you don't understand. There's gonna be a big fire there, real big."

She paused. "How big?"

"Big. You heard what's been goin' on with the trees, right?" He knew how easy it was to get disconnected from the world when you lived in the bottle.

"Yeah, I been hearin' stuff." She sounded a little more alert now.

"It's true, Jenna. They're serious. I think we're at war."

The deep voice rumbled in the background again.

"I gotta go now," she said, quietly.

"Jenna, you have to leave. I'm serious!"

"I'll talk to Bill." The unmistakable tinkle of ice in a glass chimed in Charlie's ear.

"Please, Jenna."

She paused, long. "I'll talk to Bill. Bye, Charlie."

The line clicked dead. He stood dumbly with the phone up to his ear. She wasn't going anywhere. Even if she did believe him, she'd probably stay there just to spite him, counting on luck like she always did. She never did anything for herself, just banked on the kindness of strangers and suckers like him. And now this new guy, this joker Bill. They'd probably drink their way right through the apocalypse without even noticing. Self-destructive little—

Self-destructive.

Charlie jerked at the touch of Tamia's hand on his arm.

"Did you reach your people?" she asked, tears rimming her eyes.

Charlie shook off her hand and stalked up to the pine. "You're makin' a big mistake, guys."

"Explain," said the tree.

"This isn't how it works with us," he said grimly. "You make yourselves into the enemy now, folks won't forget. Burn as much as you want, they'll just come back with something else."

"Harm to us is harm to people."

"Since when does that matter?" asked Charlie. "You been watchin' us, right?" He turned to Tamia. "That's what you said, isn't it? Why they're learning so fast? They've been watchin' us all this time, and now that they can think, they're starting to understand everything that's been going on around 'em." He addressed the tree. "So you know what we're like. Once you become the enemy, we'll fuck ourselves over just to get a swipe at you."

"No other choice," the tree responded. "We cannot wait. Your poisons kill us."

"But what if they stopped the spraying?" asked Tamia, "Would you put out the fires?"

"Fire is our last defense."

"Yes, we know!" said Charlie. "We kill you, and you kill us, and everybody's dead. But what if we get them to stop?" He stepped closer to the tree. "What if everyone could live?"

The pine didn't speak immediately. "Trees choose life when possible," it finally said. "If they stop poison, we will speak with them. Speak peace."

Charlie nodded. "You heard 'em, get on the horn," he told Tamia. "Call your people and get 'em to put a stop to this."

"Well, they're not going to stand down just because *I* say so." She crossed her arms to think. "They need some kind of proof."

Proof, he thought. Not just words, but a sign. There was only one sign he knew. He pointed at the tree. "Okay, hang on, I have an idea. But we need time to get a message to those guys in the planes. Tell your friends, don't start anything yet."

"Come on," he said to Tamia, stepping away toward the river. "Grab that machine and let's go."

CHAPTER 47

TAMIA UNLATCHED THE translator from the tree and stuffed it into her bag. She caught up to Charlie as he clomped over the wooden planks to the other side of the river. She was excited. He had an idea, and together they'd work it into a plan. The trees hadn't anticipated this, had they? They didn't think anything was actually going to happen when she found Charlie. They'd only been trying to get her out of the way. She was supposed to be their ally, but apparently that word meant something different to them than it did to her. Making peace was going to be way more complicated than she'd thought.

Still, hope bubbled up inside her as she and Charlie got into her car. She backed up and turned the wheel, taking them back toward town.

"Okay, talk to me," she said. "Where am I heading? What's your idea?"

"Where's the biggest blaze they're fighting right now? We got to go there."

"Here," she said, giving him her phone. "My browser's already on the fire map. So why the biggest blaze?"

Charlie swore quietly. "This can't be right."

"What?" She clenched the wheel, turning onto the main street of Nakalish.

"They're moving."

"What do you mean?" She glanced over, and he was shaking his head.

"There's a bunch of fire icons moving. They're multiplying."

"What?" Tamia turned on the radio, catching an emergency announcement in progress: "—in response to increasingly volatile fire activity across the state. Citizens are advised to prepare an emergency bag with food, water, and medications, keep a full tank in your cars, and stay tuned for further information. These blazes have become highly unpredictable statewide, so an order to evacuate your community could come at any moment. We advise you to look at the list of shelters on our website and note the location closest to you."

"They're starting it," he said, his voice full of anger. "Why are they starting? They're supposed to wait!"

Tamia fought down panic. "They must not be connected this far out. If we want to talk to them, we've got to get closer."

"How fast you think they can spread a message?"

"I don't know," she said. "What are you thinking?"

He turned down the radio. "You know how those trees were lying down back at the river? I'm gonna try to get the ones spreading the fire to do the same thing, a peace gesture in front of the fire crews. That should give you leverage with your people at the governor's office."

"Hold on, they fired me, remember?"

"But they still know you," he insisted. "If I can get the trees to stop for a second, that should be the proof you need to get the governor's office to listen to you. That's the best shot we got at stopping the spraying."

"You sure about this?" Tamia asked.

"Nope," he said plainly. "You got anything?"

"No." She gripped the wheel and tried to come up with a Plan B as she turned onto the highway out of Nakalish. Yellowed grass and stubby little bushes whizzed by the windows on both sides. *One spark and all this would go up in flames.*

Once they hit Pilalla City, they had a choice to make.

"Which way?" asked Tamia. "If we're going to Seattle, the 82 would be fastest."

"But there's traffic advisories for Highway 12." Charlie thumbed through Tamia's phone. "That's where the trouble is, so that's where we need to be."

Tamia turned west onto the 12, against a flood of traffic heading the opposite direction. Her stomach tightened, wondering if it was just her, or if the air really was getting hazier. She kept driving, trying not to stare at the patrol cars parked at regular intervals on the shoulder.

The nearer they got to the pass, the taller the trees on either side grew, and the closer they pressed in toward the highway. Funny, she'd always loved that about Washington, how at every turn the sheer size and number of trees reminded you that each city was a speck of civilization carved into a massive forest. That thought had never really felt threatening until now.

"Crap." She hit the brakes, stopping at the barricade blocking her lane. A trooper climbed out of his vehicle and approached. Tamia glanced over at Charlie's sullen profile. A whiff of smoke entered the car when she rolled down her window for the officer.

"Sorry, Miss, road's closed. Fire activity. You'll have to turn around."

"But, um, all our stuff's still up at our campsite."

"Sorry, outbound only, Miss. You'll have to go back and wait until we get the all clear."

"How long will that be?" she asked, already knowing what a stupid question it was.

"Wish I could say, Miss. Sorry, but you'll have to go wait it out in town."

"Okay, thanks," said Tamia, hiding her frustration. She rolled her window back up and turned around into the growing line of vehicles heading back out to the main highway. "Any other way to get close?"

"I don't know," said Charlie. "They probably got everything but the 90 blocked off by now."

Tamia held out her hand for her phone as they crawled behind a line of cars away from their goal. She checked the fire activity map. Service was slow, but the fire icons finally reloaded. Two spindly lines of activity snaked westward, toward Seattle and Olympia, a surgical strike against the largest city and the seat of government. These trees were not messing around. She clicked on the refresh button and the screen went blank. Service sputtered in and out, reloading the page in dribs and drabs. How long would it take for the fire to reach Seattle? Days? Hours?

She gripped the wheel and cursed quietly at the mass of vehicles in front of her. Behind her, officers were moving the barricade, converting the two-way highway into outbound only. But still, who knew how much time they'd lose backtracking, let alone trying to find another way to get closer to the fire. "How close do we have to be for your plan to work?" she asked.

"Hang on," said Charlie. "See that?" He pointed to a turnoff that appeared to wind back into the woods. "That's got to get us deeper in."

Tamia peered at the sign. "'White Pass Maintenance.' Are we supposed to go up there?"

"Do we have a choice?"

Tamia took a deep breath and looked around for troopers. She veered to the right onto the side road, thankful now for the wall of trees hiding them from the highway. The rusted bar gate stood upright and open, and Tamia purposely didn't look at the trespassing signs as she rolled through. She sucked in her breath as she bumped over a pothole.

"Where exactly does this go?" she wondered aloud as she rounded a curve.

"Hopefully, right up to the fire," Charlie said. "Listen." The chop of a helicopter waxed and waned overhead. Tamia stepped on the gas, hoping they weren't being tracked. A moment later, she heard the deep rumble of a big rig behind them and checked her rear view mirror. A bright red, tank-like truck crawled up the road behind her. She eased off to the side to let it pass, but it ground to a stop beside her. She heard shouting and opened her window.

A man in a yellow helmet shouted at her over the chugging engine. "There's a fire up here, Miss, I need you out of here right now!"

"Oh, sorry," she yelled back, trying to sound clueless. Exhaust and smoke wafted in through the window and she coughed.

"Turn around and get back on the highway, now!" shouted the firefighter. The massive tank on wheels pulled off, grinding uphill as Tamia rolled the window back up and snapped her vents closed.

"Shit, they're gonna send someone up here, I bet," said Charlie. "They're gonna send up a patrol to chase us down."

"Well, we just have to get to the fire before they come."

"How you gonna do that with that truck up ahead?" he asked.

Both of them looked up as an airplane flew overhead. It sounded low and out of place.

"Hang on." She shifted back into gear and rolled up to a Y in the road. The service road curved to the left and an unmarked gravel road veered off to the right. They looked at each other.

"You sure this little car can take it?" asked Charlie

"No. Maybe. I hope." She took the right fork onto the gravel road.

Tamia bumped slowly over rocks and divots, wincing at every scrape of the undercarriage. She wanted to race uphill, but this was not the time to pop a tire or disembowel her little Toyota on a boulder. Steadily they climbed, the air growing hazier as they wound their way up the trail. A few minutes later, another helicopter chopped overhead. "Is that the same one?" she asked.

Charlie craned his head around to get a look. "There's a couple of 'em. I think one's a news 'copter."

"Well, they're here for the fire, they don't care about us," she decided out loud, more for comfort than for any logical reason. The trail narrowed as her car struggled uphill. Helicopters circled and Tamia could have sworn she heard another airplane off in the distance.

"That's probably them dumping retardant," Charlie guessed.

The smoky haze grew thicker, and the ruts in the road became so large and frequent Tamia couldn't avoid them. She and Charlie swayed back and forth like they were riding in a wagon train.

"I bet we could walk faster," said Charlie.

She looked over at him. "In this smoke?"

"We got to move, I bet those copters are tracking us."

"Why would they?"

BANG!

"Shit." Both her front tires had landed in a divot extending all the way across the road. She eased her toe back onto the gas pedal and heard something scraping below. "Shitshitshitshit."

"That doesn't sound good," said Charlie. "Lemme take a look."

As soon as he opened the door, smoke stung her nose.

"Close the door!" she yelled. He slammed it shut and she looked around for something to put over their faces. A scarf, an extra shirt? No, nothing but her stash of bottled water. "Just cover your face," she said to Charlie. She handed him a bottle of water and pulled the front of his shirt up over his mouth and nose.

He stepped out. Panic rose up inside Tamia as the smell of ash seeped into the car. She climbed over the front seats into the back, hoping to find some cloth shopping bags in the trunk. She pulled the tab to fold down the back seat and fished around with her arm. Nothing. She slammed the seat back into place.

Charlie yanked open the door. "Patrol," he croaked, pointing downhill. Tamia heard the sound of a vehicle rolling up the gravel switchbacks and she scrambled out of the car. She yanked her sleeve down past her hand and held it over her mouth as Charlie pulled her over the lip of the road into a deep, eroded trench running alongside it. The approaching engine grew louder. Tamia stumbled toward a dead log at the bottom of the ditch, throwing herself down next to it and pulling dead leaves and broken pine boughs over herself.

She heard the vehicle stop. The doors clicked open and two muffled voices called out. It sounded like they were wearing masks. Tamia wished she had one too. Her eyes felt like sandpaper. She started to rub them, but the crackle of dead leaves stopped her. She held perfectly still, her tongue grating ash against the roof of her mouth. Boots crunched over gravel. Her heart thudded so hard she was afraid her whole body would start jumping.

She heard murmurs and what must have been the officers stepping around her car. One of them called out, "Sir? Miss?" and a moment later her trunk thunked open. Just then it occurred to her that she'd left the back door open, her purse inside, and keys in the ignition. They'd organize a whole search party.

"Miss! Sir! Can you hear us?" an officer yelled, closer this time. "Call in backup," he yelled to his partner.

"From where?" shouted the other. "We got all hands on evacuation."

The ground trembled. A radio blipped and the ground shook again. The officers yelled, and the earth began to churn beneath Tamia. Dirt roiled and rocks tumbled down the ditch, pelting her. She struggled to her feet and tried to climb up the slope, but the dirt crumbled away beneath her feet. She fell to her knees and looked for Charlie, finally spotting him crouched behind a boulder with his arms over his head.

The tickle in Tamia's throat intensified. She squeezed her watering eyes tight and clamped her hand over her nose and mouth, rocking with the ground. Above her on the road, car doors slammed shut and an engine roared to life. Tamia made a final dash up the slope and clutched at the edge of the ditch. As she pulled herself up, she peered over the edge just in time to see the trooper's car back into a 3-point turn. As the vehicle raced away down the mountain, the shaking subsided and finally stopped.

Tamia exploded into a wracking coughing fit, and Charlie scrambled over to pull her out of the ditch.

"You okay?" he yelled.

Tamia couldn't answer, just made a stumbling beeline for the car and wrenched the cap off one of her bottles of water. She drank and coughed and drank some more before twisting the lid off another bottle and handing it to Charlie.

"Get in," he said, pushing her gently into the passenger seat and closing the door. He jogged around the driver's side and turned on the ignition. Cool, filtered air circulated through the car.

Tamia poured water over her face to flush her burning eyes. She blinked and wiped them with her sleeve, finally able to see clearly. And then she understood what had made the officers flee. All around the car, in every direction, craters and cracks gaped where something had pushed up through the surface of the road. A huge crevasse had opened up in front of her car, and another one behind. A movement caught her eye, and she turned her head just in time to see something slip down beneath the surface of the road—something that looked like a root.

She turned to Charlie. His expression told her he'd seen exactly what she had. "Guess we're not drivin' out of here," he said.

"We need masks," said Tamia, popping open the glovebox and pulling out the first aid kit. "Why didn't I think of this before?" She wetted one of the gauze pads with water and held it up to Charlie's mouth and nose, then wound gauze around his head to hold it in place.

"Do me," she said, wetting another pad. He tied it to her face.

"What about our eyes?" she asked.

He held the gauze up to his eyes, then looked around. "You got any sunglasses in here?"

"I live in Seattle," she said, a bit of sarcasm to mask her fear.

"Guess we're out of luck."

She stuffed as much gauze, pads and water into her bag as would fit and looped it over her head. "Ready?"

Charlie nodded. "Let's go find that fire."

As soon as she opened the door, it felt like the fire had found them. A hot wind pressed against her as she got out of the car and followed Charlie into the trees on the uphill side of the road. They'd have to get high enough to spot the fire, and stay away from the emergency crews long enough to negotiate with the trees. The sound of helicopters above reminded her that they couldn't stay hidden for long.

They clambered up the slope, maneuvering over branches and underbrush, winding through cedars and firs. While Charlie stopped for a drink, Tamia climbed onto a small, flat clearing with two squat utility buildings. He joined her at the edge, where she had found a view of the valley.

A thick haze hung over the deep green carpet of treetops stretching out below them. The wind caught and bent columns of dark grey smoke rising up from the forest, carrying heat and ash for miles. A tanker plane flew in low and dumped a plume of blue retardant over a distant knot of smoke.

Tamia wiped her gritty eyes and focused on the undulating treetops. Amidst the drone of planes and helicopters, she heard the distant creak and pop of trees flexing. Haze blurred the details, but she knew what was happening. The trees were waving, bending, passing the flame from one to another, westward toward Seattle. She tried to check the fire activity map again, but it still wouldn't load.

She squinted, trying to spot the far edge of the blaze, but the smoke was too thick. She wanted to know where the fire ended, how close it was to Seattle. What if it was already on the outskirts? She imagined flames dancing through the cedars and pines in her parents' yard, licking across their lawn, crawling up the side of their home.

How far away were Mom, Dad and DeShaun right now? They'd told her they were going to head north, join the growing line of cars seeking refuge in Canada. But even on a good day the I-5 was a mess, so by now they were probably stuck in a parking lot on the highway.

Tamia imagined what it would be like when the fire got to the heart of Seattle: smoke, sirens, panic, burning buildings, streets clogged with cars and glittering with broken glass. People screaming and running for the harbor, desperate to get to the water, the city turning to ashes behind them.

Charlie crossed over to a large Whitebark pine on the edge of the clearing and stood facing it. He put both hands on the tree and leaned in toward its pale, scaly trunk. Something in his stance told her not to intrude. She took out her phone instead and typed in Governor Palmer's direct extension. She knew it from work—but she'd never dared to dial it before.

"Palmer," he answered.

Her stomach twisted at his deep, authoritative voice. "Governor Palmer, this is Tamia Bennett. We're up at White Pass, off Highway 12. We're looking right at the fire."

"Tamia? How did you get up there? Doesn't matter, you have to get out. They're evacuating."

"I know," she said. "But we can stop this. We're negotiating with a pine right now. I think we can get the trees to stop this if you call off the fire crews."

"You can't be serious. I don't have time for this."

"Please wait, sir. I am serious. The trees are open to negotiations, but only if you stop dousing them with chemicals." She glanced over to Charlie, who had wrapped the translator around the tree and was speaking into it.

"Out of the question. I'm watching footage right now. That fire's out of control."

"You're watching the White Pass fire?" she asked. She looked at the helicopters circling and thought she could make out the News 5 Logo.

"Yes, and it's a hell of a fire. We can't stand the crews down."

"Sir, you know I work with Dr. Block." Not that this was Dr. Block's plan, but it was the only thing that would get him to listen. "If we can show you something—

if we can show you that the trees are serious about cooperating, will you stop dumping the retardant?"

"If you stop that fire, we'll talk."

"Keep watching," she said, glancing over at Charlie again. "I'll call you right back," she told Palmer and hung up.

She approached Charlie and the pine cautiously. Now he wasn't saying anything at all, just resting his head on the trunk. Was that good or bad?

"Charlie?" He didn't respond. "Charlie, talk to me."

He raised his head from the trunk and walked past her to the lip of the clearing, then looked out over the valley, silent.

Her heart sank. This didn't look like success. It didn't look good at all.

CHAPTER 48

CHARLIE GLANCED OVER at Tamia, phone clamped to her ear, as he wrapped the translator around the Whitebark pine. He heard her say "Palmer." Now it was time for him to seal his part of the deal.

The pine spoke immediately. "Charlie Meninick, you must go away from fire. You must be safe."

"I'm trying to help everyone be safe. I'm asking you to stop the fire."

"Cannot. Your people are too—"

"Hang on," Charlie interrupted. He couldn't have any confusion backfiring on the Palalla. "Those people out there, the ones you're fighting right now—those aren't my people."

"You live here, live there. Over mountains and back. You choose them, live like them, only return to Palalla when you hurt too much."

The tree's words stung. "I've made a lot of bad decisions," Charlie admitted. "Yes, I turned my back on my people. Shit, I couldn't get out of Nakalish fast enough. And I said 'yes' to every bottle I drank." He looked down at his boots. "But I decided to make a change. *I* did. And that's the only way it's gonna stick, because *I* made the decision."

Charlie turned at the sound of a plane in the distance. His gut clenched when yet another plume of toxic blue retardant billowed out the back.

"Your leaders make their decision too," said the tree.

"Those aren't my leaders. I'm Palalla. But those people," he said, pointing toward the plane, "you back 'em into a corner, they're gonna keep doing more of the same. You gotta give 'em an opportunity to make the right choice."

"How you know they make right choice?"

"You talk to 'em," said Charlie. "You negotiate, you make a deal."

"And trust them?" asked the tree. "Your people, Palalla and other native species . . . in-di-ge-nous people, learn about cost of too much trust for new species."

Charlie searched for an argument. Nothing he could say about peace and forgiveness and looking toward the future could erase everything that had happened to his people since the "discovery" of America. But he had to try.

"Look, not all white people are evil. We're all the same species, and we can all live together."

"Does not matter now what color flowers are," said the tree. "Whole field needs to be resown."

"But what you're doing will wipe everyone out!"

"Most, not all. Humans are . . . resilient. You spring up again, together we reshape land, create healthier . . . environment for all. Everything . . . will be better."

Charlie looked out at another airplane approaching a plume of smoke in the valley. "Yes, humans are resilient," he said. "If anyone is resilient, *my* people are. You watched it all happen, and now you *understand* what you saw. Our land was stolen, our tribes slaughtered and torn apart, but we survived. We've come back strong and proud, more determined than ever to keep our ways alive. But our survival doesn't excuse everything that was done to us in the name of 'progress.'"

"Invasive people had wrong idea of 'progress'," replied the tree.

"But at the time," said Charlie, "they were completely convinced they were right. Do you know the term 'Manifest Destiny'?"

"'Ma-ni-fest Des-tiny' not progress. If trees could think and move then, in past, everything change, everything different today. But we cannot go back. We can only change now."

"You're right," said Charlie. "We can't go back. We've seen the evil that happens when one nation can't think of any better solution than wiping the other nations out; when people think war is the only way toward *progress*." He gripped the trunk, willing the tree to understand. "You're making that choice right now, war or peace. And once you choose, we can never go back."

The tree didn't respond. Charlie waited, more uncertain with every moment of silence. He closed his eyes and leaned his head against the trunk. The trees had to make this decision on their own time.

Tamia called his name, wanting, he knew, to hear good news. Any news.

He walked past her to the lip of the clearing, stalling for time, looking out over the valley. Hoping.

CHAPTER 49

TAMIA COULDN'T BEAR any more silence. "Charlie," she called sharply. "Talk to me."

"Now we wait."

"How long?"

He shrugged. "It's up to them."

She cast her gaze out over the valley. Trees continued to creak and pop as planes buzzed overhead. Bitter ash coated the inside of her mouth. What would happen now? Had her family gotten out in time? Wasn't there anything more she could do?

The hours passed as the sun marched overhead. Tongues of flame leapt up from the valley, and load after load of blue retardant floated down into the forest. Charlie pulled out his phone, turning away from Tamia as he dialed and waited. He spoke softly, but she still heard the message he left. "Dad, if you're still in Seattle, get out. Now."

So they'd failed. It was going to be all out destruction. Tamia closed her eyes and wiped tears off her grimy cheeks. She felt numb, helpless. She sat down on the ground and buried her face in her hands.

Then, finally, Charlie tapped her on the arm.

She opened her eyes and looked up at him. He pointed out toward the valley. The smoke billowing up from the forest had thinned a bit, enough for her to see that the trees had changed their movements. Instead of thrashing into one another to pass along flames, they were swaying gently from side to side. Tamia jumped to her feet. In another minute, the trees stopped moving completely.

Tamia scrambled for her phone. She pressed *redial* for Palmer and put the phone to her ear. All she heard was a stream of rapid, high-pitched beeps before the line went silent. *Oh no. No!* She punched her screen to call again. This time she didn't hear anything.

"Charlie, I can't call Palmer. There's no service!"

She tried again, stumbling over the buttons on her screen. No connection.

She tried again. Silence.

This couldn't be happening. They couldn't have come this close for her to fail at the very last step.

Charlie jerked into motion, digging his phone out of his pocket and handing it to her. Hands trembling, she typed Palmer's number into Charlie's phone. Her knees almost buckled with relief when she heard ringing.

The call clicked through. "Palmer."

"Governor Palmer, it's Tamia. Are you still watching the White Pass fire?" The connection was hollow and scratchy, like through a radio system. He must be evacuating, his phone forwarded to whatever car or helicopter he was using to flee.

Garbled voices rose behind his before he replied. "Yes."

"So they can stop dumping retardant, right?"

"Don't be stupid," he scoffed. "We still have to get the fire under control."

Her face flushed with anger. "But can't you use something else? Water or a different retardant, one that doesn't poison them?"

"Look, whatever you may have done to slow this down, I thank you, but—"

"What about the people?" she argued. "There are towns around here. And the waterways; didn't the Forest Service guy say—"

"Who are you to question me?"

"Call off the poison, now!" she demanded, clenching her fist. "If you don't, and the trees start moving fire again, it's on you."

"Tamia—"

"Has anything else you've tried worked?" she yelled. "Are you going to call this off and save millions of lives, or do you want to watch those trees rise up and burn the whole damn state to the ground?" Silence. "Do you really want that to be your legacy?"

She hung up and had to stop herself from throwing Charlie's phone into the valley. She slapped it into his palm and stood with him on the ledge, watching helicopters buzz overhead as the smoke died down further. They watched and waited. The forest remained still, but how long that would last was anyone's guess.

Charlie pointed toward an approaching tanker plane. Tamia sucked in her breath. She would be sick if she had to watch another cloud of blue smother the trees.

Charlie put a hand on her shoulder. "We did everything we could."

"But what if . . ." She couldn't even finish.

"The trees have given us as much room as they could," he said quietly. "Whatever happens next is exactly what we deserve."

Tamia held her breath, praying she wouldn't see blue.

The tanker doors opened, and a roiling white cloud poured out. Suspended by velocity, the churning plume of water trailed the plane for a moment before descending, clean and clear, into the forest below.

CHAPTER 50

CHARLIE SPED ALONG Highway 90 in his new Chevy Ram, its wipers batting at the rain. The truck wasn't actually new, but it was new to him. The A/C was busted and the brakes would need some work soon, but it was his.

Only forty more miles to Tacoma, according to the sign that rushed by. Urgent-sounding music blared out of the speakers and an announcer launched into the afternoon news. "The long-anticipated official launch of Tad Palmer's campaign for U.S. Senate has been pushed back yet again. The governor was called to testify once more in the ongoing investigation of ArborTech Industries."

He turned the radio off, content to listen to the *thunk* of his wipers laboring at the windshield. He was tired of hearing about the investigation and what various officials thought about who did what, when. None of that really mattered. What mattered now was that they were dealing with a whole new world. In the six months since the White Pass fire, he'd been inundated with requests to mediate between the trees and the Palalla Nation, as well as local farmers, businesses, and government agencies. After the initial distribution, the supply of translators had been restricted while the powers that be argued about who should have them and why. People who had machines, like him and Tamia, were in high demand.

And guess whose call was ringing through right now? He put Tamia on speakerphone and kept his eyes on the road.

"I can't believe you're leaving," she said. "Wish we could have said goodbye in person." A flight announcement drowned her out for a moment. He should have known she'd be at the airport. She was almost always on the road now, sporting some long job title that basically meant ambassador between the State of Washington and the trees of the Pacific Northwest. "So, my appointment's official next week," she said after the airport loudspeaker went quiet. "You sure you don't want to reconsider what we talked about?"

Charlie heard the sly smile in her voice and couldn't help but chuckle. The job offer again. "Sorry, Tamia. You sure made it sound tempting, but—"

"Come on, you're already doing the job, you may as well get paid for it. Thanks to you, we've worked out industrial zones for all of central Washington. We know where those tree communities stop and start, where we can log, how much we can take, what they'll allow."

"Now, it wasn't all me." He knew her game by now, roping folks in with praise. She was good at what she did.

"But the trees trust you. They really respond to you."

"Maybe," he said. "But you were the one who worked through all the property rights." The tree communities ran across boundaries through state, tribal, or private land, and in many cases, all three. Each deal with a tree community required agreement from multiple human entities, and Tamia made each side feel like they were making the smartest decision. *Leading from behind,* she called it.

"But we make such a great team." Her excitement was genuine, and hard for Charlie to resist. "And we're not even done yet. We still have to pin down the details."

"Just a matter of signing papers. You don't need me for that."

"Maybe, but what about the rest of the state? What about Canada? The whole border area is on standby, waiting to see what happens here."

"Okay, okay, I get it." She was relentless, in a good way. "I'll think about it. But you know, I've got some business to attend to first."

"I know. Sorry to push. It's just that we work so well together." She sighed. "And I'll miss you. Be careful out there, okay?"

"Always. You too."

They said their goodbyes and hung up as Charlie's truck trundled down the highway in the rain. He was going to miss her too. But another project was calling him now. He just had a couple more people to visit on the way.

His phone bleeped and told him to merge on to I-5, where he cursed the perpetual traffic until his exit to Tacoma came into view. The phone was another recent acquisition, and it sounded uncannily like the tree translators. It pinged and guided him through wide, tree-lined suburban streets to a house with a familiar maroon SUV in the driveway.

Charlie squirmed a little while Ricky gushed and asked him a million questions. A hero's welcome didn't sit particularly well with him, so he was relieved when the boy's grandfather interjected.

"Now, Ricky," said Dr. Nystrom, "shouldn't we offer our guest something to drink? Go get a glass of water for Charlie, please. And one for me too." As Ricky sprang out of the room, the older man quietly brought Charlie up to speed. Ricky's father was home and in stable condition. He and Ricky's mother were at one of his many doctor's appointments. And Dr. Nystrom's translator had been seized, along with Dr. Block's, as part of the investigation.

"But don't worry," the older man reassured him. "I won't ask you for yours. I seem to have a group of supporters who say they can get me a new one. Between the 'fan club' on the one side and the death threats on the other—"

"Death threats?" Charlie asked, his eyes popping wide open.

"Oh yes," he answered softly. "People are scared, Charlie. They don't know what to think. Some say this is the beginning of a brave new world, others see it as the end of days. They're looking for either a hero to guide them or a villain to blame. Eco-warrior, eco-terrorist, everyone sees what they want to see."

Ricky entered the room holding two glasses of water and gave one to Charlie. "Now will you tell me how you put out the fire?"

Charlie laughed and took a sip. "It's no secret. I just asked 'em nicely. Said please and thank you."

Ricky sighed and handed the second glass to his grandfather. Charlie sat with them a little while longer, talking about Dr. Nystrom's research and Ricky's day at school. He even let Ricky drag him to the rec room for a few rounds of Zombie Apocalypse before saying he had to go.

The rain had stopped by the time they stepped outside. Charlie shook Dr. Nystrom's hand and thanked him for his help.

"Well," said the older man, "it remains to be seen how much I've helped. I just hope I have." He looked intently at Charlie. "Be safe."

Charlie nodded. "You too." He headed down the driveway to his truck with Ricky on his heels.

"You comin' with me?" he joked.

"I could, if you want," said Ricky.

"That's all right, I think I'll be okay." He kneeled down, face to face with the boy. "Besides, your parents need you here. Especially your dad."

Ricky nodded.

"And not just your folks," said Charlie. "Your grampa needs you too. And you know who needs you the most?"

"Who?"

"The trees. You're one of their trusted ones. They told me so."

Ricky looked down at the driveway.

"I understand," said Charlie. "I mean, I think I do. I know they hurt your dad, but they didn't set out to hurt him. They were just trying to protect themselves." The boy looked up at him again. "They trust you, Ricky, and they want you to trust them too. I tell you what, I trust 'em. And I think between you and me and the trees, we can help everyone figure this whole thing out."

Charlie stood up and stuck his hand out to Ricky. "How about it, you think you can help us, me and the trees?"

Ricky twisted his lips, then nodded and shook Charlie's hand. Charlie climbed into his truck.

"Where are you going?" Ricky asked.

"I told you, to find my mother."

"I know, but where?"

Charlie thought for a moment. "I don't know, that's why I have to go look."

Ricky crossed his arms.

"I'll send you a postcard, how 'bout that?" Charlie plugged his next destination into his phone. He stuck his arm out the window as he drove away, waving at the reflection of Ricky in his rear view mirror.

As he drove, he considered what Dr. Nystrom had said about eco-warriors and eco-terrorists. People were asking him for help, and so far, he'd done his part to keep the peace. But if it came down to it, if negotiations broke down and tree vs. human tensions rose up again, which side would he take? Deep down he thought he'd probably be the first person to hand the trees a match if they asked for one, if humans needed a reminder of the alternative to peace. So what did that make him; eco-warrior or eco-terrorist?

His phone issued more directions. He'd be at Liz's place in a few minutes.

He was amazed that she'd agreed to see him, after their first disastrous date and all the chaos since. He'd been honest with her; told her he didn't really know yet where he was going or how long he'd be away. But she understood. She knew this was important. And yes, she'd told him, she would like to see him again.

He had a life now. He had money, a car, a future—and a second chance with a woman who understood why he had to put it all on hold.

Charlie glanced at his bag on the passenger seat, grateful for the translator inside, thankful for the gift it had revealed. Somewhere, far from home, a Palalla mother breathed an old prayer into an awakening forest, asking the trees to care for the son she'd left behind so many years ago.

And now he finally had a way to find her.

EPILOGUE

A HEAVY VEHICLE lumbered along a clearing at the outskirts of a Tacoma suburb, crushing saplings under its treads. Vibrations rumbled through the earth, thrumming along the root system, announcing the mobile mulcher's progress toward a spindly young pine at the edge of the subdivision.

The pine's boughs trembled, but it remained still. The community had agreed.

The mulcher operator pushed a lever to raise the mechanical arm, directing the bulky attachment at its end toward the top of the tree. With the flick of another lever, the metal head buzzed to life. Steel blades bristling with teeth whirled past one another in perfectly timed revolutions. The clean whine of rotating discs changed to a guttural stutter as the teeth bit into the tip of the tree.

The pine bravely suppressed messaging through its roots as its body was ripped apart, but it couldn't keep its chemicals from releasing into the air. The young alders closest to the pine quivered at the airborne screams. They shot a message through their roots to the rest of the community. "Can't we do anything?"

The cottonwoods joined in the messaging. "All it would take is one or two of us to fall and crush the machine." They leaned closer to the mechanical arm chewing on the pine.

"We understand this is distressing," replied the network of red cedars. "But Douglas Fir and Red Cedar have agreed upon this course of action."

The mulcher at the end of the vehicle's arm rattled and sucked pine boughs into its maw. Wood crackled as mechanical teeth chewed their way steadily down the trunk, spitting out mulch where the tree once stood.

"But, Elders, it's not too late," prodded the maples, shaking their leaves. "If we all work together; we could topple the machine with our roots."

"Maple," asked the community of Douglas firs, "are you suggesting we compromise our whole communication system for one tree?"

"No, Elders," the maples replied, pulsing sugars back through their roots toward the Douglas firs and red cedars. "Your wisdom benefits Everytree."

"This is the painful part of our agreement," messaged Red Cedar. "Humans need room to expand their communities, and in exchange we will get room to expand ours. You must all remain calm and trust us. Trees under stress don't serve the eco-hood."

Surrounding oaks, alders, and pines joined with the maples in pushing sugars toward the Douglas fir and red cedar elders. The mechanical arm lifted, its blades having chewed the pine down to a stump surrounded by a ring of needles and wood chips. The operator swung the lethal attachment over to the top of another tree.

"These trees are not being destroyed wantonly," explained the community of red cedars. "This is all according to our negotiations with the humans. We will continue to work with them on your behalf—but we trees must remain united." The cedars pulsed sugars and nutrients back toward the trees surrounding them. "We will care for you, Cousins."

The trees soaked up the elder cedars' flow of nutrients. The spinning metallic teeth began to gnaw into another pine at the edge of the clearing.

"Humans have made great strides," continued Red Cedar. "They continue to develop alternatives to using our bodies for their products, and they have agreed to restrict expansion into forestland. But make no mistake: no matter what they say to us, we must remain vigilant and united."

The Douglas firs pushed sugars out through their roots as they picked up the lecture. "Humans may try to change their ways, but they cannot change their nature. They have a pathological attraction to the smell and the feel of our flesh. Red Cedar notes their improvements, but they still use us to build their homes. They carve us up into objects to sit on and eat from, and hang their electric wires from. They cut us into 'decorative objects' that serve no purpose at all. And you have seen them on their porches with their knives, shaving away strips of our dead flesh, letting it fall to the ground, and calling the butchery 'passing the time.'"

The mulcher lifted again and lurched toward a third pine.

"Cousins," concluded Red Cedar. "We granted humans the right to take five trees from Pine. Only five, when they wanted many more. And they will always want more. They will always feel the need to tear us down and use us, and only by speaking with a strong, unified voice will we check their growth. Now, let us rest so that we may continue to protect you."

The nutrient flow from the Douglas firs and red cedars slowed, and the root system was still for a moment. After destroying the fifth pine tree, the vehicle rumbled away.

Bit by bit, normal communications between trees resumed. Water, weather, and wind. Insect and animal residents. So much to be discussed, compared, and managed.

The maples discreetly nudged some extra sugars to the pine community. Pine took them quietly, determined to grow, no matter what.

✿ ABOUT THE AUTHOR

TARA CAMPBELL IS a Washington, D.C.-based writer of crossover sci-fi. With a BA in English and an MA in German, she has a demonstrated aversion to money and power. Previous publication credits include stories in *Barrelhouse*, *Punchnel's*, *Toasted Cake Podcast*, *Luna Station Quarterly*, *SciFi Romance Quarterly*, *Masters Review*, and *Queen Mob's Teahouse*.

Originally from Anchorage, Alaska, she has also lived in Oregon, Ohio, New York, Germany, and Austria. She currently lives in Washington, D.C. where she volunteers with 826DC and the Washington Writers Conference/ Books Alive.

She is the grateful recipient of two awards from Washington, D.C.'s Commission on the Arts and Humanities, both granted in 2016.

Larry Neal Writers' Award, Adult Fiction, for her short story "Justice for Mama Jaboley"

Mayor's Arts Award for Outstanding New Artist

Visit **www.taracampbell.com** to learn more about Tara.

RESOURCES

For those who want to dive deeper into the world of TreeVolution.

Plants and Trees

TREES ARE ALL around us, and yet how much do we really know about them? This is a partial list of the key resources that shaped my understanding of the amazing powers of plants and trees.

The Sound of Thirsty Trees, *All Things Considered*, NPR, April 28, 2013: This report was the genesis of the *TreeVolution*. After hearing that we could listen in on trees and hear what was going on with them before we saw any visible indications of trouble, I was hooked on the idea of finding out what else the trees might be trying to tell us.

The Intelligent Plant, Michael Pollan, *The New Yorker*, December 23 & 30 issue, 2013 (online)

Native Trees of Western Washington, Kevin Zobrist, Washington State University, Forest and Wildlife Extension, online course and book, Washington State University Press, 2014

What a Plant Knows: A Field Guide to the Senses of your Garden—And Beyond, Daniel Chamovitz, *Oneworld*, 2013

Trees Call for Help—And Now Scientists Can Understand, Gabe Popkin, *National Geographic*, April 16, 2013 (online)

How Plants Secretly Talk to Each Other, Kat McGowan, Wired.com, December 20, 2013 (online)

Trees Are Speeding Up Their Life Cycles To Try To Keep Up With Climate Change, *ThinkProgress*, September 13, 2013 (online)
Do Plants Think? Gareth Cook, *Scientific American*, June 5, 2012 (online)
Flower Power: Genetic Modification Could Amply Boost Plants' Carbon-Capture and Bioenergy Capacity, Mike Orcutt, *Scientific American*, October 18, 2010
Mapping Tree Density at a Global Scale, T. W. Crowther, H. B. Glick, K. R. Covey, C. Bettigole, *Nature*, September 10, 2015, Vol. 525, pp. 201-205
Designing Trees, Naomi Lubick, *Scientific American*, April 1, 2002 (online)
Mother Nature Network (http://www.mnn.com)
Washington Forest Protection Association (http://www.wfpa.org)
Evergreen Magazine (http://www.evergreenmagazine.com)

Native American/Yakama History and Culture

I grew up in Anchorage, Alaska, the city with the highest population of Native Americans and Alaska Natives in the United States, and spent a good deal of my twenties in the Pacific Northwest. Even so, several site visits and a lot of research went into familiarizing myself with the particular environment and cultures of *TreeVolution*.

My upbringing in Alaska was fueled by natural resources, both in terms of family income and state infrastructure. The extraction of oil, fish, timber, etc. almost always hinged on agreements with Native tribes. Because *TreeVolution* is a novel about our relationship with natural resources, it was important to me to include an indigenous voice in the book as well.

Once I decided that the story had to take place in south-central Washington state, I researched and visited the area to educate myself about the history and culture of that particular place. The Yakama Nation became key in my research, given the size of their forest holdings and their timber industry. Washington's largest reservation in size and population, the Yakama Nation is a confederation of tribes and bands that overlaps to a large extent with Yakima County (yes, different spelling, as depicted in *TreeVolution*); and the incredible breadth and strength of their combined cultures and industries is truly inspirational.

Below is a partial list of resources about the Yakama and other tribes/Nations of the area. I decided in the end that it would be more responsible to frame Charlie's Nation in *TreeVolution* as a fictional Nation similar to Yakama, rather than presume to speak for a real Nation. If I get something wrong, it should not reflect poorly on anyone else. Any risk involved in this approach was, for me, preferable to completely excluding an indigenous voice from a novel about our relationship with natural resources.

Yakama Nation (http://www.yakamanation-nsn.gov/index.php - official site of the Confederated Tribes of the Yakama Nation)
Smithsonian National Museum of the American Indian (NMAI)
Yakama Rising: Indigenous Cultural Revitalization, Activism, and Healing (First Peoples: New Directions in Indigenous Communities), Michelle M. Jacob, University of Arizona Press, 2013
Indian Voices: Listening to Native Americans, Alison Owings, Rutgers University Press, 2011

Tara Campbell

Indian legends of the Pacific Northwest, Ella E. Clark (author), Robert Bruce Inverarity (illustrator), University of California Press, 2003

Ghost Voices: Yakima Indian Myths, Legends, Humor, and Hunting Stories, Donald M. Hines, Great Eagle Pub, 1992

Indian Country Today Media Network (http://indiancountrytodaymedianetwork.com)

Indian Country TV (http://www.indiancountrynews.com/index.php/tv/indian-country-tv-com)

NorthWest Indian News (http://www.nwin.tv/NWIN-Welcome.html)

So You Want to Write About American Indians? A Guide for Writers, Students, and Scholars, Devon Abbott Mihesuah, University of Nebraska Press, 2005

"Never Lay a Salmon on the Ground with His Head toward the River": State of Washington Sues Yakamas over Alcohol Ban. Haupt, Robert J., *American Indian Law Review*, Vol. 26, No. 1 (2002), p 67-87

Gym Shoes, Maps and Passports, Oh My! Creating Community or Creating Chaos at the NMAI? Archuleta, Elizabeth, *American Indian Quarterly*, v29 n3-4 p 426-449 Sum-Fall 2005

"This I Know from the Old People": Yakama Indian Treaty Rights as Oral Tradition. Fisher, Andrew H., *Montana: The Magazine of Western History*, 49, no.1 (Spring 1999), p 2-17.

The 1932 Handshake Agreement: Yakama Indian Treaty Rights and Forest Service Policy in the Pacific Northwest. Fisher, Andrew H., *The Western Historical Quarterly*, 28, no.2 (Summer 1997): p 186-217.

Yakama Forest Management Plan (2005), Steven Harrell, University of Washington

Yakama/Sahaptin language resources:
Yakama/Yakima Dictionary. Virginia Beavert and
Sharon Hargus, Heritage University and
University of Washington Press, 2010
Sahaptin Noun Dictionary (online) Teresa Ana-
hoo-ey Kurtzhall with the permission of Virginia
Beavert (http://www.native-
languages.org/sahaptin.htm)

39601488R00210

Made in the USA
Middletown, DE
20 January 2017